LIBERTY'S
TORCH

TONY ISABELLA & BOB INGERSOLL

D0730332

LIBERTY'S TORCH

TONY ISABELLA & BOB INGERSOLL

ILLUSTRATIONS BY
MIKE ZECK & BOB McLEOD

BYRON PREISS MULTIMEDIA COMPANY, INC.
NEW YORK

BERKLEY BOULEVARD BOOKS, NEW YORK

Special thanks to Ginjer Buchanan, Steven A. Roman, Michelle LaMarca, Howard Zimmerman, Emily Epstein, Ursula Ward, Mike Thomas, and Steve Behling.

CAPTAIN AMERICA: LIBERTY'S TORCH

A Berkley Boulevard Book
A Byron Preiss Multimedia Company, Inc. Book

PRINTING HISTORY
Berkley Boulevard paperback edition / December 1998

The Penguin Putnam Inc. World Wide Web site address is http://www.penguinputnam.com

Check out the Byron Preiss Multimedia Co., Inc. site on the World Wide Web:
http://www.byronpreiss.com

Check out the Ace Science Fiction/Fantasy newsletter, and much more, at Club PPI!

ISBN: 0-425-16619-8

BERKLEY BOULEVARD
Berkley Boulevard Books are published by The Berkley Publishing Group, a member of Penguin Putnam Inc., 375 Hudson Street, New York, New York 10014.
BERKLEY BOULEVARD and its logo are trademarks belonging to Berkley Publishing Corporation.

PRINTED IN THE UNITED STATES OF AMERICA

10 9 8 7 6 5 4 3 2

ACKNOWLEDGMENTS

No man is an island—especially in a project of this magnitude. The authors would like to acknowledge and thank the following for their help:

Keith R.A. DeCandido, editor extraordinaire and the first person to recognize the potential of the dream.

Mike Thomas and Steve Behling of Marvel Creative Services, who fought to keep the dream alive.

Morris Dees for inspiration and for fighting the good fight.

Bill Thom and Russ Maheras, who didn't think we were strange when we asked the airspeed of a laden Cobra attack helicopter or how to disable a TOW missile.

Max Allan Collins, Barbara Collins, and Nathan Collins for reasons that will become clear.

Harlan and Susan Ellison for uncountable kindnesses.

The Cuyahoga County and Medina County Libraries for having the books that we needed when we needed them.

The Comic Book Writer's Guide to Information on the Internet (http://members.aol.com/jayjay5000/WritersGuide/index.html), a wonderful web page of reference links to information sites useful to all comic book writers, because where else are you going to get information on performing CPR at two in the morning?

Mark Waid, Kurt Busiek, Roger Price, Thom Zahler, Tom Condosta, and Bill Soukup, the sounding boards who kept us on track—whether they knew it or not.

Prologue

LEGEND

It was the kind of June night that made even the most jaded of New Yorkers wonder why anyone would ever want to live anywhere else. Warm, with a refreshing breeze coming off the Hudson, and so clear that one could even see stars in the sky over the bright neon glare of the city. The streets were full of people glorying in the blazing night as they strolled to cheesecake at Lindy's or the evening performance of *Cats*. To be young and single tonight in this sleepless city was to move in the land of fairie: everything one could desire was within arm's reach.

A walk up Fifth Avenue alongside Central Park, most pleasant on a fine night like this, would lead one to a stylish three-story townhouse at Seventieth Street. The most unaware visitor to the city would undoubtedly deem the building a splendid dwelling. The more informed traveller would, of course, see it as a modern-day Camelot, an enchanted fortress in the very heart of Manhattan. Those unfortunate souls less inclined to embrace a sense of wonder would simply identify it as Avengers Mansion, headquarters of a team of costumed adventurers that others might call Earth's mightiest heroes.

Inside the mansion, Steve Rogers—six foot two, blond-haired, blue-eyed, and, to all outward appearances, young enough to fall in the upper reaches of the Generation X archetype—sat at the main computer terminal trying to come up with one last polynomial triple-encryption security code that would satisfy him. He had been working for hours in the command center and had previously programmed twelve such codes into the several Kray mainframes surrounding him; enough to keep out most prying eyes and even, he chuckled inwardly, some eyes permitted access. Hawkeye, for one, always used to complain that he couldn't access the computers after Rogers was finished, because he couldn't remember all the new codes.

Still, there were others—evil geniuses such as Dr. Doom or Baron Zemo—who would dearly love to have the information contained in the Avengers' computer banks at their disposal and who would find no challenge in anything less than the security on which Rogers insisted. Tomorrow, if the top cryptographers the Avengers employed to test their security failed to crack the new codes, *then* Rogers would be satisfied he had done his job properly.

"A little out of uniform, aren't we, sir?" said a voice from someone entering the command center.

Rogers swivelled in his chair and smiled at Edwin Jarvis. The man who had served as personal butler for the Avengers since the team first formed carried a tray into the computer room, moving with a gait that was unprepossessing yet self-assured, with a grace rivaling even Fred Astaire's best moves.

Rogers glanced down at his costume. The blue chain mail shirt with white sleeves and red and white vertical stripes around the waist, the white stars emblazoned on the chest and back, the blue pants, the red gloves and boots—the entire ensemble was all there. For a second, Captain America—the name Steve Rogers had been best known as since 1941—didn't know what Jarvis meant by *out of uniform* until he realized that his blue cowl and mask, with its proud, block-letter "A" on the forehead, was hanging from his neck behind him.

"It's Dress-Down Day, Jarvis," the Captain said with a smile. "Didn't you get the memo?"

"I'm afraid I missed it, sir," Jarvis said dryly, but with a smile of his own.

For many years now, Jarvis had worked with charges whose dress codes ranged from the Sub-Mariner's swim trunks to Mantis's revealing sarong to Iron Man's full suit of armor. Yet Cap had never seen Jarvis in anything but his ever-present coat and tails, black bow tie, vest, gray striped pants, and black patent leather shoes. To Jarvis, dressing down would likely mean wearing a clip-on tie.

Jarvis crossed the room with his tray. It was already the third time this month that Captain America had overhauled the computer's security codes; something he normally did several times each month at unscheduled intervals during any of the three-nights-per-week monitor sessions the Avenger scheduled for himself. Cap's teammates had attempted to get him to take it easy, to take more time off, but that simply wasn't the way of Captain America.

And even if it were, Captain America would still have been at the monitor this night. Two days ago, he'd been out of the country on a mission for the UN agency known as S.H.I.E.L.D. when the other Avengers were summoned to face some deadly enemy in Olympus, home of Hercules, the Greek demi-god and occasional member of the Avengers. He hadn't been able to finish his mission and get back before the others left. Now, unable to communicate with the Avengers—their communications systems were state-of-the-art, but not even they could breach the dimensional barriers that separated Earth and Olympus—and even less able to travel cross the dimensional rift and travel to Olympus on his own, he was the only Avenger remaining on Earth. Which meant that he could not "take it easy." Indeed, if anything, he redoubled his vigilance, ever alert for any sign of trouble, knowing that with his team gone, he would need to be ready to spring into action at a moment's notice, leaving Jarvis to summon Earth's other heroes, such as the Fantastic Four, if the need should arise.

"Are you finished, sir?" Jarvis asked as he placed the tray down on the computer console. He knew that as long as the Captain was modifying the security protocols, the more basic functions of the computer were offline.

"Almost," the Captain said as he glanced at the frosted glass on the tray. "And I think you've given me an idea for the final code."

He tapped out *iced tea* on the keyboard and then activated a randomizer. One of several dozen encryption logarithms would be chosen by the computer and turn the simple phrase into binary gibberish, one of several that would prevent anyone who didn't know the proper codes and encryption se-

4

quences from gaining access to the computers.

"There. Finished. The new codes should be online tomorrow. I'll send a memo listing them. For now, the old codes still work. Did you need the computer?"

"I did, sir," Jarvis said, as he sat behind his personal computer station. "I need to prepare the shopping list for tomorrow. I'm afraid our customary suppliers have ceased carrying Master Hercules's favorite brand of baklava and I must locate a new source in case he chooses to return with the others."

The Captain took a bite of the simple bologna sandwich Jarvis had prepared for him, thinking he would rather meet the Masters of Evil in pitched combat than face the challenge before Jarvis this night. Battling super-villains had to be easier than tracking down the various foods—from international delicacies favored by African princes and Asgardian gods to the little-known brand of domestic mustard the Captain himself preferred on his hot dogs—needed to satisfy the palates of the myriad heroes to whom Jarvis attended each day.

As he ate his sandwich, the Captain watched Jarvis work at his private computer station, visiting web sites on the Internet to check on the currently available foodstuff; sometimes making an order and other times leaving the page almost as soon as he entered it. He thought of the garish pulp magazines he had read as a boy: *Amazing Stories, Astounding, Doc Savage, Operator 5.* For all the wonders he found in their pages—the robots and personal flying packs and rocket ships—none of the super-scientific champions he read about had ever conceived of anything like the World Wide Web, which allowed a man to patronize food suppliers from all around the world while never leaving his own house. Every time the Captain compared the then of his youth to the now of today, it made him feel, at once, very old and very young.

The Captain turned back to his own terminal. He and Jarvis might not speak again for hours, which was in no way a reflection on the respect each man held for the other. It was a common comfort that they took together on such evenings; a quiet time to consider the events of days past and days to come.

After entering a series of complicated encryption codes known only to himself and about which no memorandum had ever been sent, Captain America opened his own personal directory and called up a file. His autobiography appeared on the screen. The Captain knew that, as long-lived as he was, he wouldn't be around forever. No one who had lived his life could believe otherwise.

He kept the book a secret from the others. He knew that if he told them about it, they would ask him why he was writing it and he had no answer to the question other than, perhaps, that he felt he owed it to his country. He had no family, no heirs, and no estate. This book might be his only legacy.

He was still wrangling over the title. His own choice, *The Autobiography of Captain America*, seemed too mundane; the title suggested by a publisher who had contacted him long ago, *The Legend of Captain America*, was too pretentious.

His actual writing was even worse than his title.

The Captain skimmed the pages he had written, the words that set forth his life. "I was a child during the Roaring Twenties," his story began. "The country had just come out of its glorious 'War to End All Wars' and was enjoying a period of unprecedented prosperity. We would soon learn that prosperity was as illusory as our belief that any war could end all wars."

The Captain read further. It was all there; all that he could safely tell, anyway. All the facts of his life, save the frequent omissions for reasons of national security.

Maybe that was part of the problem. For security reasons, his book skipped over his personal life, picking up its tale when his career as Captain America started in 1941. However, what the book could not tell, he remembered all too well. Its absence bothered him. His background was an important part of who he was and why he had become Captain America.

Steve Rogers came from a poor family on New York City's West Side; poor even during the imagined prosperity of the Twenties. When the Depression came, it hit his father hard. So hard that the man had died young, working himself to death trying to provide for his family in a time when there were no provisions. Not too many years after that, Rogers lost his mother as well.

Orphaned as a teen, Rogers had to fend for himself. It was a lonely life; the infrequency of his meals and inadequacy of his shelter made him frail, a sick and gangly boy.

The Depression dragged on, holding a nation in a grip of utter despair. But, if the news from home was woeful, the news from across the Atlantic Ocean was nothing short of monstrous. In Germany, the atrocities being committed by the Nazis horrified him, convincing him that, no matter what the Isolationists said, war with Hitler was inevitable.

When Rogers was barely old enough to enlist in the armed services, even before the sneak attack on Pearl Harbor, he went to the Draft Board. But the frailty and sickness that had plagued his youth had followed him to adulthood. To his bitter disappointment, the Army declared him 4F.

Devastated, the young man left the Draft Board. He had wished only to serve his country in whatever manner it would have asked of him. His frustration at being denied that simple ambition was writ clearly on his features.

General Chester Phillips had been in the Draft Board looking for a man like Steve Rogers. Even before the general had heard the desperate pleas to be accepted and the urgency in the young man's voice, he had known at a glance that here was the one he sought. Taking Rogers to a secluded inner office, Phillips asked the young man if he would volunteer for Operation Rebirth, an experimental and perhaps even dangerous program which would allow Rogers and others like him the opportunity to serve their country regardless of their physical limitations. Even then, Rogers was not given to hesitation. He said, "Yes," then added, "Thank you, sir," proudly saluting the General as he did so.

Rogers was taken to Washington D.C. and, for the next several weeks, he trained and studied while the great experiment was being made ready. Then—when it seemed as though the waiting would never end, that there was in fact no experimental program, that Rogers would *never* serve his country—he was taken to the laboratory of Dr. Abraham Erskine.

To Rogers, Erskine's lab seemed like something out of a Flash Gordon serial with its impressive and complicated machines and flashing lights. And what happened to him in that lab was no less fantastic.

He was injected with a "Super-Solider" serum, then exposed to some sort of radiating device that made his body, inside and out, tingle. The serum coursed through his body, its exotic mixture of chemicals aided and controlled by the mysterious "Vita-Rays," and worked its magic on the frail man. It built muscle tissue, added body mass, and actually created new brain cells, increasing his intelligence. The experiment proceeded at an incredible speed. Within moments, the sickly young Rogers had vanished, replaced by a paragon, a man as physically perfect as any man could be and yet remain a man.

Operation Rebirth had succeeded, but Rogers would be its sole triumph. Security had been unprecedented. Guards were stationed everywhere throughout the facility. Participants and witnesses had passed through multiple checkpoints. As an additional precaution, Erskine had never committed the formula for his Super-Soldier serum to anything save his own memory. And still, it had not been enough to protect the scientist's dream.

Germany had learned of Erskine's work and sent a Gestapo agent to infiltrate Operation Rebirth. The agent had carried out his mission exceedingly well; he was one of but a handful of people who witnessed the miraculous transformation at close hand.

Perhaps shocked by what he had seen and fearful of what Operation Rebirth promised for the Allies, the Nazi over-reacted. Rather than try to secure the Super-Soldier formula for his fatherland, the agent panicked and opened fire on Erskine. It happened so suddenly that no one had a chance to stop it.

Steve Rogers was the first to react. Without thought for his own safety, he leapt across the room at the armed Nazi. Minutes earlier, the young man would have been hard-pressed to subdue such a fanatical enemy. Now, his punch sent the murderous Nazi flying several feet through the air.

The assassin rose shakily, attempting to flee from the angry young man before him. In his fear, the Nazi stumbled into an array of electrical generators. It took Rogers less than an instant to reach the cutoff switch, but, by then, nature had exacted payment in full for the slaying of Abraham Erskine.

Rogers and those around him marveled at his newborn strength and agility. Even without training, he was the perfect fighting machine, the first of a new breed of warrior.

And the last.

Erskine had died before he could reveal his serum's formula to anyone else. For the next several weeks, Rogers alternated his time between training for his new role as a super-soldier and being tested by America's finest scientists. They tried to find a trace of the chemicals in him, tried to decipher what had been done to his DNA in hopes of using the young man as a template to duplicate Erskine's success. They could not. They tried transfusing his blood into others, hoping those individuals might gain a fraction of his abilities. They did not.

When it was clear Erskine's formula could never be duplicated, that there would be no other super-soldiers, the government decided to make Rogers a living symbol of the people he served. Hope was, after all, as vital a component of the coming defense of the nation as were blood and iron.

They designed a colorful costume for Rogers, patterned after the American flag. They gave him a resplendent shield made of a strange, indestructible alloy; it served as protection from enemy fire, but was also perfectly balanced for throwing as a weapon. And they gave him a name, one which would leave no doubt that he was the sum and substance of his country's dreams and hopes and ideals. They called him Captain America.

At first, before the United States entered World War II, the reborn Rogers operated only within its borders. By day, he was Private Steve Rogers, the rawest recruit at Camp Lehigh, Virginia. By night, he was Captain America, battling the saboteurs and Nazi Bundists on the home shores.

It was shortly after Rogers had been assigned to Camp Lehigh that James Buchanan Barnes, "Bucky" to his friends and the mascot of the camp, accidentally learned that the clumsy new recruit was Captain America. Perhaps because Bucky was an orphan like himself, Rogers befriended the youngster, providing him with a costume and combat training.

The Captain had seen something of himself in Barnes, the same fiery determination and sense of duty. As much as he might hope otherwise, the coming war would demand much from even the young. It wasn't long before a blue-and-red-clad thunderbolt named Bucky was sharing headlines with his star-spangled mentor and, in his civilian identity, explaining with secret amusement that he was *not* named after the Captain's masked sidekick.

Even before the U.S. entered the war, Captain America, Bucky, and their deeds had become legendary. It was with those legends that Steve Rogers had begun writing his autobiography.

From the cusp of the new millennium, Rogers tried to take his future readers back to those long-ago times and put into words how and especially *why* Captain America had come into being. And then, he tried to tell them about his adventures, though "adventures" was not how he had thought of them while they happened.

He wrote of Sando and Omar, phony psychics who used

false predictions of disaster to both undermine America's confidence and disguise acts of sabotage. He told of the Circus of Crime and its ringmaster, touring the country in the guise of a traveling circus so they could hunt down and kill individuals vital to America's war preparations. He devoted several chapters to his most persistent enemy, Johann Shmitt, aka the Red Skull—madman, murderer, and Nazi agent supreme, trained by Adolf Hitler himself to embody the Aryan *übermensch*, just as Captain America embodied the American ideal.

His book told how, on the rare occasion of an evening pass, the private and his young friend would go to the movies, a show always prefaced by the latest newsreel. Rogers was not, by nature, a conceited man. Still, when he saw the newsreels of his exploits and saw how they stirred the emotions of those watching, he could not help but feel a little pride. Captain America *was* working as the symbol he had been created to be.

In 1942, Captain America and Bucky were sent to the European Theater of Operations. They fought alongside American soldiers, taking the battle to the Axis. Their successes and fame mounted, and they inspired both the soldiers in the field and the workers on the home front.

Then, late in the war, Captain America and Bucky disappeared.

They had been sent to England on a mission to prevent Baron Heinrich Zemo, a Nazi agent and scientist, from stealing a prototype drone plane. The craft carried a bomb in its nose cone, England's answer to the German V2 rockets. As they fought their way through Zemo's troops, just seconds behind him, Zemo launched the disarmed drone toward his masters in Berlin.

With no thought of their own safety, Captain America and Bucky chased the plane on a motorcycle, leaping onto it before it flew out of reach. Because the Captain had been driving the motorcycle, he had to jump *after* Bucky; his purchase on the plane was not as secure as that of his young ally.

Despite his strength, he could not hold on and fell from the drone into the frigid waters of the North Atlantic. His last sight before hitting the water was of Bucky activating the bomb, making certain the weapon would never be used against the Allies.

Captain America drifted deeper into the cold waters and might have died, had he not gone into Diver's Reflex; his brain storing oxygen even as his body slipped into hypothermia. Even then, he would have died, had not the Super-Soldier formula maintained him, allowing him to live at an impossibly lower metabolism for longer than anyone could have imagined. Long enough for the freezing waters to form a block of protective ice around him. It was as if Providence itself had decreed his survival.

He stayed in this suspended animation for decades, until found by the Avengers. The heroes had been searching for Prince Namor, the Sub-Mariner, sometimes foe and sometimes friend of the surface world. They had recognized Captain America's costume, revived the legendary soldier, and brought him back to New York. They offered him a place to live and a spot on their team. Impressed by their bravery, the Captain accepted.

Since that day, Captain America and the Avengers had battled side-by-side against Kang the Conqueror, Graviton, the Masters of Evil, and countless other would-be tyrants. The Captain felt honored to stand with such courageous men and women. His fellow Avengers were proud to have him in their ranks.

Around the country, men who had served in the war remembered the Captain and relived their past glories in his new adventures. Fathers and grandfathers passed on the stories of Captain America's war efforts to their children and grandchildren, as those children would someday tell stories to their sons and daughters. The legend of Captain America lived on.

• • •

The Captain turned off his computer in disgust. It was all so lifeless. Oh, the facts were all there—the memory of this eternal warrior was as impressive as his physical prowess. Still, that was all they were: cold, dry facts. Something was missing, a spark to the writing.

There was so much he could not bring to the mute keyboard before him. The emotions of the times. The heroism and tragedy he witnessed during the war. The horror of seeing his closest friend die. The oblivion of his decades-long sleep. The amazement and loneliness he felt at waking to a new and wonderful world, decades distant from his own. The first visit to his parents' graves after his waking and the futile wish that they could have lived to see the man he had become and he could tell them once more how much he loved them. His friends. His foes. This world.

Captain America was not one to beat his own chest. Still, he knew, all humility aside, that his was an incredible tale. One deserving of a far better wordsmith than he. One who could make the words sing and bring life to his story in a way he could not. Perhaps another time. But not now.

The Captain picked up the new detective novel he had brought with him when he came on duty, the latest Nick Hale novel by Colin Maxwell. Though his duties as an Avenger did not leave him much time for pleasure reading, the Captain made sure he read each Hale novel as soon as it was released, buying it in hardcover instead of waiting for it to come out in paperback. He had been one of Maxwell's regular readers for years now, following the Hale series almost from the first modestly successful paperback originals to the current marginally more successful hardcovers.

Rogers opened the book and began to read. Tonight was not a night for being alone with his thoughts. It was a night for being with a friend.

1
IDOL PURSUITS

everal years ago.

With little success, Colin Maxwell was trying desperately not to be embarrassed. Not so much embarrassed for himself, although there was certainly room aplenty within his tortured psyche for that, as he was for Jackie Schnoop, the owner of the Poison Pens bookstore. When Maxwell's second Nick Hale novel, *Stolen in the Night*, won the Trenchcoat Award, it had seemed to the schoolteacher and part-time writer from Iowa that he had arrived. After all, he had two successful books and a contract for the next three in the series, plus a promise from his publisher that if the third Hale book did as well, the fourth would be released in hardcover. When Jackie phoned him, told him she was his biggest fan, and then asked him to do a signing at her mystery bookstore in Manhattan, he agreed as quickly as he could without seeming too anxious.

He had flown to New York, taking the shuttle to Des Moines, putting up with the usual crying baby in the row directly behind you on the flight to Chicago and then a different, but in no way less resonant baby on his connecting flight to La Guardia. When he arrived at Poison Pens, he found a small card table in the back of the very small store, expectantly set up next to a very large pile of books. He dutifully sat behind the table, pens at the ready, and waited. And waited. And waited.

After several hours, Colin had signed, perhaps, half a dozen books—and that was being optimistic—warded off three would-be novelists who wanted to tell him the plots of their own works in progress—progress being a highly relative term in their cases—and suffered the indignant looks of the man who seemed mightily offended at the writer's lack of enthusiasm when told that, "writing is simple, I got a hundred books I could write if I had the time," and offered the golden opportunity to turn the man's stories into bestselling novels on which he the "too-busy" man would split the enormous profits. However many people Jackie had been expecting to enter her shop seeking Colin's signature, and taking into account the copies of *Stolen in the Night* rising from the floor next to him, clearly it was several dozen more than had shown thus far.

Colin knew he wasn't what one could call an imposing figure seated behind the card table. Hell, at five foot seven, he wasn't exactly imposing when standing up. Add to that a medium build, nondescript, close-cut brown hair, and thick glasses, and, Colin knew, there was little about himself that would make him stand out in a crowd.

Back in Iowa, Colin was something of a local celebrity from his novel sales; the hometown boy made good. But, here, in New York City, he couldn't even attract readers to a bookstore. Hardly surprising. What with the Fantastic Four, the Avengers, Spider-Man and, if the reports of recent months were true, the revived Captain America all running around in hyperkinetic activity, Colin Maxwell wasn't just small potatoes, he was a single french fry.

It was, in many ways, very different from Colin's first trip to New York City.

He had decided to set his Hale novels in the New York City of the 1940s. Raymond Chandler and Dashiel Hammett had pretty well mined the midcentury detective novel in Los Angeles and San Francisco, and he wasn't sure about setting the series in Chicago, for fear publishers would expect the Roaring Twenties. So New York it would be.

However, to write about New York, he had to know New York, and to write about New York of forty years ago, he had to know the city as it was forty years ago. Which was difficult for someone who had lived all his life in a small Iowa town.

Colin saved his money and during one spring break from his teaching job took an extended vacation in New York City, a busman's holiday in which he would attempt to get the feel of how that city had been four decades earlier.

The trip had not started well. Numerous travelling difficulties, both in the air and on the ground, left him exhausted and hungry by the time he reached his Times Square hotel. He had spent almost all of the money he carried on the cab fare. All he wanted was to have room service bring up a simple meal, so that he could eat, watch TV, and relax.

Although Colin got his meal, the table wasn't big enough to hold the tray; he had to balance his plate on his lap. And as for watching TV, well, the set wasn't wired for cable, and the neon lights of Times Square caused such interference as to make a decent VHF picture impossible. After trying every channel and every conceivable position of the contrast button, the best picture he could find alternated between ghostly images and purple-skinned people speaking Spanish. Colin Maxwell decided that, those bouncy tourism ads notwithstanding, he did *not* love New York.

The next day, Colin wandered the streets of Manhattan, trying to imagine what the city had looked like *before* the gleaming metal and glass of the CitiCorp Center, the Trump Tower, and the World Trade Center replaced their brownstone and granite predecessors. He met with little success. He spent the afternoon, and another small fortune, in the library making copies of photographs of New York City as it had looked in the '30s and '40s. He went back to the hotel with plenty of reference material, but still no feel for the city.

On Sunday morning, Colin decided to visit Saint Paul's Chapel, the oldest church standing on Manhattan. He took the C train down Eighth Avenue to the World Trade Center and walked one block over to St. Paul's. He strolled the Wall Street area leisurely, his already well-worn guidebook in one hand. His neck threatened to stiffen as he looked at the buildings towering above him. He was so absorbed by the immensity of this steel-and-stone forest that he didn't even notice the little old man standing next to him, until the man tugged on his jacket and spoke.

"Would you like to see Little Old New York?" the man asked, his smile that of a grandfather asking his grandchildren if they'd like some candy. And the old man knew what Colin's answer would be before the writer fully grasped the question.

Colin looked at the short, withered old man. The man was gray—there was no other way to describe him. Thinning gray hair, gray jacket, gray pants. Even the man's skin held a grayish pallor, as if he had lived in the shadows of these Manhattan skyscrapers all his life, never exposing himself to the sun. The man was stooped over from a spine bent and curved with age and he shuffled as he walked, as if he was no longer strong enough to lift his feet from the ground. He looked like a question mark as he slid along the sidewalk. But there was a sparkle in his eyes, a shine of life that defied his wizened body.

Again he asked: "Would you like to see Little Old New York? You look like a tourist. You got the guidebook and the crinked neck. But I can show you things that are in no guidebook. I can show you the *real* New York."

Colin and the old man spent hours wandering through the lower portion of Manhattan. The man walked six or seven steps in front of Colin, always beckoning Colin to follow. He never walked fast, never straightened from his hunched-over gait, save when he neared something special to him. Then the man stood erect and strode with pride, as he showed it off to Colin.

Together they saw the Battery, Greenwich Village, and Soho. They strolled through Washington Square Park and under its famous arch. Columbus Park, Seward House, Knickerbocker Village, Stuyvesant Town. The man showed Colin his favorite jazz club (a hole in the wall on Bleecker Street), his favorite restaurant (a quaint, but surprisingly good French restaurant in the Village that got the French bread exactly right, the perfect crispiness to the crust and softness within), his favorite open-air market (in Union Square, where Colin got some of the best apple cider he'd ever drunk).

They went to the cemetery where Mother Goose was buried and the house where Teddy Roosevelt was born. They stood at the tip of Battery Park and looked out toward Ellis Island, where, for so many immigrants, their new lives in fabled America had begun. They sat together in St. Paul's Chapel, where the man called Colin to join him in kneeling on what had once been George Washington's personal pew. Outside, Colin asked his guide if St. Paul's was his church. "No," the man answered. He gestured with his arms, spreading them so wide as to figuratively encompass the entirety of Manhattan. "*This* is my church."

When he and the old man had finished the tour, Colin, whose own smile had broadened with each new sight, shook his guide's hand. Finally, the writer had a feel for New York, a sense of the life and history of the city, and he had this man—this little gray man—to thank.

"Listen, I don't know how I can thank you for this," Colin said. "Is there anything I can do to repay you? Buy you dinner or something?"

The old man looked up at Colin with an expression turned flat. The sparkle had left his eyes and he stared blankly at the writer for a moment, no more than a second, really. Then, he walked away. Colin tried to follow, but the man turned a corner and, when Colin came round it, he was gone. Vanished as if he had become one with the gray night and the gray buildings.

Colin had insulted his guide. He hadn't meant to, but he had. Colin never saw the old man again, a regret that never diminished with the passage of time. He was never able to apologize or thank the man, the man who had given him so much—who had given him New York City. And Colin *loved* New York.

Colin glanced up at Jackie—she was gazing out the store's picture window at the people walking past, people who were neither window shopping nor stopping in to buy—and wondered whether he had been premature in asking Barb to marry him based on the success of his first two books. Still, he had a contract in hand for the next three Hale books and a moderately large advance check to deposit in his bank. Provided, of course, he ever got out of the store. With no customers, time wasn't merely dragging, it was locked in cement at the bottom of the East River.

To keep busy—he and Jackie had both run out of small talk two hours ago—Colin was signing the books that lay in the pile beside him. He hoped Jackie could sell them as autographed copies later and recoup something from this disaster. When he finished, he'd find some excuse to beg off of the dinner she'd promised him—he could save her a few bucks, at least—and grab a cab back to his hotel. Of course, he thought with little humor, the way his luck was running today, his cab would likely be eaten by one of the Mole Man's giant slugs.

It was while he was signing the books that Colin Maxwell first noticed the arresting individual standing in front of the table. Actually, *arresting* did not do this man justice. This was a tall man with movie-star blond hair and leading-man features. He wore a nondescript blue suit that seemed old and out of fashion, but it didn't look retro on him, it looked . . . right. The man beneath the suit was powerfully built, possibly a devotee of the new Solo Flex craze.

This man had also made it all the way back to the table before Colin had noticed him. Colin knew that his attention had been diverted as he signed the books, but only a little. He had made sure he was aware of any customers coming up to him, wanting to greet them with an immediate smile and "thank you" and let them know he appreciated their patronage. And yet, this individual had managed to approach without him noticing at all. He wondered how anyone so large could move so silently, then mentally chastised himself for sounding like a *Doc Savage* pulp magazine.

It was then Colin noticed that the man was holding out for him to sign, both a new copy of *Stolen in the Night* and an obviously well-read copy of *True Facts*, the first Hale novel. The man didn't say anything, which was as strange as his sudden appearance. Colin had not had a great deal of experience behind an autograph table, but had learned the usual autograph seeker wasn't shy. Usually, they spoke right up, asking for the autograph and engaging in some small talk, as if by doing so, they could claim some sort of friendship with the autographer. This man said nothing. He simply held out the copies of Colin's first novels in a silent and, it seemed, almost shy request for his signature. Despite his imposing size and stature, this quiet man was strangely reserved.

It was the man's eyes that truly intrigued Colin. They were blue eyes, as deep blue as the ocean, and probed as deeply as their color. He recognized in those eyes what he had seen in his own eyes, the ability to scan a room while taking in every detail. Anyone who wanted to write, especially someone who wanted to write at least halfway decent detective novels, needed this ability. And though this man did not appear to be a writer, his were eyes that didn't merely look at things, they observed them. They *saw*.

Something clicked inside Colin Maxwell's mind. This man was more than he seemed, much more than a shy, silent autograph hound. If he could somehow get the man to open up, to break his reserve, Colin sensed the result would be a most fascinating conversation. And, if the man wouldn't speak to Colin, then it was up to Colin to speak to the man, even if the only thing he could think of to start the dialogue was every syllable as trite as one's asking an author where he got his ideas.

"So . . . what do you think of my books?"

The man smiled. In fact, Colin thought, he more than smiled. He visibly relaxed. It was as if he were honored to be asked his opinion by a writer whose work he so obviously admired. Colin had not read the man incorrectly, but still mentally kicked himself for his pride.

"I liked them quite a bit," the man said. "I thought you captured the period quite well, and the 1940s aren't the easiest era to get a handle on. A lot of writers just ape Raymond Chandler's style, figuring that would capture the feeling of the times. But Chandler's books didn't work because of the *way* he wrote, but because he understood the times he wrote about. Copying his style without his understanding results in words lacking either conviction or feeling.

"You, on the other hand, seem to truly understand those times and you bring to those times your own style without doing Chandler. It's refreshing to see the modern point of view and sensibilities brought to an accurate depiction of the forties. Very refreshing, indeed, to see a young person with a sense of history."

"*Young* person?" Colin asked, looking up in puzzlement at a man who couldn't possibly be any older than he was.

"I'm older than I look," the man said with a grin.

"Listen, uh . . . say, what *is* your name?"

"Rogers. Steve Rogers."

"Would that be like . . . 'Bond. *James* Bond'?" Colin asked in an exaggerated British accent, only to be surprised a second time by the baffled look on Steve's face.

"James Bond?"

How strange, thought Colin. How could a man as obviously well-read in mysteries as Steve appeared to be, be confused by the reference to James Bond? Colin let the question go. Not everyone had the same literary tastes; it was possible Steve had never read the books or seen the movies. Colin didn't want to risk running Steve off by pointing out his literary deficiencies; he wanted to get to know this man. He changed the subject.

"Steve, at the risk of sounding presumptuous, you strike me as someone I have a lot in common with. How about we grab some dinner after I finish up here?"

"It would be an honor."

An honor? Perhaps. But Colin wasn't sure for whom.

The meal wasn't fancy—just two guys eating and talking in an diner on Ninth Avenue—but it *was* memorable. Over fare no more elegant than BLTs on toast, they ate and talked and passed the night better than if they'd been dining on the crown rack of lamb at Lutece.

Steve told Colin that he had enjoyed the first Hale novel and was looking forward to reading this new one. He hoped that would be soon, but, as he explained, his schedule was erratic. He could go for weeks without any time for pleasure reading. Colin recalled the ragged copy of his first novel that he had autographed for his new friend—a copy that had clearly been read several times. Colin knew the expression, "I'm your biggest fan," was a cliché, but he believed it might well apply to Steve Rogers. The man might not have had much time for reading, but, judging from the condition of that book, Steve spent much of that precious time reading and rereading Colin's novel. It was the greatest compliment anyone had ever paid the writer.

As the night wore on, Steve mentioned a few factual errors in Colin's novel, insisting all the while they had not diminished his enjoyment. "Even with the little mistakes, it felt right. You did your research and you carried it over to your writing. Your book was more than research in service of a plot, you managed to bring the New York of 1940s to life. Almost as if you'd lived it. Or, at least, had a great love of the city and the time."

"I had a unique and special experience once," Colin responded. "It gave me a love for this city."

"I thought so," Steve said, smilingly knowingly, and didn't pursue the matter further. Most people would have asked about that experience. However, Colin sensed, his dinner companion was a man who understood secrets, knew the value of private things, and would not intrude unless upon them unless invited.

Steve went on to explain the "minor mistakes" in Colin's novel and the "major blunders" he had found in other authors' books, the mistakes which had kept him from enjoying those books. As Colin listened, he was impressed, even amazed. Steve was a virtual encyclopedia of New York City in the 1930s and 1940s. Colin wondered whether the man might not be a history teacher or a librarian.

An idea hit Colin. "Steve, you sound like you've lived in New York City all your life, but have you ever really *seen* this city? Or are you like most of the natives, never getting around to seeing the sights, because you figure there will be always time enough for that later?"

Steve smiled. "I'm afraid you've got me pegged. I was on my own a lot while I was growing up, never got the chance to explore the city, not the way you mean, anyway."

Colin beamed.

"Steve, would you like to see Little Old New York?"

Steve made a quick phone call first—he said something about checking the office—then joined Colin outside the diner. As they walked, Colin told him about the little gray man. "Other than the day Barb agreed to marry me, it was the best day of my life," Colin said. "And I've always known I should share it with someone. When someone does you the type of favor that man did for me, you owe him an obligation to pass it on."

Together they wandered lower Manhattan, Colin showing Steve what he had been shown and Steve adding his own information to what the old man had told Colin. They visited the sites Colin had seen before and new ones that looked interesting.

They were especially fond of a little pool hall that hadn't been redecorated since 1944. They played for hours. During his college years, Colin had been good enough at the game to pay his tuition. Steve was better; he told Colin he'd learned the game after realizing that calculating the angles and rebounds could be useful in his work. Colin didn't ask.

They wandered the city all night. At breakfast, Steve excused himself again, saying he had to "report in." It surprised Colin. Steve hadn't mentioned a girlfriend or wife to whom his comings and goings were accountable. However, just as Rogers had respected his privacy, Colin would respect Steve's.

Later, after Colin checked out of his hotel and as he prepared to board the bus for La Guardia, he and Steve said their goodbyes. When Colin mentioned he was coming back to the city in the summer to research the next Hale novel, Steve suggested they get together again. And, if Colin was interested, Steve would be honored to assist with the research. Colin readily agreed and they exchanged phone numbers.

Several months later, as Colin was preparing for his trip, he pulled Steve's card from his Rolodex and dialed the number written there. The proper British voice on the other end of the line took the writer by surprise. So much so, in fact, that it took him a long moment to grasp what that voice had said on answering the phone. The sudden realization left Maxwell speechless. The voice repeated the greeting.

"Avengers Mansion. How may I direct your call?"

2

HELL UP IN
HARLEM

T *oday*.
        Captain America was falling. Four stories straight
        down to the unforgiving street below. And it was all
the Falcon's fault.

The Captain and his sometime partner had been going
through a training exercise, mock combat on and above the
tenement rooftops of Harlem. As usual, Cap was getting the
better of the session. So, as a diversion, the Falcon ordered
his trained falcon, Redwing, to buzz the Avenger—distract
his sparring partner long enough for the Falcon to use his
talon. The grappling hook line housed in the winged hero's
glove would ensnare the Captain, allowing the Falcon to get
the upper hand for once.

True to the command received through the telepathic link
he shared with his master, Redwing swooped toward Captain
America's face. His claws were extended as if to rake the
Avenger. The sudden movement did distract the Captain, so
much so that he reeled backward. But Cap had been standing
at the edge of the roof and the step backward led to naught
but empty air and a short trip to the ground below.

The Falcon launched into action. He was across the building on the other side of the roof from where Captain America
had fallen, but his solar-powered glider wings were capable
of reaching speeds of one hundred and forty miles per hour.
With the cybernetic circuitry in his mask, he rotated the ma-
neuvering turbines concealed beneath his wings until they
pointed straight behind him, and then accelerated toward his
imperiled friend as quickly as his equipment could manage.
The wind beat against the skin not covered by his costume,
whipping his face, burning his bare arms and chest. He
stretched his arms out in front of him, his body forming a
flying wedge to cut through the air. He pushed the miniature
turbines to their maximum.

The Falcon reached the end of the roof in perhaps two
seconds, but it seemed an eternity; he was sure Captain
America was little more than a stain on the street below. He

flew over the edge of the roof, angling his flight so he would be heading down toward the Captain. As soon as he had a clear line of fire, he could activate his talon and snare Cap. If, by some blessed miracle, he wasn't already too late.

The Falcon cleared the roof, looking toward the street below in search of Captain America.

He saw nothing.

That was when the Falcon heard a thud and felt something heavy hit him in the small of his back. Then, two powerful legs wrapped themselves around his body. The remote imaging sensors in his mask allowed the airborne hero to see in all directions, but he didn't need them to know what had just happened.

Resisting the urge to mutter a Homer Simpson–esque "D'oh!" the Falcon asked Captain America if he would care to go two falls out of three.

Later, after the second fall of the afternoon, the two friends relaxed on a rooftop and discussed the session. Several times a month, Captain America and the Falcon trained together. Sometimes, they used the high-tech facilities of the Combat Simulation Room of Avengers Mansion, where any environment and any scenario could be created. Other times, they trained in the streets of the Falcon's Harlem neighborhood. When Cap brought the new encryption codes to the Falcon's, or, rather, Sam Wilson's office in Harlem, the two decided to take advantage of the opportunity to hold one of their no-frills-but-no-less-intense uptown training sessions.

The Falcon, like Captain America, stood at six foot two inches and had a ruggedly handsome face. One couldn't help but notice it because, in or out of costume, Wilson always looked you straight in the eyes when he listened or spoke to you.

"You were never really falling," he said to Cap. "You scammed me to lure me into position. What did you swing around on?"

Cap smiled. "A fire escape. It always pays to know your surroundings."

"Up, around, and—bam—on my back," the Falcon continued, playing it out in his mind. "You taught me everything I know about combat, Cap, but, just when I think you've taught me everything *you* know, you open a new wing to the library. This is my turf. *I* should have had the home field advantage, but you know my neighborhood better than I do. Are you ever gonna let me win one of these?"

Cap grinned. "You've come closer than almost anyone else, Sam, except maybe Hawkeye . . . and he cheats. Besides, if I *let* you win, you know you wouldn't find it satisfying."

The Falcon grinned back. "I'd be willing to risk that."

Their training in Harlem was important to Sam Wilson; he tried to maintain a high profile in his community. When he first began his costumed career, he established himself in Harlem. He wanted the Falcon to be a presence there, to be seen and known and, most of all, respected. Not just for *who* he was, but for the ideals for which he tried to stand.

That was why he redesigned his costume a few months after his debut. It had to be *his* design, not something thrown together from whatever scraps he could find lying around on the Caribbean island where the Falcon was "born."

He had chosen a red-and-white motif. Even when he redesigned the costume to incorporate the latest enhancements and weapons that Stark Enterprises could offer, he kept those colors.

Yes, it was true that red and white were hardly synonymous with the bird of prey from which he derived his *nom de guerre*. But, for standing out as a symbol of hope to this community, they would do just fine. The Falcon wanted to be visible and available to the people he served, both in his role as a super hero and in his civilian identity of Sam Wilson, social worker. He was working to insure a brighter future for his friends and neighbors in this community. It was his calling *and* his dream.

He turned to the man who had been his best friend for many years and was about to suggest going another round when he heard the all-too-familiar sound of sirens cutting shrilly through the air. He was about to look around for their source when he realized that Captain America—ever alert, always aware of his surroundings—had already fixed on it.

The Falcon followed the Captain's stare. Several blocks to the north, in a neighborhood of stores and homes, smoke billowed up, choking the afternoon.

The Captain moved his head in the direction of the fire. That was the only exchange the partners needed. Their communication, though not as miraculous as the telepathic link the Falcon shared with Redwing, was no less complete.

Captain America ran to the roof's edge as the Falcon flew into the air. The Captain hit the parapet edge running and leapt from it, the Falcon swooping down to catch his partner in midair. They flew toward the fire.

The Captain knew that, even with his extra weight, it would not take the Falcon long to fly them to the fire, but he wanted to be informed of the situation before they arrived. He activated his Avengers communicator.

"Jarvis, we're over West One Twenty-seventh and Douglass Boulevard. Report."

There was a moment's silence, barely perceptible. The Captain realized Jarvis must have been attending to one of his many other duties.

"Sorry, sir. I'm obtaining a police report even as we . . . yes. It was—dear Lord—a firebombing. A transient hotel on One Thirty-fifth and St. Nicholas Avenue. The blaze has spread to nearby dwellings. None of the others have returned from Olympus," Jarvis added, anticipating the next question. "My call to the Fantastic Four has thus far gone unanswered. I'm afraid it will be up to you, Master Falcon, and New York's Finest."

The Captain had noted Jarvis's initial apology, as if Jarvis was somehow at fault for not anticipating the fire and waiting by the communications console for the Captain's call. He would have a word with Jarvis when this was over.

There was such a thing as taking too much responsibility on oneself.

Before them, a growing cloud of black smoke spun on the updrafts that bounced between the buildings and swirled in the air like some obscene tornado. A hideous red-and-orange blaze lit up the afternoon sky as if hell itself had broken through the earth's surface. They followed both the light and the darkness back to their source.

Captain America and the Falcon landed next to several fire engines. Most of the apartment buildings on the north side of One Thirty-fifth were burning. These were old structures, several decades or more, some dating back to the last century. Of late, they had been neglected, neither improved nor maintained by absent and uncaring owners. Inhabited by people who had neither the money nor political voice to make their complaints or concerns heard, the buildings were left to rot around the people who lived within them. Safety codes were ignored, trash collected only occasionally. The buildings were firetraps, the urban equivalent of drought-dried forests, needing but the slightest spark to ignite them into disaster.

And here was that disaster. All around them, the block was an inferno. Further complicating matters, the trash that littered the streets around and between the buildings had also ignited, forcing the firefighters to divide their efforts and keep both building and street fires from spreading further. They were understaffed and underequipped and they knew putting out these fires was impossible. They also knew there were people trapped within those doomed and crumbling buildings.

Captain America had made his way to the lieutenant in charge of the efforts. The firefighter's skin was leathery, tanned by the heat of too many fires, black soot mottling it further. From behind that face, however, bright and blue eyes shone, showing a grim determination.

"What can we do to help?" Cap asked.

The lieutenant looked grimly back at the blaze in front of

him, already spreading along the street. "We need to get the people out. We can't save the buildings, they're like tinder. Hell, the hotel where this started is already gone," he said, pointing at a burned-out skeleton in the middle of the conflagration. It hadn't been much when it stood, an old, dilapidated building that had likely danced on the edge of being condemned for decades, but, to the people who lived there, it had offered a modicum of warmth, shelter, and hope. Now it was rubble, ashes, and smoldering wood, an obscenely large campfire.

"I think we can contain the fire long enough to get the people out and keep it from spreading any further," the lieutenant said, "but we don't have enough ladder units."

"Tell us where to start."

That was all Captain America had to say. The firefighter pointed to a building a few doors down and said, "That one. We've barely begun on that one."

"What channel are your walkie-talkies set at?"

"Channel 40."

The Captain pulled out his Avengers Com Card, noting that the Falcon was reaching for his own card as well. The Avenger reset the card's frequency so it would broadcast and receive on the same channel, then started to move toward the building.

"Cap!" the lieutenant called after him.

Captain America turned back to the lieutenant to see him holding out an oxygen tank and face mask. Another firefighter was running up with a second set of equipment. Cap took it and strapped it on as he ran toward the apartment.

The Falcon refused the bulky gear. The apparatus would not fit over his wings. He did take a small rebreather tube like those used by scuba divers for short work and that the firefighters kept for use in areas too cramped for full tanks. Then, instructing Redwing to wait for him outside, he flew after the Captain, catching up to his partner just outside the building.

Fortunately, it was only a four-story building. That limited the number of possible causalities.

"I'll check the first and second floors and work up," Captain America said. "You start on the fourth and work down."

They entered the building. Around them, everything burned. Flames ran along the floor and jumped out from the walls. Above, a sheet of fire seemed to dance across the ceiling from one end of the hallway to the other, oddly beautiful as it moved gracefully down the corridor.

A wave of heat crashed into the Captain like a sucker punch from the Hulk, almost forcing him to his knees. Though the special weave of his costume protected his as well as a firefighter's turnouts, the heat hammered at him. He had fought against the subterranean Lava Men, creatures capable of generating body heat of near-magma temperatures. This was hotter.

He did not stop. The Captain put his shield in front of him, blocking the waves of heat as he ran down the hallway.

There were four apartments on this floor, two in the front, two in the back. The Captain saw that one of the rear apartment doors was open. He verified that it was empty, then turned his attention to the other apartments. He kicked into the second of the two rear units and found, to his relief, that its occupants had apparently also fled to safety, as had those of one of the front apartments.

In the second, he found a desperate family trying to gather a few belongings before they fled.

"You don't have time to take anything," he shouted. "You need to get out of here *now*!"

The family stared at him, shock and disbelief evident on their faces. The mother clutched a varied bundle of her family's clothes to her chest, the father was dragging a heavy tool chest, a young boy was juggling toys and comic books. They froze.

"Take what you already have and follow me," Captain America compromised. They still hesitated. Then the Captain noticed the woman's eyes dart sheepishly to a table holding a small fish tank. He understood what was needed to get the family moving. He ran to the tank and picked it up.

"I have them," he said. "Now follow me."

The Captain led them out of the building, hurrying them while taking care they did not drop anything. When he got them safely behind the firefighters' line, he ran back through the flames.

The Falcon hadn't been as lucky as Captain America. Like his friend, he had felt the heat of the fire smash into him, and like Cap, he ignored the heat as best he could, flying up to the roof and through the stairwell access down to the fourth floor.

Two of the apartment doors were open, and a third was unlocked. He flew through the tiny dwellings at top speed and found them all abandoned.

It was the fourth door that troubled the Falcon. It was not only closed, but locked. No one fleeing a fire would bother to lock a door behind them. He felt the door; it was not hot, which meant there was no fire burning out of control behind it. He could open it without a dangerous backdraft leaping out of him. Fearing the worst, he broke the door down.

He found the old woman on the floor of her living room. He knelt beside her. She wasn't breathing. There was no pulse. He didn't know how long she had been that way or whether she would last long enough for him to fly her outside. He acted immediately.

The Falcon pulled the rebreather from his mouth. He tilted the woman's head back, lifted her chin, and pinched her nose closed. He covered her mouth with his own and breathed into it. Once. Twice. When she didn't respond, he placed his hands in the center of her chest, right on top of left, and began the rhythmic thrusts of CPR.

"Come on! Breathe, *breathe*!" he commanded as his eyes blinked and burned in the heat. The woman was not responding.

* * *

Captain America bounded up the stairs to the second floor. Fortunately, as on the first, three of the apartment doors were open and the units empty. The fourth door was closed, but, when he entered the apartment, he found it bereft even of furniture.

Since he hadn't heard from the Falcon, the Captain didn't know whether or not the upper floors were empty. He decided to continue his efforts on the third floor.

The Avenger didn't like what he saw. Tongues of flame lapped at the stairs up the entire length of the stairwell. As the fire used up the oxygen of the lower floors, it shot up through the shaft in a relentless search for both fuel and air. It was a thing alive, a beast greedily consuming everything in its path.

He had no way of knowing how safe the stairs were, but if he were to continue looking for anyone who might be left in the building, he also had no choice but to climb them. He started up the stairs, his booted feet kicking up showers of red-hot cinders flying with each step.

The stairs trembled under the Captain's legs. What support they had offered was being eaten away beneath him. They wouldn't last much longer. Ignoring the flames reaching up for him through the stairs, he ran up, taking two and three stairs at a time.

He was fast. The fire was faster. As he neared the top step, the stairwell let out a loud whine, as if to protest his weight upon them, and then crumbled beneath him. Two stories of stairwell cascaded down. Stairs and bannister crashed, still burning, on the first floor, forming a fiery mountain of debris.

Captain America fell back toward the death that burned out of control below.

3

EXTREME
PREJUDICE

"**A**vengers Mansion. How may I direct your call?"

"Good afternoon, Jarvis. Is Captain America there?" Even as he spoke, Colin Maxwell noticed that his own voice was flat and businesslike; there was none of the friendliness or the sparkle it usually carried when he spoke to Jarvis.

"I'm afraid not, sir. He is otherwise engaged."

"Will he be back today?"

"I expect so, sir."

"Jarvis, do you recognize my voice?"

"Of course, sir. You're Mr. Ma—"

"I'm staying at the Day's End Hotel on East 40th near Grand Central Station," Colin interrupted, not wanting his name thrown out over an open line. "When Cap returns, have him call me here. Ask for Lew Archer's room. Do you have that all?"

"I do, sir. Rest assured, I shall relay the message exactly as you presented it."

"Thank you, Jarvis."

Colin had to give Jarvis credit. *Everything* about Maxwell's phone call was wrong. He had never asked for Captain America before, always calling for Steve. He always stayed at the Embassy Suites because he enjoyed the luxury of setting up the living room as an office, rather than trying to cram everything into one room. And he always used his own name, since he wasn't famous enough to require travelling incognito. But Jarvis reacted as if it were just another call from one of Cap's acquaintances.

Colin wasn't so vain as to assume his one phone call was the strangest thing the butler for the Avengers had ever experienced, but those other things were likely more in the nature of demigods, galactic heralds, and high-tech audio-animatronics. His call was more personal—a one-on-one rarity which Jarvis likely would have found very odd—yet the butler had expressed no surprise.

Since Steve—Captain America—hadn't been at the mansion, all Colin could do was wait.

Colin walked over to check the deadbolt for the fourth time that hour, noting as he did how quickly he could cross the small room. Again he resented that the nature of this business required he travel undercover and stay away from the comfortable suite that was his usual Manhattan port of call.

Like so many hotel rooms in this city where space was at a premium, this one was small and cramped. There was barely enough floor space for a lone double bed, a dresser, an aged TV and stand, a tiny formica table, and a single chair by the window. Colin's notebook computer and printer filled the table so completely he had to spread out his new book on the bed. The room was barely serviceable, and the wallpaper, a hideous mixture of purple and green in ugly madras patterns that resembled a lunatic power tie, almost destroyed even that bit of utility. Colin wondered how the Day's End had rated even two stars in his guidebook.

The room was mostly shadow, illuminated only by the floor lamp next to the table and a wall lamp over the bed. There was no overhead lighting. Another time, Colin would have opened the curtains to the afternoon's natural sunlight. This time, he could not, feeling it wiser to keep the curtain closed, his presence in the room unseen.

He crossed back to the table and sat down by the computer, intending to work on the new Hale novel. What he actually did was sit in front of the computer watching the cursor blink on the otherwise blank screen. There was too much on Colin's mind, too many distractions. Whatever words he had hoped to write would not come. He closed the document.

He started to phone Barb. He had called when he first checked into the hotel, but had gotten their answering machine. Then, remembering Steve might call him back at any time, he realized he had to leave the line clear. Maybe it was just as well. When he left the message that he had arrived safely on the machine, he had, he hoped, successfully kept the tension he felt out of his voice. He wasn't certain he could fool his wife in an actual conversation.

Colin decided not to check his e-mail either, logging on just long enough to send a quick note. When he was finished, he turned off the lights, arranged his book into a somewhat orderly pile, and stretched out on the bed to wait for Steve's call.

The world knew him as Captain America, but Colin rarely thought of him by that name. After all, it had been Steve he'd met and befriended all those years ago.

Shortly after that first meeting, Colin realized that, while Captain America had a great many friends in the government, law-enforcement, and super hero communities, the man behind the mask had very few.

Steve's boyhood and wartime acquaintances were either dead or so old Rogers could not look them up, for fear of having to explain how he had remained so young. And most of the people Steve had met since his return knew him as Cap. Only a select few knew the "real" Steve Rogers, and Colin prided himself on being one of them.

But, on this trip, it wasn't his friend whom Colin had called, it was Captain America. Because, this time, he needed the legend. And so, he feared, did their country.

Colin picked up a few pages from the pile of notes beside him. *So much over a single novel*, he thought with a grim smile. *You'd think I was Salmon Rushdie or something.*

It was almost a year ago that Maxwell had started work on his new Hale book, a novel he thought would be his best in the series to date. He'd come up with a twist for this book, a change of pace that excited him. Instead of a period piece set in the 1940s, this book would take place today, with a retired, happily married Nick Hale enjoying his senior years in a quiet midwestern community far from the big cities and *noir* locales of his youthful exploits.

Colin realized that even the most desperate clients would not be seeking to hire a retired detective, so he needed to find a mystery Hale would go to on his own. Colin found it in the pages of his daily newspapers. Where his previous Hale novels had been conceived in dusty history books and old magazines, this newest tale owed its inspiration to the morning headlines.

Ruby Ridge. Waco. Oklahoma City. The names of these places and the events associated with them had awakened in the American people an awareness of the hidden armies among them: the militias. Homegrown paramilitary organizations that were very much in the news and yet still the stuff of mysteries.

There were many catchphrases that had come to signify the fear people had of America's large urban centers: muggings, carjackings, gangs, drive-by shootings. These buzzwords went to the hearts of the people, burrowing to tap into their most primal fears. But, for all that, they remained words associated with cities. This fear had not penetrated the small towns and farmlands idolized in the Disneyesque concept of Main Street, USA—until recently.

Another word had been added to the lexicon of America's fears: *militia*. Colin knew many of these militias were harmless, perhaps little more than social clubs for the ineffectual and disgruntled. But there were also more radical groups whose members believed in violence—and who acted on those beliefs.

Unfairly or not, *militia* had become a buzzword equating *all* such groups with the relatively few violent ones. This newest of catchphrases was every bit as commanding as *drive-by shooting*, but far more universal. This was a fear of homegrown terrorists at war with the government and willing to accept civilian casualties as an acceptable consequence of their righteous struggle. It was not a fear reserved for the larger cities, for New York or Los Angeles or Chicago. Smaller metropolitan areas, like Oklahoma City, and even rural areas, such as Waco or Ruby Ridge, were as likely to be staging grounds for the violence of these self-styled patriots.

It was the stuff of mediocre action flicks, short on wit and long on fireworks. Indeed, for a time, the militia groups in their infinite variety had threatened to supplant super heroes, cheating spouses, and makeovers as *the* hot topic of the syndicated talk-show circuit.

To Colin, a radical militia group had seemed like a good contemporary topic, an interesting and even educational challenge for an aging gumshoe and his readers, educational in that the writer intended to be fair in his approach and make it clear that not all such groups advocated bombing office buildings. He would research his subject thoroughly, both the standard militia groups *and* the more radical ones.

That was when he learned about Liberty's Torch.

There were, in the spectrum of the militias, groups that were mainly political in nature. They conducted peaceful protests and tried to sway their fellow citizens to their viewpoints. There were groups that prepared toward the day, which they fully expected to come, when they would need defend their viewpoints against some foe, whether that foe be a foreign or a federal one. And there were groups demanding compliance with their beliefs, even if that compliance was achieved through violence.

And then there was Liberty's Torch.

Liberty's Torch was to radical what molten lava was to *warm*. Taylor Douglas, its founder, had been a weapons manufacturer who'd made his considerable fortune when the cold war was still hot and the military lusted after his wares. But even then, he was openly critical of what he considered the over-regulation imposed on his trade by the government with its support of the United Nations and many foreign aid programs. Douglas said America was selling out her people to foreigners and he said it as frequently and as loudly as he could.

Douglas's unremitting criticisms were not accepted cheerfully by the government that was his leading customer. When communism toppled and the U.S.S.R. broke up into its component states, the Joint Chiefs of Staff informed Douglas that our armed forces no longer required his weapons. The U.S. was at peace and the funds that had been spent with his companies would be better used to fund social programs. Whether the government actually intended to spend that money on such programs was immaterial. It had, in effect, invited Taylor Douglas to succeed elsewhere.

Douglas responded by moving to a small community in upstate New York and establishing Liberty's Torch, the militia organization of which he was commander-in-chief and treasurer. From the pulpit of his command, Douglas spoke. When he did, he did not beseech others to join him, did not attempt to sway them to his viewpoints. He demanded. Demanded America stop supporting foreigners over her own sons. Demanded America dismantle the useless welfare programs that siphoned resources from its productive citizens and squandered them on people clearly incapable of contributing anything of value to "our" society.

And Douglas did more than demand. He assured all and sundry that if the federal government did not see the wisdom of his counsel and do exactly as he dictated, there would be bloody and violent revolt. Oh, he was always careful not to counsel or foment that revolt or break the law by urging his followers into action. He only predicted revolt would come unless the government heeded him.

When the Alfred P. Murrah Federal Building in Oklahoma City was bombed, Douglas could scarcely contain the glee in his voice as he proclaimed that "true" Americans now stood poised to regain the rights stolen from them by the government. And, when the aftermath of that slaughter did not spawn that revolution, it did not deter him from further forecasts—still careful not to urge violent action, only predicting it would come.

Financed by Douglas's personal fortune, branches of Liberty's Torch opened up all over the country. He made it his business to travel the country keeping in physical contact with his followers, always present when a new branch opened, always ready to welcome his new allies with substantial funds.

Douglas barely acknowledged the subsequent loss of his family. His wife didn't even contest the onerous prenuptial agreement she had signed; she simply wanted to get away from him as fast as possible, taking their children with her.

Colin realized Liberty's Torch was exactly the type of militia he needed for his book. He read as much as he could about militias in general and Liberty's Torch in particular. Under assumed names, he joined several groups, including the Iowa chapter of Liberty's Torch. He didn't attend any meetings—best to leave that for his fictional alter ego—he merely wanted to receive their newsletters and pamphlets.

Which was how he met Paul Storrie.

Colin was picking up his mail in the post office. The stack included a recent *Liberty's Letter*, the Liberty's Torch newsletter. Storrie entered carrying an armful of sorted newsletters to be bulk mailed and noticed the issue in Colin's pile.

"Hey, I see you got the end-of-the-month issue," Storrie said, pointing to the pamphlet on top of Colin's mail. He held up his bundle with a flourish. "I've got the new one right here. Got some extras back in the truck, if you don't wanna wait until these government boys get around to delivering it."

Colin studied Storrie. He was a short, scrawny man, five-foot-five at best, and with less meat on his bones than a week-old Thanksgiving turkey. As he spoke, Storrie's eyes darted about like a moth flitting indecisively between two lights. He wouldn't—or couldn't—make eye contact. A half-smoked cigarette hung from his lips, but he never seemed to draw from it or inhale the smoke. It simply hung there, the ash growing in length until it fell.

As a boy, the Liberty's Torch member had likely been as gangly and stunted as he was now, his slight stature an invitation to any bigger kids looking for obvious prey. Colin guessed the guy had spent his life as a hanger-on to people he thought were big, hoping to gain respect by association. Maybe Storrie even believed he had finally achieved that respect in the ranks of the Torch.

Colin smiled widely at Storrie. He felt a brief pang of guilt over how easy this would be.

"Hey, that would be great! You must be pretty important for them to trust you with delivering the *Letter*. Probably quite a few folks who'd like to stop the truth from getting out—if it weren't for you making sure it does."

Colin remembered teaching his son how to fish. Use the right bait, he'd told Nicholas, give the fish enough play, and it'll set the hook right into itself. It didn't matter what kind of fish. The basic principle was the same.

"That's for sure," Storrie replied, his chest swelling out as he spoke. "It takes more than a pickup that'll get ya from here to there, to do *this* job. Y'know, I don't think I ever saw you at any meetings," Storrie continued, relishing even this small bit of attention from another human being. "I'm Paul, Paul Storrie; folks call me Pauley. Pleased to meet— Say, who are you?"

"Hell, I'm no one special," Colin said with mock humility, seemingly dismissing the question with a wave of his hand, the hand holding his mail. The gesture afforded Colin a quick glance at the name on the label of his *Liberty's Letter*. When he had subscribed to the various militia publications, he had used a different name for each group.

"My name's Diamond, Dick Diamond. I'm actually not a member, Mr. Storrie. I'm just a writer doing some research for an article I'm fixing to write."

A taste of the truth. More bait for the fish.

Storrie's smile faded. "You figuring on writing some stab-in-the-back hatchet job on my boys?"

"Hell, no," Colin said, shaking his head wildly and imitating Storrie's own expression. "Those things give me a pain where the sun don't shine. I'm fixing to write my article for— Well, actually, I don't *have* a publisher for it yet. I'm hoping it'll be good enough for one of the really good magazines, *Soldier of Fortune*, or something like it. Maybe you can help me. A man as important as you knows a lot of things I could put in my article. You know, the kind of personal interest stuff that would give it heart. Let people know what Liberty's Torch stands for.''

''I don't know if that it'd be such a good idea,'' Storrie said, trying to sound discouraging without appearing *too* negative. ''Yeah, I know important stuff, but it's stuff that shouldn't appear in some magazine.''

Storrie fancied himself a fisherman, too, it seemed. He was clearly trolling for a strike. Colin knew the best way to reel him in was to take the errand boy's bait.

''It'd be your call where we should and shouldn't go, that goes without saying. And I'd be willing to pay you for whatever help you gave me. A guy like you, your time's valuable.''

''Well, I guess it'd be okay, just as long as we steer clear of where I say we shouldn't go. It'll give us a chance to get our story out the right way. Not like those big-city papers twist everything all around.''

Storrie met with Colin a few times over the next couple weeks, Storrie spilling whatever he knew about Liberty's Torch. It did not surprise Colin that Storrie never once pulled back from any of his questions. As the writer had suspected would happen, Storrie was very willing to talk about the sensitive areas; it allowed the errand boy to show Colin how important he was to the organization.

Storrie may have thought he was privy to vital information, but it was just bits and pieces; scraps of conversations the poor sap had overheard while policing the grounds for butts and emptying waste baskets. It wasn't enough to give Colin a clear picture of what was going on with the militia group.

Still, there was a certain intensity to those bits and pieces. It was as if something big was in the works, as if Taylor Douglas was moving beyond merely predicting a revolution.

As to what he could do about it, that wasn't nearly as obvious to Colin. From his research, he'd learned that police departments had been infiltrated by militia members. Storrie had hinted that Liberty's Torch, too, had people in police departments all over the country.

Colin wasn't sure he could safely bring his suspicions to the police. But, he realized, there was one man in whom he could put his complete trust: Steve Rogers.

No, not Steve Rogers. Not this time.

After all, what could Colin tell the police, even if he felt he could talk to them? Misgivings he had developed by listening to the comments of a minor member of a picayune local branch? Would anyone take them—and him—seriously? Unlikely.

But if Captain America thought the bits and pieces added up to something, then there was a chance those suspicions could be acted on before it was too late. And if they didn't, if Colin was just being paranoid, Cap would tell him that, too, and Colin would believe it.

Less than forty-eight hours before he called Avengers Mansion, Colin had decided he had enough to take to Cap. He was about to phone his friend to let him know he would be coming to town when he noticed the car parked outside his house: a nondescript black sedan sitting across the street from his house. It did nothing suspicious, but it gave the writer the same sinking feeling as when he listened to Storrie's offhand comments about Jews or blacks or other "foreigners."

Colin's wife was at her job and his son was at school. He sat in his living room staring through the sheer, translucent curtains that covered the window. It was daytime and all the light was on the outside. He could see out; no one could see in. For almost an hour, he did not move.

Neither did the car.

Colin tested his suspicions, getting into his car and driving around town on assorted errands. The dry cleaner, the grocer's, the bookstore so he could buy an out-of-town newspaper and read the reviews of his latest novel. Whatever was on his to-do list, he did, but always with an eye in his rearview mirror to see whether the sedan was following him.

It was.

He didn't drive fast, never tried to lose his tail, never let them know he knew they were there. They followed at a distance, but they were there. When he returned home, they circled the block twice and then again parked across the street.

Colin had to see Captain America immediately—and secretly. He researched flight times and Manhattan hotels with an online travel service. When he was done, he left the house again. He went to a movie theater for a matinee, but spent several minutes of the feature using a pay phone to call a travel agency and book tickets and reservations in the name of Lew Archer.

After the movie, Colin went to his bank, withdrew enough cash to cover the tickets, and asked Ray Marks, his old fishing buddy and the bank's manager, to messenger it to the travel agency. An accompanying note explained ''Mr. Archer'' would pick up the tickets at the airport. He went back home.

Back in his living room, Colin called his usual travel agency and booked tickets to Los Angeles on the same airline, departing a little earlier than Lew Archer's New York flight. When Barb came home, he explained that his agent had called, a movie studio wanted to option one of the Hale novels, and that he had to fly out in the morning. That was Hollywood, he told her, everything was a rush, everything had to be done last week.

The next morning, with Barb and Nicholas safely on their way to work and school, Colin took a cab to the airport. He checked in on his Los Angeles flight, but did not check his luggage. He would need it in New York.

A few hours later found Colin Maxwell—or Lew Archer—sitting in his Manhattan hotel room waiting for the phone to ring. What he heard, however, wasn't a ring, but the grate of a passkey sliding into the lock of his door and turning. He picked up the phone on the nightstand; it was dead. And, before the writer could think to do anything else, the door was pushed open and he saw Paul Storrie standing in the hallway.

Colin knew something was wrong as soon as he saw Storrie; there was no cigarette in his informant's mouth. He also noticed the large purple bruises on Storrie's face and the two men standing behind him. One of them was Ray Marks.

They pushed Storrie into the room and he fell to the floor in front of Colin's bed. The men locked the door behind them. Marks was a big man; his companion was bigger. Both were over six feet. Ray wore a black T-shirt; the other man a combat fatigues shirt.

They each carried a weapon: Ray had a Glock 17 auto pistol; the other one had a Ruger P-85—both nine millimeters, both equipped with silencers. And both meant business.

Ray picked up Storrie and held him by the back of his collar. "Aw gee," the man said in a rough tone, "looks like Pauley's fallen down and hurt hisself. Maybe he better lie down and rest."

Marks pushed Storrie onto the bed. The pages of Colin's novel scattered about the room.

Colin looked at his old fishing buddy. Marks was ten years younger than him, had played football in high school and college and, as Colin knew all too well, spent hours each day on a weight machine to maintain his powerful, sculpted muscles.

"Now look at what you done," Fatigues said. This man was in his mid-thirties with muscles almost as well sculpted as Ray's. He, too, had probably played football in college and high school, had, no doubt, been a star. But that had been more than a few unforgiving years ago. Now Fatigues was losing his hair, his face was starting to go jowly, the once-firm muscles of his body were starting to sag. He was not a man likely to age well. By the time he was forty-five, he would be fat and bald and bitter.

"You made Pauley go and mess up the big-time author's

papers. I gotta tell you, I hate it when some freakin' hump comes along and messes up *my* paperwork.''

Fatigues swung his right arm down and struck Storrie with his gun, knocking Storrie onto the floor.

"Pauley, pick up the man's papers."

Storrie scuttled across the floor like a cartoon crab, picking up the scattered pages, tucking them in a crumpled mass between his left arm and his chest. When he finished, Storrie started to give them to Colin.

"Pauley, where are your manners? You can't go and give the man his papers all out of order and ratty like that. Here, give 'em to me."

Storrie handed the pages to Fatigues. The man skimmed several of them and then looked up at Colin.

"Hey, these are good. You write these? They got—ah, whadda ya call it? Style. They got style. Hey, Ray, I want you should give a listen to this stuff.

" 'Freedom's Torch called itself a patriot's dream,' " Fatigues read aloud, " 'like in the song, but it was more like a nightmare. It was the serious look on the doctor's face just before he tells you the worst possible news. It was a virulent cancer crawling through the body and soul of the American people.' I mean, that's good. Ain't that good, Ray?''

"Like Shakespeare," Marks answered.

Fatigues sat heavily on the bed next to Colin, holding out the manuscript with one hand. "Thing of it is, 'Lew'—you don't mind me calling you 'Lew,' right, even though you paid for 'Lew's' room with Colin Maxwell's credit card like you wanted to make *sure* Ray over there could find out where you was staying—you got a bunch of wrong stuff here. You need to get yourself a, whaddayacallit, a research assistant. Hey, Pauley, you got any ideas about that? You maybe know where 'Lew' could find someone dumb enough to shoot off his mouth about the Torch?''

Sweat poured down Storrie's face as he stammered, "No, Norm, I don't know anyone who . . .''

"Shut your freakin' face!" Fatigues—Norm—shouted.

"You sell us out to this dirtbag, and then think we're too stupid to figure out what you done? I don't know which of you humps is worse, a traitor to the cause or a traitor to his country. But, I guess it don't matter much, bein' as how the penalty for treason's the same either way."

Norm pulled the trigger. A soft *fup* sounded and a red dot appeared on Storrie's forehead, spreading outward like a blossom opening in the spring. Pauley's mouth formed into an *O* as his eyes glazed over. It was if he were looking at something very far away, just before he fell wetly to the floor.

Norm got up, wiped off his gun, removed the silencer and put in it his belt. Then he took Ray's gun.

"Get the computer."

Ray packed Colin's laptop and printer into their carrying case. Norm gave Marks the manuscript.

"Get outta here, then call Andy on his cell phone. Tell him he can reconnect 'Lew's' phone."

Marks left. Norm moved to where Storrie had been standing before he died and pointed Ray's gun at Colin.

"Know what really frosts me? That alias of yours. Like we're not supposed to figure that one out. Like we're too freakin' stupid to read."

He pulled the trigger. Another *fup*, and Colin felt the bullet hit him in the chest. He fell back on the bed paralyzed and knew he was dying. He could not move as the gun that had killed Paul Storrie was placed in his hand and his fingers were closed around it.

Colin could have written this scene himself. The other gun, its silencer also removed, would be found in Storrie's hand, making it appear they had shot each other.

Colin heard Norm say something from the doorway—"I'll remember you to the Pulitzer Prize Committee, ya hump"—and then he heard the door slam shut.

Colin's gaze was fixed on the phone sitting on the table. His dying thoughts were ones of regret: that the last time his wife and son would ever hear his voice would be on an answering machine, telling them he had arrived in Los Angeles safely, and that those last words to them were a lie.

Hours later, the phone rang.

No one answered.

4
SAYING GOOD-BYE

Captain America's red-gloved hand shot up through the smoke. The landing on the third floor was just above him and, if he could grab the floor of that landing, he could catch himself and stop his fall. But, as fast as he was, the pull of gravity was faster. His hand missed the landing by inches, brushing futilely against the hard, smooth wall.

He fell, but did not panic. He twisted his torso, rotating his body. As he turned and fell, he pulled his shield arm back toward his head. Then, when he had rotated one hundred and eighty degrees, he swung his shield arm toward the wall that blurred past him.

His shield was made of an indestructible alloy of adamantium and vibranium, far stronger than the plaster of this old building. It struck the wall with the force generated by Captain America's powerful muscles. The edge of the shield cut into the stairwell's plaster wall and the wooden latticework supporting that wall, embedding itself firmly enough to support the Captain as he hung by the straps on its underside.

With his feet, the Captain pushed off the wall, curling into a ball to flip himself up and over his shield. He shot his legs out and down. They struck his shield and bounced off it as if it were a diving board. A perfect somersault carried him to the third-floor landing. He leaned back over the stairwell, reached down, and pulled his shield out of the wall. Then he moved down the hall to the front apartments.

The fire roared around him, burning out of control and with a deafening noise that sounded like the cry of a jungle beast on the prowl. The heat rose up and swirled around the Captain, attacking him as if he were that wild beast's prey. The smoke, black and thick, filled the hallway from end to end.

As the Captain moved toward the apartments, he heard another noise above the thundering whoosh of the fire—faint, at first, then louder. Someone was banging on a door,

54

shouting as best he could with the smoke making his every breath a struggle.

"JaWanda! JaWanda, girl!" A cough. "Open the door! Open the—" another cough "—door!"

The Captain pressed through the smoke to the rear units. A young man in his twenties, with a shaved head and wearing a crimson jogging suit, stood by a closed apartment door. No, not stood, the Captain realized, at least not alone, for the man supported himself on two crutches. The man leaned on his left crutch, letting it hold him up as he banged on the door with his right hand.

"JaWanda!" Two more coughs. "Come on, girl. We got to get *out* of here now!"

"Take this," said Captain America, as he held out the oxygen mask he had removed from his face.

The man turned suddenly, with a speed and agility that belied his obvious need for the crutches. He coughed twice more, then took the offered mask. He breathed deeply, sucking real air into lungs mercilessly assaulted by the smoke.

As the man breathed deeply, he looked at the Captain with deep brown eyes that were set so far back in his skull they appeared to be floating in dark caverns. In those eyes, the Avenger saw the same look that he'd seen in the eyes of too many young GIs in the European Theater. Eyes young as their owners and old for having seen more conflict and fighting in their short lives than a dozen men should have seen.

For a moment, the man stared at Captain America, but only for a moment. In that moment, the Captain saw the look of an awestruck boy. Then the eyes glazed over, becoming cold, hard, piercing orbs that saw much but reacted to little. It was their natural state; a defense against what they encountered every day.

"What's your name, sir?" he asked of the young man.

"G-Roc. Um, that is Ordell."

"Who's in there?"

"The Walkers," Ordell answered. "Mrs. Walker and JaWanda. JaWanda's only six. Everybody else on this floor jetted. They on the curb. But I didn't see Mrs. Walker or JaWanda, so I come back in. Found they door locked. You can hear JaWanda crying. I been tryin' to get her to open up so we can get gone, but she too scared, won't even answer me.''

''How about you? How well can you maneuver?''

''Got capped in the back in a drive-by. Legs ain't useless, but they can't support me. That's why the crutches. But I still get around pretty good.''

Captain America looked at the door. It was old, but sturdy, built back when things were made to last. He could knock it down easily, but he didn't want to do that if he didn't have to. Something told him it would be better to have the door intact and serve as a barrier against the fire. If he could manage it, he wanted the door opened from the inside.

''JaWanda? Listen to me. This is Captain America.''

The Captain looked at Ordell then nodded at the door.

''Word up, JaWanda. He be the article. *The* Avenger. The Flag Man hisself.''

While Ordell spoke, Captain America searched for a memory from three lifetimes ago, from when Steve Rogers had been a boy, not any older than JaWanda, and his parents were alive. A storm, a bad one, had knocking out the power to their building and was shaking the walls with thunderclaps that sounded like the monstrous boom of some giant cannon.

The noise and the dark scared young Steve, terrified him, and he had locked himself in the bathroom. His mother's urgent pleas for him to come out went unheeded; Steve was too afraid to open the door and be taken by the monsters waiting in that dark and terrible night. Then he heard his father's voice.

''It's all right. Steve. Your mother and I are here. Nothing else. Nothing in the dark, son. Nothing to be afraid of. Nothing that can hurt you. Just open the door. Come out to us and you'll be fine.''

Joseph Rogers spoke softly, but his voice filled both his son and the locked room. His tone was calm, no sense of urgency in it at all, but it carried the soft, calm reassurance with which it was spoken. It filled Steve with confidence, with the knowledge that what his father said was true.

Steve opened the door. Holding his father's hand, he sat with his parents and waited out the storm.

It was one of Captain America's few memories of his father; Joseph Rogers died a year later. Even now, several decades later, he remembered the incident exactly and remembered the voice. Remembered how his father had spoken, the tone, the inflections, the timbre. All that had convinced his younger self to listen and believe. He closed his eyes, wrapped himself in the memory, and began to speak to another frightened child.

"JaWanda. Listen to me. We have to leave. I know the fire is very bad, but if you come with me, I promise it won't hurt you. I won't *let* it hurt you. I need you to come to the door, JaWanda. Can you do that? Come to the door and unlock it. Don't open the door, just unlock it. Remember, unlock it, but don't open it."

Several seconds passed; it seemed nothing was going to happen. Ordell steadied himself on his crutches and lifted his hand to pound on the door again. But, before he did, he looked at Captain America. The Captain shook his head.

"Wait," he said, and Ordell lowered his hand.

They heard the lock turn and the deadbolt slide.

Captain America took off his glove to feel the door. It was cool. Whatever fire was inside the apartment wasn't burning out of control and wouldn't flare up into a lethal backdraft when the door was opened.

"That's good, JaWanda," he said. "Now I need for you to back away from the door. Go into your kitchen. I'll be coming in, but I want you away from the door."

The Captain waited a brief moment, then opened the door. He and Ordell entered the unit, closing the door behind them to keep as much of the fire outside as they could.

He looked around the apartment quickly, assessing the extent of the fire within and how quickly they would have to move. As he did, the Captain's eyes took in the details. It was a sparsely furnished unit. What it held was battered, chipped, broken, or threadbare. It reminded him very much of the apartment where he and his parents had lived, not because of its impoverished state, but because of the photographs hung or placed all around it. As with his own family, the only wealth to be seen here was in the images of loved ones.

"Can you help my mommy?" the Captain heard a small voice ask. He turned and looked at JaWanda Walker. She was small for her age, with thin spindle arms and legs. Her long black hair was done up in several strands of tight curls. Her black eyes were too big for her head, overwhelming her face with their beauty. The bright pinks and blues and yellows on her Big Bird shirt jumped out, even through the smoke floating in the apartment and the soot covering her clothes like a carbon paper stain. JaWanda reached up, took his hand, and urgently pulled him to the bedroom.

"Please, can you help my Mommy?" she asked again. "She and me were takin' naps and now I can't wake her up."

The Captain went with her to the bedroom. He saw Mrs. Walker lying on the floor, her arm outstretched from where JaWanda had been pulling on it in a futile attempt to wake her. He felt bile rise to his mouth as he saw how still the woman lay. He knelt by the woman and felt for a pulse.

There was none. During the war, he'd seen death more times than he cared to remember, seen that blank look on the faces of the dead. He knew JaWanda's mother was dead.

"JaWanda, we've got to get your mother and you out of here. Do you know what a fire escape is?"

"Yes, sir."

"Is there one outside your window?"

"No, it's down the hall at the back."

"Okay. We can't go down the stairs, so we'll have to go down the fire escape. Do you understand?"

"Yes."

"How about you?" the Captain asked Ordell. "Can you manage the fire escape?"

"Man, to get out of *here*, I could shimmy down the Statue of Liberty."

Captain America picked up Mrs. Walker and carried her to the living room. He placed her on the floor and felt the door again. It was hot. Too hot.

"Ordell, JaWanda, the fire's bad outside. Wait here a second while I see if we can go down the hall. Will you be all right while I check that?"

Ordell knew the question was meant more for the girl than him, but nodded anyway, trying to force as much confidence as he could into the gesture so that JaWanda wouldn't see his own fear. He looked at her and realized she had none. She merely smiled at Captain America and said, "We'll be all right."

She *knew* he would get them all out of the building.

The Captain opened the door and moved quickly into the hall. He looked toward the fire escape. The fire burned out of control. The hall was impassible.

The Falcon didn't know how long he'd been applying CPR to the woman, only that it hadn't been long enough. She still wasn't breathing.

Breath, breath, pump the chest fifteen times, check for breathing. When he found no response, he repeated: breath, breath, fifteen pumps on the chest.

He knew that below were firetrucks and rescue vehicles with defibrillators and other equipment for reviving the injured. But he also knew that if he stopped what he was doing and tried to move her, she would not survive long enough for any of the equipment to do her any good. Her only chance was for him to revive her there and now.

There was still no response. He started the cycle again: two breaths and fifteen rhythmic pumps.

"Come on—breathe! I haven't lost a patient yet and I'm not about to start with you! Breathe!"

The woman coughed, hard, and shook spasmodically, as her lungs forcibly expelled the smoke that she had drawn into them. Then she breathed. Once. Twice. Steady.

The Falcon smiled. He gently placed his rebreather tube into the woman's mouth and grinned with satisfaction at the sound of her breathing in the air compressed in the small tube.

He knew the woman was still in danger. She would need medical attention as soon as possible and he wanted to get it to her faster than by flying her down the stairwell and out the door. He picked up a chair lying near them and threw it through a window.

The chair smashed through the glass. The fire burst into new life, fed by the outside air. Flames took hold in the window frame and the wall surrounding it.

The Falcon picked the woman up, activated his turbines and flew through the window at maximum speed. Fast enough, he hoped, that the fire wouldn't touch them as they passed. He felt the heat on his bare arms and chest, hotter than anything he had ever felt before. Were *they* on fire?

As he glided to the street, he looked at the woman in his arms and breathed an audible sigh of relief. She may have been burned, but, thankfully, her clothes were not on fire.

Emergency services and rescue vehicles were waiting just a few yards beyond the firefighting effort, waiting for any victims to be brought to them. The Falcon swooped to the closest one and landed before an astonished paramedic.

''This woman needs medical attention!'' the winged hero shouted. The paramedic quickly regained his composure, helped lay the woman on a stretcher, and immediately started tending to her.

The Falcon watched anxiously for several long moments. Then, the paramedic turned to him with a smile. ''She should make it.''

The Falcon closed his eyes, releasing a slow exhale of relief. His eyes still watered from the heat and smoke. His chest pulled with each breath. His shoulder burned where a stray flame had tasted him. But, seeing the woman smile weakly at him as she was lifted into an ambulance, he was humbly grateful for the providence that had spared them from the inferno.

With the ambulance safely on its way, the Falcon sought out the lieutenant he and Cap had spoken on their arrival. The firefighter brought him up to speed quickly.

"We have the fires under control. They won't spread anymore. Now we're trying to put them out, hopefully before the rest of the block comes down."

Suddenly, the Falcon looked around anxiously. He didn't see a familiar red-white-and-blue costume anywhere.

"Where's Cap?"

The lieutenant shook his head. "Haven't seen him. But, with the way everyone's been in and out of these buildings, I haven't been able to keep track either."

"You mean he could still be—"

The Falcon's question went uncompleted as he took to the air, heading back toward the inferno he'd just escaped.

Captain America closed the door behind him. The apartment was full of smoke. He had to make sure as little more as possible came in while he figured out another escape route.

"JaWanda, where does your mother keep the towels?"

"There's some in the kitchen," the girl answered, pointing the way as she did.

The Captain found the towels in a drawer next to the sink. He ran them under the faucet, then went back to the door. He lay the soaking towels on the floor to cover the space between the bottom of the door and the floor, then wedged them tightly into that crack with his shield.

He moved to a window at the front of the apartment. The fire was blazing all around it. He would not be able to get JaWanda or Ordell through it without burning them.

He rushed to the bedroom window, which looked out on an alley space between the burning buildings. He looked down, past the web of clotheslines that hung between the buildings.

The alley burned, piles of trash having ignited as the fire from within the buildings sought the freedom of the open air. But, though the ground itself was a deadly inferno, there were no flames around the bedroom window. They could pass through it safely, but then what?

The Captain took out his comm card and activated it.

"Cap! Where are you?"

The Falcon's reply came through the miniaturized speaker on the card and, even filtered as it was, Captain America could hear the urgency in his friend's voice.

"Third floor, front apartment. The bedroom window on the east side of the building. We need help."

"On my way."

The Captain ran back to the living room, where he found Ordell balancing precariously on his crutches while holding JaWanda close to him.

"JaWanda, Ordell, we've got to go to the bedroom window. Someone will be there to take you down."

"What about Mommy?" the girl asked.

The Captain picked up the body of Mrs. Walker. "I have her," he said reassuringly, "Let's go!"

He followed JaWanda and Ordell into the bedroom; the Falcon was already at the window.

"JaWanda, this is my friend, the Falcon. If you just hold on to his neck as tightly as you can, he'll fly you down to the street and the firemen."

The Falcon picked up JaWanda tenderly, tucking her head within his wings, and flew her out the window.

Captain America turned to his remaining companion.

"You're next, Ordell."

Ordell's gaze was on the limp body in the Captain's arms. The Avenger answered the young man's unspoken question.

"She was dead before we came into the room. I didn't want to tell JaWanda. Is there a father?"

"Yeah. Crackhead fool who only show up when the relief

checks comes. You don't want to be leaving her with him. Mrs. Walker got a sister over to Jersey somewhere. Good folk. They's the ones you should get to look after her. Don't know for sure where they live, though.''

"Next," the Falcon said at the window.

The Captain helped Ordell into the Falcon's arms, then handed the young man his crutches. He watched as the two flew upward through the smoke. Once they were above the flames, the Falcon would turn and carry his passenger to safety.

He looked into the face of the woman in his arms, the woman he had arrived too late to help.

"I will find your sister for JaWanda," he promised her. "I won't fail you there, too."

When the Falcon returned to the window, the Captain handed him Mrs. Walker's body. The Falcon objected.

"Cap, this fire is burning out of control! She's dead! I've got to get you out of here now!"

"Take her, Sam. I can't leave her body here to burn. I won't allow that to be JaWanda's last memory of her mother. I'll be fine. Take her."

"But—"

"Please, Sam?"

The Falcon took the body and left. Captain America looked back and saw the fire burning out of control in the apartment and spreading into the bedroom. He was no firefighter, but he knew he couldn't stay here any longer.

He dove out the window and grabbed onto a clotheslines that hung between the buildings. For a second, it supported his weight. Then it broke. As it did, he swung off it, reaching out and grabbing the one next to it. It, too, held for an instant and then snapped as quickly as the first. But the Captain was already repeating the maneuver, swinging off and reaching out to clutch the next line. This rope, which was already burning at one end, broke immediately, before he could swing to the next one.

Even as he fell, the Captain pulled on the rope he still

held, yanking it hard. The rope was tied to a hook screwed into the decaying mortar of the building. The force of his pull jerked the hook out of the mortar and away from the opposite wall.

He cast the free end of the rope up and out in the manner of a trout fisherman, whipping it so that it had a downward momentum. The rope shot out and over the last of the lines hanging between the buildings, hitting them with the downward whip the Captain had imparted to it. The rope and hook wrapped around the last of the clotheslines, ending his fall with a sudden jerk.

Until the last clothesline also broke and he fell toward the fire burning in the alley below.

The Captain turned his head toward the front of the building. He couldn't see anything through the thick smoke swirling around him, but he could hear the familiar sound of the Falcon's wings. Like a well-practiced trapeze artist, who knew when to reach out for his catcher's arms, the Avenger shot his own arms up over his head. He felt the Falcon's strong hands grasp his wrists.

"Thanks, Sam. One more stop. Take me down so I can retrieve my shield."

The Falcon didn't attempt to conceal his admiration.

"I'm beginning to wonder if it's your *nerves* that are made of adamantium, Cap, and not that shield. Without a doubt, you are the coolest man under pressure I have *ever* seen."

"What pressure, partner? I knew you'd be there."

The Falcon smiled.

"Just the same, at our next training session, I think we need to work on our timing."

The next few hours were agonizing for Captain America. Not trained as either a firefighter or a paramedic, he knew he could serve best by standing and watching as others did what they had been trained to do. The Falcon pitched in to help the firefighting effort by flying hoses above the buildings, where ladders could not reach, and spraying the fires. The Captain could do little more than help move people out of the way.

Although he did what he could, for the most part, he watched. He especially watched the ambulances and emergency vehicles. Each time he saw a paramedic smile or indicate that a patient would pull through, he wanted to cheer, no matter how undignified it would be. Each time he saw a sheet pulled up over the head of anyone who had died, either one of the tenants or one of the firefighters, he felt a little piece of himself dying, too.

After several hours, Captain America saw a black sedan pull up to the fire. This was not a firefighting or rescue vehicle, but it had gotten past the roadblocks posted at each end of the street. He stared at the car and his suspicions were confirmed when two figures, one tall lanky man, another shorter, broader man, both wearing dark suits, exited the vehicle. They were federal agents.

The Captain felt the muscles in his stomach clench into a knot. The FBI wouldn't bother with a simple neighborhood fire, no matter how widespread, not unless there was something far more serious and sinister behind its origin.

The Captain looked around him. He saw the determined faces of firefighters, who still fought the blaze and could not yet grieve for their fallen comrades. He saw the sad faces of people who had so little to begin with and who watched what they had consumed before their eyes. He saw the hysterical faces of those who had lost more than mere possessions. He saw all of it and the awareness that the grief and loss was not simply an accident, was the aftermath of a cruel and inhuman act, turned the knot in his stomach into a fire of rage that swept over him as quickly as the fire outside had overwhelmed these buildings.

This, he grimly realized, was an area in which he *could* be of use. He moved swiftly to the agents.

The short one, his hair nearly as dark as his suit, flipped open a carrying case to show Captain America his badge.

The gesture was more one of respect than identification.

"Captain, I'm Special Agent Mack. This," he said nodding at the taller one, "is Agent Hattori."

He nodded to acknowledge the agent's courtesy. "Your presence tells me this wasn't an accident or even arson."

"An anonymous call came into the *Daily Bugle*," he confirmed. "The caller didn't identify himself or his organization. He said that the firebombing of the 'welfare hotel' was a 'warning to the unproductive mongrels infecting America, siphoning away our vital resources without giving anything back.' "

The proffered "motive" sickened the Captain. A hate crime couched in economic terms was no less a hate crime. There was nothing he could do at the moment, but he promised the FBI agents that his help was theirs for the asking.

The trio watched silently as the firefighters completed their work. At one point, the Captain turned and studied the faces of the FBI agents, not surprised to see in their eyes a mix of the same rage and determination he felt in his own soul, though, given the situation, he could take little comfort from it. When the fires were at last extinguished, the agents went to speak to the lieutenant in charge while he tracked down the Falcon.

"You've got a long day ahead of you, Sam."

The Falcon looked at the federal agents, also realizing what their presence meant.

"Yeah. The Falcon won't be needed in a federal investigation, but Sam Wilson is going to have his hands full finding shelter for these people."

"Do me a favor then, Sam, let *me* find JaWanda's aunt. It's the least I can do for her mother."

The Falcon nodded. He realized only some kind of action could even begin to ease the pain he saw in his friend's face.

"You got it, Steve."

"Thanks, Sam."

• • •

It was still another hour before Captain America returned to the Avengers headquarters. Jarvis met him almost as soon as he had set foot in the mansion.

Jarvis could smell the strong odor of smoke and sooty carbon that clung to the Captain's uniform. "Your attire needs cleaning, sir. I'll attend to it immediately."

"Thank you, Jarvis."

As the Avenger removed his garb, Jarvis told him that Colin Maxwell had called while he was out.

"Colin? That's strange, I didn't even know that he was coming to town. How is he?"

"That's what I'm not sure about, sir," Jarvis said and told the Captain about the odd phone call he had received.

"That is unusual," Captain America said, trying not to show his concern. "I'd better return his call right away."

As the Captain changed into a new uniform, leaving the old one for whatever miracle Jarvis would work on it, he turned on a nearby speaker phone and tried to return Colin Maxwell's call. That no one answered bothered him, but he realized Colin might be out getting a bite to eat or buying his wife and son some of what he called "guilty traveller" presents.

The hotel switchboard operator was clearly annoyed when the Captain asked to leave a message.

"Tell Mr. Archer—" The Captain paused a second, realizing that he didn't want to leave either the name Steve Rogers or Captain America with this desk clerk. Just in case. "Tell him, I returned his call."

"You gonna maybe leave a name?" asked the gruff voice on the other end of the speaker.

"Mr. Archer knows who I am. Tell him I'll be home all day and that he can reach me here."

Before the desk clerk could ask anything more, Captain America hung up. Then he sat down at the computer terminal in his room and switched it on.

As soon as the computer finished booting up and connecting with the Avengers' network, the system told Captain

America he had one hundred and fifty-six new e-mail messages. He didn't bother retrieving any of them; he couldn't deal with the usual requests from charities looking for donations or law-enforcement seminars looking for speakers. Not now. He needed to find JaWanda's aunt.

It wasn't the type of search to which he was accustomed and he made several false starts. JaWanda's birth certificate had listed her mother's name, but said nothing about a sister.

He hit upon the idea of searching the city records for wedding licenses, learning Mrs. Walker's maiden name was Parks. Another check of birth certificates brought him the name of JaWanda's maternal grandmother, Lillian. A search for Lillian Parks's other children brought him to Florence Parks, who—back to the wedding licenses—had married a Lionel Evans.

The Captain used his Avengers clearance to access the Internal Revenue Service records to find the most recent return of Lionel and Florence Evans, feeling somewhat guilty that he was accessing such private information. He looked no farther then the Evans's address and phone number.

He called Florence Evans and gave her the tragic news of her sister's death, assuring her that JaWanda, at least, was alive and unharmed and could be found through Sam Wilson, a social worker who would be expecting her call.

Their conversation was a brief one; Florence wanted to get to JaWanda as quickly as possible. There would be time enough for her own tears when she had seen to her niece.

The Captain was shaken. Remarkably, in all the years since he had first donned his colorful uniform, with all of the tragedies he had witnessed, he had never had to make such a phone call before. He hoped it would be the only one.

The phone buzzed, pulling the Captain his melancholy thoughts. He picked up the receiver anxiously.

"Colin?"

"I'm sorry, sir," answered Jarvis, "It's a Detective Briscoe on the phone. He is seeking the party who called a 'Mr. Archer' from this number."

The Captain quickly searched his memory. He had, of course, met many of New York City's police officers in the years since he had returned, but he had no memory of ever having dealt with a Detective Briscoe.

"I'll take it, Jarvis," the Captain said and waited for Jarvis to switch the call to him. When he heard the click indicating the transfer was complete, he said, "This is Captain America, how can I help you?"

"Captain Am— Cripes, what the hell was this guy mixed up in?"

The astonishment in Briscoe's voice was obvious. Then the detective caught himself and his tone became more professional.

"Listen, Cap. My partner and I are investigating a double homicide at the Day's End Hotel. Do you know this guy, this Lew Archer?"

The detective's words hit the Captain hard. He felt as he did more than fifty years ago, when he was sinking into the North Atlantic toward what he was sure was his own death, but unable to think about anything other than that his friend Bucky Barnes had died.

"I think so, Detective. That is, I know the man who was using that name."

"A phoney name, right. I figured you were going to say that. Look, maybe you'd better come down to the morgue so you can give us a positive ID on this guy."

The morgue was cold and dark, and the cold made Captain America think again of that horrible day when he sank into the icy water off the coast of England. He met Detective Briscoe, a heavy-set man whose girth probably pushed the outer limits of what department regulations allowed, and his partner, Detective Logan, a smaller and much thinner man. The Captain noted that, were the partners combined and divided evenly, the result would be two normal-sized men.

He followed the detectives into the morgue, where the rows of stainless steel drawers set into the wall waited ominously. Briscoe nodded to one of the attendants, who pulled open one of the drawers for them.

The Captain looked down at the dead, white face within in the drawer. He had known, deep in his soul he had known, what he was going to see—*who* he was going to see—and was still not prepared for it. He felt his knees buckle slightly, then he closed his eyes and breathed deeply.

It was Colin Maxwell.

After he made the official identification for the detectives, he asked whether anyone had informed Colin's wife.

"No," Detective Logan answered. "We had two names for him, the name he checked in under and the name we found on his driver's license. Until we were sure who was dead, we weren't prepared to notify anyone."

"I should be the one who calls her," the Captain said and the detectives nodded. As homicide investigators, each of them had no doubt performed that unpleasant duty more times that they cared to count. They were obviously grateful when someone offered to do it for them.

The Captain asked Briscoe how it happened.

"It's supposed to look like a double murder," Briscoe said, as he handed Captain America several photos that had been taken at the scene. The snapshots showed Colin and Paul Storrie lying dead in Colin's hotel room. Briscoe continued, "It's supposed to look like your friend and this other guy—name of Paul Storrie—got into some kind of beef and popped each other."

"Supposed to?" the Captain inquired.

"We're not entirely convinced," Logan said. "I mean, it seems to be all there. We recognized the name Colin Maxwell; Briscoe's even read a couple of his books." The fatter man nodded. "And we checked up on this Storrie to see whether there was any connection between him and Maxwell. There was.

"Storrie was making some pretty decent deposits into his bank account, amounts that corresponded with withdrawals from Maxwell's account. We had the local cops check out

Storrie's home. They found papers there concerning some scam about selling movie rights to one of your friend's novels. We think it's supposed to look like Storrie was blackmailing Maxwell. Maxwell gets tired of it, decides to have it out with the guy. It gets out of hand and they shoot each other.

"Thing is, it doesn't add up. They both lived in Iowa, so why travel to Manhattan under an assumed name and have a meeting here? Also, the ME thinks the entry wound angles don't match where the bodies fell—she'll know more after she does the autopsy."

The Captain looked back down at the body of his friend, which would soon be cut apart for the medical examiner's autopsy. Of course, *he* knew Colin could not have killed Storrie. He knew his friend would never pay blackmail and the notion that Colin would resort to murder was unlikely to the point of absurdity. But he was pleased the detectives had not been taken in by whoever had murdered the two men— and angered at the killer's arrogant attempt to deceive the police and besmirch the memory of a good man.

Captain America shook hands with the detectives, promising to assist their investigation in any way that he could. When he again returned to Avengers Mansion, he told an ashen-faced Jarvis what had happened and steeled himself for the unpleasant task of phoning Barbara Maxwell. Although it was the second time that day he would make such a call, it was not any easier.

In between her choked breathing and anguished sobs, Barbara told the Captain she would catch the very next flight to New York. He convinced her to remain in Iowa and asked for the number of a friend or family member who could come to her.

"Barbara, you're needed there for your son, your family, and your friends," he told her. "I'll arrange to have Colin sent home to you."

Through her tears, the widow of his friend thanked the

Captain for his help, which only left him with the empty wish that he could have done more.

He pressed the cradle on the phone to disconnect, then called Sam Wilson. They spoke briefly. Sam had talked to JaWanda's aunt and uncle. They were making immediate arrangements to get the girl and move to adopt her. At least something had gone right on this miserable day.

He hung up the phone and, as he did, his eyes fell on the computer keyboard on the desk next to the phone. He remembered the accumulated messages waiting for him and decided that reading e-mail, doing something mechanical and mindless, was exactly what he needed right then.

He typed in the commands and ordered his computer to display his waiting e-mail. Several new messages had arrived; he now had one hundred and seventy-seven messages. The list filled the monitor screen.

As was his practice, he first scanned the entire list to see if any of the messages seemed of particular import or demanded his immediate attention. His eyes moved rapidly down the register, checking the entries under SUBJECT and SENDER with a practiced assurance. He stopped with a gasp when he focused on one particular entry, felt the blood rushing from his brain as the cursor blinked mockingly at him.

It was a message from Colin Maxwell.

5

A GOOD START

Time stood still. It was just an expression, yet for Captain America, that is what seemed to happen. For a timeless eternity, he could only stare at the computer screen. For a mad second, his friend was alive, but that hope vanished as rapidly as it had come to mind.

It wasn't a new experience, the thought of someone coming back from the dead. He couldn't count the number of times the Red Skull had appeared to die, only to reappear, having miraculously cheated death again. He thought Sharon Carter, a S.H.I.E.L.D. agent and former lover, had died, but her "demise" had been part of a covert mission gone terribly wrong. Wonder Man, one of the Avengers' earliest foes, had died, only to be reborn and become one of their mightiest members. Even he himself had been presumed dead in the past, but had returned hale and hearty.

Still, those were other heroes or villains, others in the game, as it were. Colin Maxwell did not wear a costume or use a colorful codename. And, scolding himself for thinking otherwise, even for the briefest of moments, Captain America knew Colin Maxwell was dead.

The explanation was in front of him. The time/date stamp on the message showed that Colin had sent the e-mail earlier that day, shortly after he had checked into the Day's End Hotel and shortly before he was murdered.

When he left the morgue, the Captain had been given a business card with Detective Briscoe's name and cell phone number on it. He quickly retrieved the card and dialed the number.

After the phone rang a few times, the Captain heard the detective's gruff voice, "Briscoe."

"Detective, this is Captain America."

"Something you forgot this morning?"

"Not exactly, but when I logged on to my computer just now, I found an e-mail from Colin Maxwell waiting for me. He sent it to me at 10:47 this morning."

"That's interesting—especially since we didn't find a

computer in the room," Briscoe said. "So, unless he donated his laptop to the Boys Club or someone on the hotel staff had the stones to lift evidence from a double homicide, then someone else was in your pal's room and took the computer. That means, if nothing else, we got a witness flyin' around somewhere."

"Do you have an e-mail address, Detective? I can forward the message to you."

Briscoe rattled off his e-mail address and even remembered to thank the Captain for the tip. The Captain put the detective into his mail reader address book. Then he opened the e-mail and read what turned out to be a short note . . .

STEVE, I'M IN TOWN. IT'S IMPORTANT WE TALK ASAP. CALL ME. DAY'S END HOTEL. ASK FOR "LEW ARCHER." APOLOGIES FOR THE CLOAK-AND-DAGGER STUFF. YOU'LL UNDERSTAND IF YOU GO TO: HTTP://WWW.CITIZENSNET.ORG/ LIBERTYTORCH/

He read the message a second time and then a third. Maxwell had known that he might be in danger and had sent this to Captain America just in case. It wasn't quite the dying clue popularized by decades of mystery writers, but it would suffice.

Captain America started to forward the e-mail to Briscoe, then noticed something he'd almost forgotten to do. He changed the *Steve* to *Cap* before he clicked on the SEND icon. True, the security safeguards in the Avengers computer would not have allowed him to transmit the e-mail until he had made the change, but he was glad he had caught it himself. Reliance on outside safety checks made a man sloppy.

The Captain then clicked on the URL that Colin had included in his message. The computer automatically started up the Stark Solutions web browser. The mansion's fiber-optic line connected him to the web page Colin had given him instantly, sparing him the wait that conventional modems required.

What appeared on the screen, however, was something the Captain would gladly have waited to see.

A logo reading, THE LAND OF THE FREE was emblazoned across the top of the screen in large and fiery red letters. This was the home page of a group that called itself Liberty's Torch. Below the logo was a question:

ARE YOU A REAL AMERICAN?

PROBABLY NOT.

ARE YOU ON WELFARE? ARE YOU ONE OF THE LAZY, UNSKILLED, UNWILLING TO BE TRAINED, AND UNWILLING TO WORK? DO YOU SUCKLE AT THE PUBLIC TEAT WHILE WE, THE real AMERICANS, WORK HARD EVERY DAY TO PUT THE BREAD ON OUR TABLES THAT YOU STEAL FROM US?

THEN YOU ARE NOT A REAL AMERICAN.

DO YOU SEND JOBS, JOBS NEEDED BY REAL AMERICANS, TO THE CHEAP LABOR OF MEXICO OR ASIA, JUST SO YOUR PROFITS WON'T SLIP? DO YOU HIRE ILLEGALS BECAUSE YOU CAN PAY THEM LESS?

THEN YOU ARE NOT A REAL AMERICAN.

DO YOU SUPPORT NAFTA AND APPLAUD WHEN COUNTRIES THAT WANT TO DESTROY OUR WAY OF LIFE ARE AWARDED MOST FAVORED NATION STATUS? DO YOU SHOP AT THE KOREAN MARKET BECAUSE IT'S A FEW STEPS CLOSER?

THEN YOU ARE NOT A REAL AMERICAN.

DO YOU SUPPORT A GOVERNMENT THAT DOES ALL THESE THINGS AND FAR WORSE?

THEN YOU ARE NOT A REAL AMERICAN.

The Captain didn't like what he was reading. He had seen it and heard it all before. From Adolf Hitler and the Red Skull. From Baron Heinrich Zemo and Baron Wolfgang Von Strucker. The same nauseating bile and dogma. The same inflammatory invectives. The same hatred he had defended his country against in the War. But it hadn't ended with the War.

He still heard it, still saw it: the same stomach-churning vomit spewed from the evil paper-hanger and his self-proclaimed "master race." From the Sons of the Serpents, from the people who had worn the mantle of the Hate-Monger, from the far-too-many sociopaths he started fighting on the day he first donned his costume and was still fighting decades later.

And now from Liberty's Torch. Yes, their hatred seemed to be based more on economic fears than racial or religious hatred, but it looked and smelled the same.

It always did.

The Captain had no desire to read or hear it again, but knew it was necessary. Somewhere in this vile web site was a link to whoever had killed Colin Maxwell and why.

BUT IF, BY CHANCE, YOU ARE A REAL AMERICAN, YOU CAN NO LONGER SIT BACK. IT IS TIME YOU JOINED US, LIBERTY'S TORCH.

LIBERTY'S TORCH IS DEDICATED TO PRESERVING THE FREEDOMS OF REAL AMERICANS. TO DEFENDING THE CONSTITUTION OF THE UNITED STATES OF AMERICA AND REAL AMERICANS AGAINST *ALL* ENEMIES, BOTH FOREIGN AND DOMESTIC. TO PROTECTING OUR WAY OF LIFE FROM A TYRANNICAL, OUT-OF-CONTROL GOVERNMENT THAT CON-SPIRES TO BETRAY ITS OWN CITIZENS AND SURRENDER CONTROL OF ALL WE HOLD DEAR TO THE UNITED NATIONS.

THE BEST DEFENSE, THE *ONLY* DEFENSE AGAINST THIS CONSPIRACY IS A WELL-ARMED, WELL-PREPARED MILITIA OF THE CITIZENS OF THE UNITED STATES—PATRIOTS WHO KNOW THE CONSTITUTION GRANTS ALL THE GOD-GIVEN RIGHT TO BEAR ARMS AND COMMANDS YOU TO USE ANY MEANS NECESSARY TO RESIST A GOVERNMENT IF IT IS TYRANNICAL, EVEN IF THOSE MEANS ARE VIOLENT. LIBERTY'S TORCH *IS* THAT MILITIA, THE LAST LINE OF DEFENSE IN AMERICA.

IT'S *YOUR* CHOICE: JOIN THE ARMY AND SERVE THE UN, OR JOIN LIBERTY'S TORCH AND SERVE AMERICA.

There was more. An address to order booklets promising to show proof—fully researched and documented, of course—of the extent to which the country had been misled by the government, which had violated its contract with the American people. A page offering books on how to prepare for and survive the coming uncertainty, as well as foods and other products necessary for that survival. A page that contained both mailing addresses and e-mail addresses of Liberty's Torch branches across the country and information on how one could join the branch closest to them.

Captain America had more than his fill of the site by the time he scrolled to its last page. He'd wanted to depart the site many pages ago, but he couldn't. Not if it contained anything having to do with Colin's murder.

But, that last page was different. It did not contain more of Liberty Torch's manifesto and hate-filled philosophy. It contained a single sentence:

THIS STORY WAS WRITTEN BY ONE OF OUR OWN MEMBERS. WE KNOW IT'S ONLY A WORK OF FICTION—UNFORTUNATELY —BUT WE THOUGHT YOU WOULD ENJOY READING IT AS MUCH AS WE DID.

Below the sentence was a title in blue type, indicating a link to another page. The Captain clicked on the link and began to read a story called "Targets."

TARGETS by I. M. America
Laid off.
Fifteen years of working my tail off for them humps and that's the thanks I get. I'm laid off.
Oh, excuse me, "laid off" isn't politically correct anymore. Now, we're "downsized." Fifteen years and then because some mook in a suit decides profits are down a little and he might not be able to afford a new Mercedes this year and Heaven forbid that he should have to suffer by driving

last year's model. So he and the other suits downsize the entire factory and move production to some nowhere town in Mexico, where the local peons are willing to work for the price of a bottle of bad tequila, but leaving me without a job.

Downsized. No, even that isn't the correct buzzword anymore. Now we're being "rightsized," meaning, I guess, we was the wrong size before. Like there's something wrong with a guy trying to earn enough to put a roof over his family's head, give them three squares a day, and hoping there's enough left over to make this month's payment on the 1989 Ford Piece-of-Crap I got at the used car lot on which I can't even turn off the heater in the middle of summer.

Yeah, laid off. Downsized. Rightsized. Why don't they just call it what it is? I was fired. Me and the entire plant. Thrown out on our keisters so some coat and tie can go visit the plant in Mexico, stop off for a quick R&R in Acapulco and deduct the entire thing as a business expense.

And just try to get another job while you're hoping the factory comes back. You ain't a woman, an alien, or a minority, and you got about as much chance being hired as a pig in a luau. Apply for a job as a middle-class white guy and you'll find out you can't even get hired to ask, "You want fries with that?"

So now it's me and the entire plant trying to make ends meet on unemployment, which there's about as much a chance of as the Pope giving up kielbasa for Lent. Guess this would be that rainy day we all been saving for, if we had anything to save. But after they get done withholding all the withholdings from our pay, there ain't enough left to save to get us past "partly cloudy."

But, they keep withholding. After all, they got to pay for welfare, with my money. Like it's my responsibility to support all the mooks who are too lazy or too stupid to work. And the ones who aren't too lazy to work, don't report that they are working, so they can double dip, work and welfare. They use food stamps to buy filet, while I'm eating Tuna Helper and day-old bread from the Safeway.

And don't even get me started on foreign aid. It's not bad enough that the government sends food to foreign simps too dumb to move out of the desert, while all they can manage to send to the hungry in this country is extra cheese, but then they got to start using that fat broad from All in the Family to cry on camera and make us feel guilty that we're not sending our own hard-earned money to feed a bunch of strangers over in some country we ain't never going to visit. Hell, if that broad just sent overseas what she probably eats in one day, not even those people would go hungry for a month!

It's like we're targeted or something. Middle-class Americans are the only people you can dump on without you get some bleeding heart complaining that you're insensitive to the plight of the underprivileged. So we're the target of every dump that every hump in the world can come up with. And our government lets them, because, hey, better that than risking one of them should get mad at us, so they won't let us trade with them no more and let us run up our trade defect.

Hey, is this a great country or what?

The story continued in like manner, crude and bigoted. As the "plot" unfolded, the angry narrator suffered what he considered one indignity after another. The local bar stopped running a tab for him because, now that he had lost his job, it feared he wouldn't be able to pay it. The bank froze his credit cards because he was over his limit and missing payments. His car was repossessed. His wife, described as "being as supportive as last year's Dr. Scholl's Foot Pads," left him.

The narrator took no responsibility for himself. It was all the fault of some vast conspiracy—the international bankers, the Trilateral Commission, whomever could be conveniently blamed—that was working hand in hand with the American government to strip the common man of everything that made life worthwhile.

The story wasn't set in any one city or any one state. It was supposed to be universal, to represent the plight of every common man victimized by this great conspiracy being carried out against them. As it progressed, the narrator's life continued to worsen. Sometimes little and by degrees, sometimes in quantum leaps, but always worse and worse and worse, until his existence ultimately "scraped bottom like the rotted-out muffler" that was falling off his Ford. As ever, the narrator refused to accept any responsibility for his own life, blaming it on society and a federal government that permitted "life forms one rung above the sponges to fall back and sponge off the few decent people left in this country, siphoning away our resources without giving anything back."

As he read the words, the Captain started. He recognized the phrase from the anonymous note Agent Mack had said the *Daily Bugle* had received after the firebombing. Suddenly, he took a new interest in the story.

The story moved forward to a scene in which the narrator built a small, powerful firebomb, actually giving detailed instructions on how anyone could build a similar device using materials found in most hardware stores. The narrator drove to the inner-city of the state capital and walked into a welfare hotel. The setting may have been fictitious, but the story itself could have been a blueprint for this morning's all-too-real fire.

They let the sponges come and go here, living without any fixed address, staying just as long as the month's check holds out. They offer aid and comfort and a roof to the enemy. Yeah, enemy. Because this is war, and, in a war, offering aid and comfort to the enemy is treason . . . and treason is a firing squad offense.

I put the bomb in the basement, set the timer and went across the street to watch. I used a good American clock for the timer, not one of those cruddy Taiwanese jobs they're always trying to palm off on you at the local five-and-dime, which, by the way, was probably bought off by the Japanese last year. Anyway, because I used a good American clock, at precisely 12:01, just like I set it, the bomb went off.

Whoever said fire is a thing of beauty must have been watching something like what I saw, 'cause this thing spread fast and, pretty soon, the whole building was dancing with orange and blue flames. And I watched it all.

Watched as the people came scurrying out like rats leaving the Titanic. Watched as the building disappeared in those beautiful orange and blue flames. Watched the building as it burned to the ground, leaving behind one less place that would offer aid and comfort to those who would destroy us.

Most of the people that lived there made it out. But not all. A few of them died. Not all, but a few. And it put me to mind of that old joke . . .

"What do you call a bus load of lawyers at the bottom of the ocean?

"A good start."

6

BURNING TORCH

DEPARTMENT OF SOCIAL SERVICES

Shortly after Captain America made his shocking discovery on the Liberty's Torch web page, he called the federal agents he'd met at the scene of the fire. He told them he had some information that might help them in their investigation and suggested they meet to discuss the situation.

Mack and Hattori agreed to the meeting. When someone with the Captain's credentials called with information, you didn't transfer the call to the Hot Tip Line nor did you have your assistant make an appointment.

"I can be at your HQ within an hour," the Captain said.

"How about we come to your place?" Mack said, and the Captain could sense the sheepish smile the agent must have worn as he spoke. "This may be my only chance to see what Avengers Mansion looks like on the inside."

The Captain agreed, smiling as broadly as he imagined Mack was smiling. The agent said he and his partner would be at the mansion in half an hour. The Captain then asked how they took their coffee, knowing Jarvis would want to have something waiting for them. After that, he called the Falcon to bring him up to speed.

"Steve, I'm sorry about Colin," the Falcon said, speaking less as the Falcon than as Sam Wilson—friend to not just Captain America, but also to Steve Rogers. "I only spoke with him a few times, but he seemed like a square guy."

"One of the best." Sam was one of Cap's closest friends; he knew the Captain as well as anyone, better than most. And, for the first time that day, the Avenger let his guard down. He could be the man, Steve Rogers, and not the legend. His voice cracked ever so slightly as, for those few precious moments, he talked about the friend he'd lost. Then it was back to business.

"I've got those FBI agents coming here in an hour. I figured you would want to be here."

"You kidding? Wild horses couldn't keep me away, not even if they could fly alongside me."

"Actually, Sam, I *have* seen a flying horse or two in my time, but I get your drift. I'll get the coffee going."

The Captain pressed the intercom button.

"Sir?" answered Jarvis.

"We'll be having company. The Falcon should be here in twenty minutes."

"I'll have his special blend waiting for him, Sir."

"Two FBI agents will be joining us. One black with one sugar, the other cream, two sugars. They should arrive in half an hour."

As the Captain suspected would be the case, the Falcon arrived long before Mack and Hattori. After all, Sam could fly above the worst traffic even Manhattan could spawn. They went to the public conference room. The Captain called up the Liberty's Torch site on the computer, displaying it on an oversized wall monitor.

The Captain watched as the Falcon read the web page at his own pace. He didn't need to look at the screen itself to see what Sam was reading. He could track his friend's progress by how the look of disgust, and then anger, grew more pronounced on the man's face.

That look was still there when Mack and Hattori arrived. The Captain brought them to the conference room and related the day's events. Then he let them read the Liberty's Torch page. As they did, Mack's and Hattori's faces remained stolid, without betraying what they thought about the venom found there.

It was when the agents thanked Captain America and said they would have to discuss the case with their boss before investigating further, that the Falcon exploded.

"Hold it—you're saying that you're not going to do *anything* about it?"

Across from him, Mack and Hattori were unperturbed. They stood impassive, their arms folded across their chests and practiced expressions on their faces. Their seeming lack of basic human decency only served to make the Falcon yell louder.

"Cap hands you practically everything you need to proceed, and you're not going to do a thing?"

"Falcon, that's enough," Captain America said to his partner, trying to calm him down.

"No, it's *not*!" the Falcon protested. "Not by half, it ain't! These are people being killed by these Liberty's Torch creeps, *my* people!" He fixed his eyes directly on Mack and Hattori, then added, "Maybe if it was *your* people dying, you'd—"

The Falcon's voice broke as he let the sentence die without completing it. "I'm sorry," he said, hoping he sounded sincere as he intended, even though his voice wasn't one-third as loud as it had been.

Captain America reached out and placed his right hand on the Falcon's shoulder. He squeezed the shoulder tightly.

"We know, Sam."

"Mr. Wilson, don't confuse our inability to act at this moment with any lack of desire," Hattori said. "We *want* to act on this, probably more than you realize."

"Then what's stopping you?" the Falcon asked.

Hattori took a breath. "You've heard of Ruby Ridge," he said, not waiting for the obvious confirmation. "Randy Weaver was an avid gun enthusiast who had been arrested on federal weapons charges for selling a pair of shotguns that were one-quarter inch less than legal length. He didn't show up for his trial. Weaver and his family retreated to their home in Ruby Ridge, Idaho. For eighteen months, they were kept under surveillance, but no one ever acted. Then, in August of 1992, Weaver spotted some of the Bureau of Alcohol, Tobacco, and Firearms agents keeping watch on his place. In the shootout that followed, Weaver's pregnant wife and fourteen-year-old son were killed. Kevin Harris, a man living with the Weavers, shot and killed a U.S. Marshall. Several days later, Weaver and Harris finally surrendered. They were charged with murder, conspiracy and assault, and Weaver was charged with failing to appear for his first trial.

"The trial was a fiasco. Harris was acquitted of all charges and Weaver was convicted only of failing to appear for his original trial. Because of the shootout, Weaver and his remaining family members collected over three million dollars in damages from the government. It wasn't our finest hour.''

Mack took over, ''Now think Waco.''

''The Branch Davidians compound,'' was the Falcon's immediate response.

''Bingo,'' Mack continued. ''The first raid was a botch. Worse than Ruby Ridge. It turned into a shootout that killed several Branch Davidians and federal agents and then it became a standoff. Only this standoff—''

''Only this standoff lasted more than a month,'' the Falcon continued. ''When the FBI tried another raid, the entire compound burned, killing almost everyone there.''

Mack nodded. ''You remember the date it happened, that second assault?''

''April 19, 1993,'' said the Falcon without hesitating.

From across the room, the Captain added quietly, ''Oklahoma City.'' His voice was soft and deliberate, outwardly calm, inside he shuddered with anger and outrage. It was a date the Captain swore he would never forget.

''Give the man in the bright blue mask a cigar,'' Mack said. ''April 19, 1995, the second anniversary of Waco and Timothy McVeigh parks a truck full of explosives outside the Murrah federal office tower. When the dust cleared, one hundred sixty-eight people were dead, among them several children who had been in the building's day care center. That date wasn't a coincidence. It was McVeigh telling us he remembered Waco and that there would be an eye for an eye. And maybe they didn't come right out and say it, but there were a lot of other sickos who stood up and saluted what he did.''

''Can you see,'' Hattori asked, ''why we're reluctant to proceed without more information? Given the potential for retaliation, we have to be sure of our facts before we act. Someone could have read that lousy story off the web page and thought it would make a great plan. It doesn't mean that someone was a member of Liberty's Torch.''

"So what *are* you going to do?" the Falcon asked.

"Gee, I don't know, maybe we start an investigation? I mean, that's kinda why they call us the Federal Bureau of *Investigation* and not the Better Business Bureau. We investigate, we learn things. We learn enough things, we can act. And, before you ask, yes, there is something you can do to help our investigation.''

Captain America asked, "What would that be?"

"Pretty much whatever you want it to be. This isn't *Murder, She Wrote* and we're not the police telling Angela Lansbury to stop sticking her nose in our business. We're underpaid, understaffed; we'll take all the help we can get. Besides, it's not like we could stop either of you. You have a vested interest in this thing and, given your records, we'd feel real stupid telling you to leave it to the pros.''

Mack extended his hand to the Falcon.

"You help us, we help you. We get these bastards and then we have a few beers to celebrate.''

The Falcon shook Mack's hand enthusiastically.

"I'll buy the first round.''

"Who knows," Mack added, as he wiggled his fingers to get some circulation back into them. "Maybe Congress will write some us new guidelines. Let us bury them so deep that not even the Mole Man could find them.''

Over the years, much to his regret, Captain America had lost contact with Hiram Riddley. Now, here he was, thinking of the boy, who was probably well into his teens now, and realizing how long it had been since they had last spoken.

He had first met Hiram, "Ram" to his friends, when a clerical error brought Steve Rogers a check for one million dollars. The higher-ups in the Army knew Rogers was really Captain America and that the soldier had no family. When Captain America disappeared in the 1940s, the Army failed to close the book on Steve Rogers. Why bother? If one was dead, so was the other.

Since Rogers had no family, there was no one to notify of his death. And, since the Army never completed the paperwork on him, he was never officially listed as dead or discharged.

Years later, someone in the Army realized Steve Rogers was still alive and still, technically, a member of the Army; a member who hadn't been paid since 1945. The bureaucracy decided it couldn't simply decide not to send Rogers the money, even though Steve himself had insisted that was what he wanted. They sent the surprised Avenger a check for one million dollars in accumulated back pay and interest.

Steve didn't need the money—his room and board were provided for by the Avengers—but he decided Captain America could use it to good purpose. He used the money to set up a national hotline, a telecommunications center with a toll-free number people could call to request his help.

The number was connected to a bank of computers with voice-recognition programs that would transcribe the calls. In this way, the Captain would have hard copies of every call that came in, copies that could be assessed for importance.

The system was not without problems. It couldn't classify the calls, only transcribe them. It couldn't separate the crank calls or trivial cat-in-a-tree requests from the important calls and the real emergencies.

It also couldn't insure its own integrity. Within two days of his launching the hotline, the Captain found someone tapping into the computer that answered the calls.

A telecommunications system designed by the best technicians that Tony Stark had to offer did not come without some security, including the ability to trace the offending call back to its source almost as soon as it was made. That the call originated in the suburban neighborhood of Montclair, New Jersey did not set the Captain's mind at ease. He had learned, over the years, that evil could hide anywhere and in any community. He'd once found a bar in Medina County, thirty miles south of Cleveland, Ohio, that catered exclusively to super-villains. He went to the house in Montclair expecting the worst only to learn, to his astonishment, that the "arch-fiend" who had bypassed his security was a twelve-year-old boy.

Ram came from a broken home; his parents were divorced and he lived with his mother Holly. For a long time after the divorce, Ram's attitude was sour. He was listless, even contentious. His grades suffered and his mother feared the worst.

Then Ram discovered Captain America. In the absence of a dad, the Captain became, even *in absentia*, the positive male role model the boy lacked. He learned of other Cap fans who, like him, had computers. They formed a network, a club that used the Internet to keep in contact with each other and share the Captain's adventures. When they learned about the Captain's new nationwide hotline, they realized it would the perfect way to keep up-to-date on his exploits. They hacked into the hotline's computer system and used it to collect data about the Captain, which they, in turn, used to keep track of his activities. Ram even wrote a computer program that searched the hotline phone calls for key words, correlated them, and displayed extracts on the computer.

Rather than be upset with the invasion of privacy, the Captain realized Ram's program could sort the hotline's phone calls. The young man and his friends, now calling themselves the Stars and Stripes, could access the calls, digest their content, and sent the extracts to a portable computer system the Captain carried. In that way, he could instantly obtain info on the calls coming into his hotline and in a way most useful to him.

This system worked very well for several months, until the Commission, a presidential task force whose purview was to oversee the activities of America's super-powered citizens, entered Captain America's life. It claimed that, since Operation Rebirth had been a governmental program and the Cap-

tain its only success—a success who had signed a contract
to serve his country as the symbol of the American spirit
until such time as the President himself relieved him of said
duty—that he should be working for the government; specifically for the Commission.

They argued that the Captain's independent activities
since he was revived—as an Avenger or an occasional operative of S.H.I.E.L.D.—commendable though they might
be, did not constitute an acceptable alternative to fulfilling
his sworn duty. The Commission took the position that Captain America's name, costume, even shield were all government design and issue, owned and paid for by the
government. It further insisted the Captain have all his activities coordinated and assigned by them.

Captain America refused to surrender his autonomy. He
chose, instead, to relinquish his name, his costume, and his
shield. For the first time in nearly half a century, he became
Steve Rogers again.

Ultimately, when the replacement the Commission had
chosen to be *their* Captain America proved to be an inade-
quate substitute, and the head of the Commission was revealed to be an agent of the Red Skull, the task force
relented. It returned his name, his costume and his shield,
free of all demands he work for them.

Captain America was again Captain America.

But, in the interim, some things had changed. The Commission hadn't allowed their Captain America to take requests from ordinary citizens; they wanted his services
exclusively. They disbanded the hotline and the Stars and
Stripes with it. And, when the Captain regained his mantle,
he lacked sufficient funds to reestablish it.

So it was with some embarrassment that Captain America
found himself outside the simple Montclair split-level where
Holly and Hiram Riddley lived. It had been some time since
he had last talked to Ram. Not that he hadn't been busy, but
that was no excuse for not having called Ram. Even Captain
America should make time for his friends. He hoped Ram

wouldn't resent his suddenly showing up again and asking for his help.

"You're kidding?" Ram said, when Captain America explained what he wanted from the lad.

Hiram had grown up well. When he had first met him, he barely reached the Captain's chest; now he stood shoulder tall with the Avenger. The thick, horn-rimmed glasses had been replaced with a more stylish frame and the crop of what had been unruly red hair was now neatly trimmed and styled. There was even a faint smell of aftershave on him. In the intervening years, Hiram Riddley had discovered girls and they him.

"My apologies, Ram. I realize I couldn't expect that you had kept your network intact. I just hoped . . ."

"Intact?" Ram interrupted. "Cap, I made it *better*. Pentium II three hundred. T1 line. Six-meg hard drive with two megs of it partitioned, just waiting for this day. And the other members of Stars and Strips have done pretty much the same. I've even updated the keyword scanning program three times. It's all here; just say the word."

The two friends grinned broadly at one another. Then, Cap's expression grew serious.

"One condition, Ram. The people I'm asking you to track are dangerous. All I want is for your network to scan the available news reports and gather information on anything that looks like it might be the work of Liberty's Torch. I don't want any of them getting involved. That's *my* job."

"I thought you said you didn't get out much, Cap," Ram said, stifling a laugh.

"I don't catch your point, Ram."

"Courageous teenager hacks into the bad guy's computer, learns their plans and goes off to fight them with guns a'blazing? Anyone else but you, I'd say they'd been watching too many lame-o movies. I'm not exactly the athletic type. I figure the biggest health risk I face is carpal tunnel syndrome and I'd kinda like to keep it that way. Still, there is *one* thing I want from you."

"What's that?"

"A new Stars and Stripes jacket. The last one you gave me ripped when I tried to wear it one year too many."

The Captain laughed. "That I can promise," he said. "Just get me everyone's size and they're as good as yours."

"Sure I saw 'em," Ordell said. "But I don't care that you the Flag Man's ace cool, an' I don't care if I did eye them two—I ain't droppin' a dime for no one. I may not run with the Blood no more, since I don't run, but that don't mean I ain't lettin' them have they own with those wack mothers if they fool enough to come back here."

The Falcon was afraid of this—the Blood was out for blood. He had heard rumors of a couple of strangers, white men who'd been seen in the neighborhood shortly before the hotel fire started, strangers that Ordell had claimed to have seen. If that were the case, the local gangs would want their piece of the men, should they ever return. He had gone to Ordell hoping that the former gang member felt gratitude toward Captain America, that he might give them the info they needed to track the men down. Unfortunately, Ordell wasn't being cooperative.

"And what about Cap? Don't you owe him for your life? Isn't that worth something?"

"It worth what it worth. Ain't denyin' that. But ain't no 'thank yous' gonna change what it be and it be personal. They did to us and, if we see them, we do to them."

"What if you don't see them?"

"Huh?"

"What makes you think they're going to come back here? Let me tell you who we think they are." The Falcon told Ordell what he knew about the bombing, the web site, Liberty's Torch, and the story. "But, here's the thing," he continued, "there's no record of any local branches of Liberty's Torch in New York City. So they're not local. What makes you think they'll come back here?"

"They don't come, they don't come."

"And if they go to the Bronx or Bed Stuy? What goes down then, Ordell? These guys aren't targeting just you. They're going after anyone who's poor or foreign or just someone they don't think belongs in *their* country. We need to know who we're looking for; you can help us. If you won't do it for me, or even for Cap, then do it for the other folks that might die if you *don't* help us. Help us keep any other JaWandas from losing their mommas."

Ordell muttered an expletive under his breath, thought for a moment, and then spoke. "I don't know who they are, but I can tell you what they look like. But no way I'm goin' down to the police station to talk with some fool sketch artist."

"What if Cap came to you? It's not common knowledge, but he's a pretty fair artist himself."

"You straight?"

"Yup."

"Fine. He comes and I'll help him draw pictures of them two. But we see them first and they ours. That's the deal. You call the Flag Man."

The Falcon started to walk off.

"One more thing," Ordell said. "That stuff about some other JaWandas and they mommas. That be cold. You don't fight fair."

The Falcon looked grimly at Ordell.

"Neither do they."

A day later, Captain America and the Falcon had sketches of their two suspects. One was a young white man with close-cropped hair, the other was an older man, balding and fat.

They gave copies of the sketches to Agents Mack and Hattori, and to Detectives Briscoe and Logan. They had used the Avengers computer network to circulate the sketches to every metropolitan area within a three-hour drive of a known

Liberty's Torch camp. They distributed the sketches to every station house and every precinct in the five boroughs. And they waited.

They didn't have to wait long.

7

HATE CRIMES

I t was as if the concept of *hate* had taken on material form and declared war on New York City. And the first week of this war went very badly for the innocents caught in its wake.

In Greenpoint, a city mission was firebombed. By the time the blaze had been extinguished, the shelter for the poor and homeless was uninhabitable.

In Beechhurst, a Korean grocery store was robbed. The masked robbers did not stop at taking the money in the register and safe. Instead, they took delight in smashing every counter, tipping over every cooler, and throwing the rest of the grocery's merchandise against the walls and floor. They torched the tiny store and, as it burned, they beat the owners. The blood gleamed in the light of the flames.

In Prospect Park, a United Nations translator from Sri Lanka was mugged during her after-breakfast run. Found by other joggers, she was admitted to the hospital as a ''Jane Doe.'' Her wallet and identification had been taken from her and she'd been beaten almost beyond recognition. When she finally regained consciousness, she was blind in one eye and would walk with a pronounced limp for the rest of her life.

In SoHo, a warehouse being converted to apartments by its new Chinese owners was destroyed. The vandals placed a firebomb in each unit, all of them timed to go off simultaneously. When they did, the building vanished in a flash of light and a roar of thunder

In Castle Hill, the target was a soup kitchen. They contaminated the food, destroyed the kitchen equipment, and smashed every pot and pan beyond salvation. That evening, while the wounds were still fresh, while the operators of the kitchen were wondering how they could possibly go on, someone slipped back into the building to set off a firebomb.

In Battery Park, a South African diamond courier was beaten. He was battered with bats and blackjacks, and sliced with a straight razor. Almost as an afterthought, his attackers stole the diamonds he had been carrying.

On the campus of Empire State University, the chair of the black studies program never saw who hit him as he opened the door of his car after teaching a late-night class. They knocked him to the ground and kicked him until he blacked out.

On Staten Island, a truck owned by a Hong Kong emigré was hijacked. The police, responding to a report of a vehicle on fire, found it later that day. Its cargo of electronics and computers was gone, on its way to the black market, but a dozen Japanese-made TV sets had been left behind to burn.

In Howard Beach, a Coptic Orthodox church was violated. Any icons that contained gold or other precious metals were taken. The building was torched.

In Tremont, an Equal Employment Opportunity Commission branch office was bombed. The fire spread to a bank and a T-shirt store on the same block.

In Harlem, where it all started, a legal clinic burned to the ground. Its impoverished clientele watched helplessly as their dreams of justice turned to ashes before their eyes.

On Embassy Row, several members of the Costa Verde delegation to the United Nations were dragged from their limousine and beaten. With each blow, with every kick, their assailants loudly claimed payback for a newly signed free trade treaty that promised millions to assist the small Latin American nation establish itself as a industrial power.

Captain America suspected the hand of Liberty's Torch in each incident, for each represented the fulfillment of the slogans found on their web page: "America for Americans" and "America for the Working." The rallying cries of Liberty's Torch had moved beyond mere propaganda, beyond euphemisms for what that vile organization perceived as wrong with the country. They were marching orders for hatred and bigotry.

The incidents were not limited to New York. Through Ram and other Stars and Stripes members, the Captain had been kept informed of other attacks in Chicago, Billings, San Francisco, San Antonio, Jacksonville, and too many other cities—all similar atrocities, all occurring within the week.

In most cases, the targets were social welfare programs and the individuals who administered them. In others, the victims were targets of opportunity.

Captain America fumed. Though he suspected, even recognized, the hand of Liberty's Torch at work, he was able to do nothing. Each news report, each Stars and Stripes communication, represented another assault he hadn't foreseen and couldn't stop, outrages that could be reacted to but not prevented.

The Captain shuddered as he contemplated what he must do. He needed to predict where and when Liberty's Torch would strike. And, in order to accomplish that, he would have to swim through the fetid sewers that were their minds.

He wasn't sure where or how to start. Though he had fought others like Liberty's Torch in his past, the Captain did not know how to think like them. He knew the type, he understood what they did and, on an intellectual level, even why they did what they did. But he couldn't understand them on an emotional level, could never comprehend the bigotry, the hatred, that filled every centimeter of their beings and drove their every action.

It was then he realized his friend Colin Maxwell could help him, even from beyond the grave. In his books, Colin had shown an uncanny ability to re-create a long-gone era. He'd had an eye and ear for details so refined that, through his research, he had gained an understanding of the 1940s and the ability to portray it as accurately as someone who had lived then, even though the era had passed into memory before Colin was born.

Colin also had an equal facility with characters. He had written about the criminal mind for years and had shown an almost frightening ability to climb into those minds and explore their motivations; to understand and empathize with them and then, in his fiction, to bring them to life for his readers. It was what made his writing so remarkable: even his villains were fully-realized and not simple caricatures created to advance a plot. If Colin had researched the Torch with his usual enthusiasm, perhaps his notes could help the Captain understand the enemy.

The Captain picked up the phone, hesitating for a long moment before he dialed. Then, realizing Colin's widow would want to help him, he made the call.

If Colin had any research materials for his new novel, Barbara hadn't found them. When they were first married, one of Colin's earliest and most explicit instructions to her was that, when he died, for her to burn his unfinished manuscripts. He never wanted the bits and pieces of his false starts to live beyond him. It was Colin's finished works, the books he thought were worth completing and which he had completed, that he wanted to represent him. His body of work, for good or for bad, would be entirely *his* work and not include posthumous collaborations with other writers, no matter how skillful those writers might be.

Colin had made Barb promise that she would destroy all of his unfinished manuscripts and notes. True to her word, Barb had spent the days since his death going over his papers, determining which were unfinished manuscripts or notes and which were not. She had not found any notes at all on Liberty's Torch or a modern-day Hale novel about a militia group.

Barb Maxwell could hear the Captain's disappointment over the phone and wished she could do something to help.

"Maybe we're not looking in the right places," she suggested. "After all, Colin flew to New York under an assumed name. He even called you using it. Maybe he suspected these people were on to him. Maybe he hid his notes somewhere."

The Captain admired Barbara Maxwell's determination. Despite her grief, she was thinking clearly, putting together everything her years of marriage with Colin had taught her about her husband, adding up the pieces, figuring out what he had done.

Barb considered and discarded several possibilities. Colin would not have left any notes with a friend, for fear of putting that friend in danger. And, for the same reason, he wouldn't have hidden them in their house. Then she remembered, shortly before he died, Colin had gone to their safety deposit box. And, thinking back, she also remembered that she couldn't think of any reason for him to have done so. They hadn't received any important papers, no stock certificates or bonds or contracts or any of the other papers they usually stored in the bank.

That had to be it, Barb decided, promising she would call the Captain back soon. He tried to urge caution, but the only response to his appeal was a dial tone.

True to her word, Barb called the Captain back an hour later. She had found several floppy disks in the safety deposit box. She had no idea what they were, but she would read them immediately and let him know what was in them.

"Don't," the Captain said.

"What?"

"Barb, if those disks are what I think they are, Colin was murdered because of them. It would be safer for you if you didn't read them."

"But I have a right to know—"

"Yes, you do," the Captain interrupted. "And you will know, I promise. When this is over, I'll give them back to you so that you can do whatever you want with them. But, for now, for Colin, for your son, *please* don't read them."

Barb heard and understood the urgency in the Captain's voice and realized he would not make the request without good reason. She agreed to do as he asked.

At the Captain's urging, Barb e-mailed copies of the files to Cap, and also placed the floppy disks in an envelope and sent them by ordinary mail to Steve Rogers at a post office box he kept up for personal correspondence on those occasions when he didn't wish to use the more conspicuous address of Avengers Mansion.

Finally, he gave her the address of a Stars and Stripes member who lived in a neighboring town. The boy's father was a retired S.H.I.E.L.D. agent, someone the Captain had worked with shortly after his return to action. He knew Barbara and her son would be safe with the man and told her to go to him at once. The Maxwell family would suffer no further harm from the murderous thugs who dared call themselves patriots.

Within the hour, the Captain received the files. As he had hoped, they were indeed Colin Maxwell's notes on Liberty's Torch. He printed the pages out anxiously. Even though the Avengers' printer could process ten pages per minute, it was too slow for him. He grabbed each page as it emerged, reading faster than the printer could keep pace.

When he finished reading the notes—the biographical data on founder Taylor Douglas, the interviews with Paul Storrie, the articles and accounts Colin had accumulated on militias in general and Liberty's Torch in particular, the Captain was left with the same overriding feeling that had brought Maxwell to New York. Liberty's Torch was planning something big.

Colin had predicted the flurry of Liberty's Torch activity, predicted the beatings and bombings and robberies and burglaries against the welfare agencies and the foreign-born. Although many of these crimes would appear to be random acts of violence against "targets of opportunity," the author was convinced that they were really blinds.

These "random" acts, he wrote, were designed to draw attention away from the robberies and burglaries by making them appear to be nothing more than a part of a wave of hate crimes. The robberies and burglaries, on the other hand, would be carefully planned against specific targets chosen to help raise money to finance the larger operation Liberty's Torch had planned.

Colin had gotten into the minds of the Liberty Torch members as skillfully as if they were characters he'd created for a novel. Every item and prediction he made in his notes was coming true with alarming accuracy. The Captain e-mailed Colin's files to Agents Mack and Hattori and to Briscoe and Logan for whatever assistance the information might offer their investigations. Then he called the Falcon. It was time for a strategy conference.

"Bottom line? We let the wave continue."

The statement might have been an oversimplification, but it summed up the course of action Captain America and the Falcon had reluctantly chosen to follow. They could not predict where or when the next random act of terrorism would come, but the robberies that the violence was meant to cover were another matter.

The robbery targets had two key factors in common: they had to involve large amounts of cash or jewelry that could be added to the war chest Liberty's Torch needed to finance its ultimate objective, and they had to be associated with victims who fit the group's profile. The most likely targets were certain social programs and foreign-owned businesses.

Realizing this did little to narrow down the list of possible targets. In a city like New York—with its large population of immigrants and the socially disadvantaged—the phone books were filled with potential targets for Liberty's Torch. Trying to pick the right target from the myriad possibilities would be as futile as trying to predict the Torch's random targets.

The Falcon suggested they divide their efforts. Both in his costumed identity and as Sam Wilson, he had contacts in the poorer neighborhoods, the frequent targets of these attacks. Meanwhile, Captain America could pore over the data the Stars and Stripes had collated for whatever leads it might offer.

Hours later, they reunited in the shadows of a free clinic in the Bronx. The Falcon had sought out every snitch he had, every contact he made as a super hero or from the time he spent as a gangster in his youth. He talked to them all, asking what they had heard or seen. He didn't make requests for specific information. He wanted to learn as much of what was being talked about on the streets as he could, without limiting it by having his sources disregard anything not fitting neatly into the hate-crime pattern. As he collected the information, he noted several possible targets. But one item in particular seized his interest.

Two men, strangers, had been seen hanging around a free clinic on Westchester Avenue in the South Bronx. The clinic cared for a variety of patients from expectant mothers to recovering addicts. There were often strangers loitering outside it, people working up the nerve to ask for treatment or waiting while a friend was being treated. *These* strangers, however, didn't look like the type who would be going to the clinic for treatment. They were older than the usual clientele and looked to be in good health. The scuttlebutt was that one of the men was somebody's father, a father who suspected that his son or daughter was in trouble and going to go to the clinic for help. The word spreading on the street was that anyone thinking of going to the clinic should be careful, because their father might be waiting for them there.

The Falcon suspected the men had another agenda. The clinic had large supplies of methodone on hand, which could easily be sold to raise money.

It was a perfect target for Liberty's Torch.

Captain America had reached a similar conclusion from his own investigation. Stars and Stripes members had forwarded transcripts of police radio calls overheard on their scanners. He had noticed several calls directing patrol cars to look for two men loitering in front of the same free clinic, noting with extreme interest that, each time a patrol car responded to the calls, they found no trace of the strangers.

The men casing the clinic were careful. Whenever they thought they may have been spotted, they left the area before the police could arrive. But, even without seeing the men, it wasn't difficult for the Captain to assess their intent. A free clinic that supplied medical help to the poor and downtrodden and kept easily marketable drugs on hand fit both aspects of the target profile he and Sam had developed from Colin's notes.

The Captain made a call to Detective Briscoe, who reported the Avenger's suspicions to the city's hate-crimes unit. Briscoe also passed along the request that the Captain and the Falcon be allowed to stake out the clinic that night sans a police presence that might deter their prey. The commander of the hard-pressed and understaffed unit readily agreed.

The two heroes were prepared to spend as many nights inside the clinic as necessary, but they caught a break: Liberty's Torch struck the first evening.

The Captain was aware of them first, though not by much. Decades of preparation, of living for exactly this sort of mission, had given him an almost preternatural ability to sense the moment *before* something happened. Even before he saw the flashlights and heard the locks on the doors being jimmied, he sensed the approach of their prey.

As the door opened slowly, Captain America studied the four men entering the clinic. They were all of similar age and type, mid-twenties to early thirties, and built for speed and muscle. They each wore a black T-shirt and army fatigues. Each of them held a large, nine-millimeter, semi-automatic pistol, and, from the steady, practiced manner in which they held them, each of them also knew how to use his weapon. There would be no second chances with this quartet of seasoned killers.

The Captain motioned to catch the Falcon's eye, nodding almost imperceptibly. No speech was necessary for them to communicate, the result of countless training sessions.

Beneath his mask, the Falcon wrinkled his brow tightly, the "on" switch he'd developed for a different sort of communication. He closed his eyes for a second and then something large flew into the free clinic from an unseen perch above.

"What the hell?" one of the men shrieked as Redwing darted in front of the man's face, his claws momentarily gleaming in the beam of a flashlight.

"It's some kind of bird!"

"Shoot the thing!"

The men raised their guns to shoot the bird, only to discover that they no longer *had* their guns. As they raised their arms to fire, something large had cut through the air and knocked the guns from their hands. The men turned to follow the path of the object. Their eyes widened and their stomachs rose in their throats as they saw Captain America effortlessly catch his famous red-white-and-blue shield.

Standing next to the Captain was the Falcon, his clenched fists poised like jackhammers and his crimson eyes burning through his mask. For the thugs of Liberty's Torch, their worst nightmare was complete.

The Captain spoke in a tone like bottled thunder. "Gentlemen, office hours are over."

The four members of Liberty's Torch looked at their guns lying in fragments on the floor, looked at the two costumed heroes, then looked at the door. But before any of them could even think of moving, Captain America and the Falcon were on them.

The fight, what there was of it, didn't last very long. The Captain leapt into the air, performing a perfect forward flip and landing in the middle of the four men. As he expected, they ran in different directions, two of them toward the waiting Falcon.

The Captain swept his legs out to trip one of the men, throwing his shield into the ankles of another. As the men went down, he glanced out of the corner of his eye and saw the Falcon moving in front of the third man.

The Captain lifted up the first man and delivered him into unconsciousness with an uppercut. The Falcon used a right cross to put down his man just as quickly.

Cap's second man scrambled to his feet, moving toward the door. Cap vaulted over the fleeing man's back, landing in front of him. The man stopped in his tracks.

The Captain and his quarry didn't move as the Falcon finished off the fourth Torch member with a rapid punch to the stomach and a left uppercut. The man hit the floor with a slap.

"Falcon?" the Captain asked, pointing to the only member of Liberty's Torch still standing.

"I've had my two, Cap. He's all yours."

A quick jab to the militiaman's chin sent him down in a heap. And, although the Captain was a firm believer in not letting one's emotions distract one from the job at hand, he had to admit that *this* punch had been uncommonly satisfying.

The battle was over in less than five minutes and—save for some sore jaws, all belonging to the Liberty's Torch members—no one had been seriously injured. More importantly, nothing in the free clinic had been disturbed. Come morning, it would open as per usual and again begin to care for its patients.

"Unfortunately, our perps have lawyered up, but good."

Briscoe was standing outside the observation room belaboring the obvious to his partner Logan, the Captain, the Falcon, and the just-arrived Mack and Hattori. Inside the room, where he had been sitting since his arrest at the free clinic, was one of the Torch members. The other militiamen were in separate holding cells. It had been a most frustrating five hours since the heroes had called for a wagon to pick up their catches.

"All four of them have been vigorously exercising their Constitutional rights. I'm starting to think 'right to counsel' is their personal mantra or something. We have, likewise, exercised all the various legal techniques at *our* disposal to convince them that cooperating with us would be in their best interests, but no soap. They ain't talking."

The Falcon turned to Detective Logan, who nodded in agreement. "We won't get anything out of them. They haven't accepted public defenders or asked to call their own attorneys. I don't believe they plan on doing so any time soon."

Captain America looked through the one-way glass into the interrogation room, where the Liberty's Torch member pulled idly on the handcuffs locking him to the table.

"They think it's a war," he said, "and that they're soldiers. We won't get anything more than their names, ranks, and serial numbers out of them. If that much."

"We can't offer a whole lot more," said Mack. "We ran their prints and did come up with a couple matches. But it's all small-time stuff, nothing to connect them with the militia. We can track their backgrounds and movements, try to find a link, but it *will* take time."

A grim Captain America stared through the observation window, wondering how many innocents had already died at the hands of the prisoner within and how many more would die at the hands of his fellows in the days to follow.

"Time," he said, and every man outside the observation room knew exactly what that one word meant.

8

TARGET: CAPTAIN AMERICA

Two hundred miles north of New York City, the immense house of Taylor Douglas sat high on a hill overlooking the eastern shore of Lake George. For sheer size alone, the house would have stood out even among the mansions of Beverly Hills. It was much more out of place here, where people usually came to get away from their own large homes and other so-called burdens of being rich and famous.

Nestled in these centuries-old, virgin forests on the eastern edge of the Adirondack Mountains, Lake George was a vacation mecca of upper New York State. People built small summer homes here, tucked away cozily in the trees, but close enough to the lake's thirty-two-mile shoreline to allow them access to the amenities it offered. They came here on the weekends or stayed a few weeks, the luckier ones managing a month. In the summer, they had their choice of the crystal blue waters or the golf courses and amusement parks that had followed them here. In the winter, the ski slopes beckoned to them. Whatever their specific agenda, they always came to play.

Not Taylor Douglas.

Douglas had come here to escape that which he despised with all his heart and soul: New York City. Once his home, the place was now overrun with the poor, the homeless, the welfare supplicants—the people those less honest than he called *the needy* but he recognized for what they truly were.

How he hated those importuning slackers who had, by sheer persistence, managed to foster in other people—people who actually worked to build decent lives—a misguided sense of guilt and then used that guilt to grab the fruits of those labors for themselves. Indolence, laziness, and grasping was their lifestyle, take and take and take and never give anything back to those from whom they took. And whenever the taking slowed or threatened to stop, they moved on to extortion—increased crime and violence, perhaps a riot— until the fools restored the largess to its former levels.

It sickened Douglas to watch it happen, to watch the enabling imbeciles encourage more taking, more giveaways, in an ever-increasing cycle toward certain destruction. Eventually, there would not be enough left to meet the demands of those slothful parasites. The so-called ''have-nots'' would again resort to their usual violence to extort what they wanted from the ''haves.'' But, someday soon, he felt sure, there would not be enough left to satisfy their demands and the violence would not stop. Eventually, all the cities would burn—and he had no desire to be there when they did.

He had moved out of New York years before, buying dozens of acres near and around Lake George. He built an estate where he and his family could be protected from the inevitable collapse of the cities. When the violence came, they would be so far away that it would never reach them.

The mansion he built had every appointment to make him and his family comfortable. It drew swift criticism, and even outrage, from the vacationers and the few year-round inhabitants. The monstrous size of ''the Douglas fortress,'' as they called it, did not fit into this prosperous-yet-restrained community. But ultimately, nothing could or would be done to deny Taylor Douglas his desire. And what he desired was no less than his own kingdom.

At first it was just Douglas, his family, his servants, and their families. His sons he sent to the finest boarding schools in New England—for his staff's family, he built a one-room schoolhouse. For a time, he was content in being the country lord from whom all good things flowed. But, then, he would look toward the south, remember the foul cancer that lay festering and multiplying there, and know he could not remain content.

Douglas abandoned his business concerns to underlings, using his wealth to build and finance Liberty's Torch. He invited others to live on his estate, like-minded patriots who came to live in the wilderness and train for the battles to come.

From his private study on the top floor of the house, Douglas could see Fort Ticonderoga. In 1775, the former

British enclave on nearby Lake Champlain had been captured by Ethan Allen and the Green Mountain boys. That had been one of the earliest battles in the Revolutionary War and Douglas considered it a fitting symbol of the new war of independence he and his fellow patriots would fight to free themselves from a government that had become every bit as tyrannical as the British government under King George III.

After Douglas's wife left him, he dismissed all his servants, replacing them with members of Liberty's Torch. In other wars, the generals had those who served them behind the battlefield, and he would be no different. Traditional servants were a luxury; he needed to conserve his vast resources for the coming war.

Still, he kept the Lake George house and all the land he owned around it. Over the years, as more and more branches of Liberty's Torch were commissioned and the organization spread through the country, Douglas knew his activities would attract the attention of the tyrants in Washington. Liberty's Torch would need to hide and there could be no better place than in plain sight.

The house, highly visible and notorious, was a perfect decoy. Douglas announced to those few members of the press who considered him, in those earliest days of the Torch, to be newsworthy, that he was building a major addition to his property. On the far end of the mansion grounds, he would raise a building to hold his growing collection of Revolutionary War memorabilia and he would open this museum to the public.

Over the following months, construction vehicles came and went from Douglas's property. The men of Liberty's Torch were building a fine museum. But, at the same time, through dummy corporations and fictitious identities, Douglas purchased additional land near his home, amassing several hundred acres of undeveloped woodland. He built on this land too, secretly diverting excess materials, equipment, and labor from the museum. As the museum was going up, the secret Torch headquarters was going down, constructed in vast bunkers deep within the land.

When the museum was finished, so was the new headquarters, unseen and unsuspected. It was powered by a hydroelectric plant that tapped into a waterfall on land Douglas had chosen carefully for just that purpose. And, while not as large as the Pentagon, the bunkers would serve him well.

His mansion would draw the scrutiny of the government. Washington would watch it, monitor it. He would allow them this invasion of his privacy. After all, they would never see anything more than weekend warriors playing soldier.

The real work of Liberty's Torch would never come near the house. From deep in the underground bunkers, Douglas and his loyal followers could meet in secret and create, in their own image, the future of the United States of America.

Douglas was not in the bunkers when he first learned what had happened at the clinic in the Bronx. For his house to serve as the misdirection he intended, he had to live and spend much of his time there. That was what he told his followers and, for the most part, it was the truth. What he didn't say was that he *liked* living in the mansion. It was large and luxurious, the result of his years of hard work. All the comforts of home—every one imaginable, several most people couldn't begin to imagine—were there for him. The bunkers were, of necessity, far more spartan. The simple truth was he enjoyed being pampered in the elegance of his own home.

He woke up that morning, as he did most mornings, in the four-poster, Louis XIV bed of his master bedroom suite. As ever, the elegance of the satin sheets and silk pajamas afforded him a most restful night. He may have demanded military precision in his daily routine, but there was no reason it couldn't be combined with simple comfort.

He rose from bed and studied the matinee-idol image reflected in the large mirror with its ornately scalloped frame that hung over the equally ornate dresser against the far wall.

It was not vanity, but a reaffirmation. He knew a leader of men had to look the part—even the most eloquent of trolls would have difficulty attracting people to a cause—so he worked to make sure he looked the part. Even at fifty-five, his hair was still thick and full and blond, no graying, no thinning, a mere trace of receding hairline. His thin moustache was perfectly trimmed. His frame, honed and shaped by his daily exercise routine, was thin and muscular. He would accept no less of himself.

His ex-wife had not been as disciplined. She had hated it in the house, whining that there was nothing to do up here "in the middle of nowhere." And, then, as if to prove the veracity of her complaints, she allowed herself to go to seed. Joyce Douglas knew neither sufficient exercise nor restraint, adding ten pounds to her weight in the first two years they lived at the mansion. By the end of the third year, it was apparent to Taylor that she would never regain the trim shape he'd so admired during her modeling days. When she left him, he let her go without a fight, even allowed her to think it was her own idea to file for the divorce. He'd already made quite certain her attorney wouldn't press for an unreasonable settlement. She'd served her purpose and he was more than happy to see her go until such time, if ever, as he might want her back.

He walked barefoot across the carpet so warm and plush that he never wore slippers, not even in winter, and moved toward his bathroom. As he did, he was surprised by a knock on the door.

His hand-picked staff knew his regimen, knew he awoke every morning at precisely 0530 without need of an alarm clock, so they knew he would be awake. But they also knew he preferred not to be disturbed until he'd finished his morning exercises—unless, of course, it was an emergency. Sighing wearily, he put on the monogrammed bathrobe his sons had given him on their last Christmas together, then opened the door.

"Yes, Sergeant?" he said to the uniformed man knocking

on his door and let more than a slight trace of his exasperation slip into his voice. He expected to see a sheepish expression on the man's face and hoped it would grow even more so, as the annoyance in his voice sank in. Instead, it was Douglas who grew annoyed, for chagrin was definitely not in the man's demeanor as he snapped to attention, saluted sharply, and said, "Sir, I regret to inform you that last night's mission was a failure."

"Failure?"

"Yes, sir. Captain America and the Falcon intervened in the operation, sir."

"And the men?"

"Captured, sir."

Douglas took a slow breath in through his nose, then exhaled it even more slowly through his mouth. He never took his eyes from the sergeant who, true to his training, remained at attention, awaiting orders from his commander. For a few moments, Douglas was silent, considering what those orders should be. Then, he spoke.

"Send my plane to New York. I want our lawyers apprised of the situation and bail obtained for our men as soon as the courts open. The men are to be brought back here— discreetly—to be debriefed. Tell the plane not to wait. I want the pilot to bring me all of the morning editions: the *Times*, the *Bugle*, and the *Globe*. After that, he will refuel and return to Manhattan for our men. Tell my chef I will have breakfast early this morning. Then, inform Colonel Paris that he will be joining me for breakfast at 0800 hours."

"Yes, sir."

"That will be all, Sergeant."

"Yes, sir."

Douglas returned to his room and shut the door behind him. So *they* had finally become involved, those interfering, super-powered meddlers. He knew it was inevitable and now had to determine how best to proceed.

He couldn't concentrate fresh from his bed, still rubbing the crumbs of sleep from around his eyes and shaking the cobwebs from his mind. He needed to get his blood pumping and his heart racing, even faster than usual. His typical morning exercise regimen lasted anywhere from two to three and one-half hours, sometimes even four. He didn't set a limit. He simply exercised until he felt he had done enough.

This morning, he would cut his regimen short. Two hours was all he could spare.

Douglas was not late for breakfast. The Torch leader ran the full gauntlet of the obstacle course several times, until his pulse raced within him so hard and so fast that he could feel it moving through his neck without placing his finger against his artery. He ran home and continued to jog in place as he stripped, not stopping until the cold, pulsating jets of the massaging shower head pounded at his muscles. He shaved, dressed in a dark gray, pinstripe suit, and then walked down to breakfast.

Colonel Norman Paris was waiting for him in the cherry-paneled dining room, seated at one end of the twenty-foot-long, solid mahogany dining table. The moment Douglas entered the room, the colonel stood and came to attention.

"Sir! As I assume the general has been informed, last night's *soirée* in the South Bronx got fouled up worse than a plugged sewage pipe."

"Not now, Colonel," Douglas said and shook his head, as much because Paris was allowing himself to become crude as because his officer had breached established etiquette. Paris's manner of speaking was effective in the proper circumstances, but he found it coarse and uncouth. How ironic that this man had proven invaluable as Douglas's second-in-command. Still, Douglas wished he could imbue *some* refinement in the man.

"There will be time enough for that later. We're not quite at war yet. We *can* observe some of the amenities of life before we get down to business. In this case, breakfast. Your preference, I recall, is onions, cheese, bacon, and tabasco sauce."

The commander and his second sat down as two orderlies brought in omelets perfectly crafted to be light and fluffy, two glasses of freshly squeezed orange juice, and two cups of coffee; black for Douglas, cream and three sugars for Paris. They ate in silence. Then, after they finished, Douglas read about the failed mission in the newspapers flown in just minutes earlier.

One by one, he read the accounts. Outwardly, his expression was stoic and focused. He didn't even raise his head when Paris left the dining room for a few moments to take a call. But internally, Douglas seethed at the front page of the *Daily Globe*. Above a gaudy photo of Captain America and his mongrel sidekick was a sensationalistic rhyming headline: CAP TRAPS MILITIA RATS.

Each account made him more angry than the one before; not only because his plans had been denied additional funding but also—and this was even more infuriating—because each account made it appear that Captain America and the Falcon had not had much difficulty in defeating his soldiers.

Douglas put down the papers, wiped the newsprint off his hands with a steaming towel, and looked across the table at the returned Paris. "This is most distressing."

"Distressing? That flag-desecrating traitor and his lackey take down our troops and all you have to say is that it's 'distressing'? I'll give you 'distressing.' I just got off the horn with our overpriced shyster and guess who didn't earn his big fat paycheck? The FBI and the Avengers ganged up on the judge, convinced him our guys represented a threat to national security. They're being held without bail."

"Our contacts in the police department?"

"They can't do diddly, not without attracting attention and blowing their covers all to hell."

"I thought as much. We've been noticed sooner than I'd hoped. We'll have to move up the timetable on our plans."

"You really think we're ready for that?"

"Ready, Colonel? The American people have been ready to take their government back from our so-called 'elected' officials since their predecessors first sold us out to the enemy in Yalta. It was simply a matter of waiting until the time was ripe. It is time, my friend, to pluck the fruits of our patience. We need a dramatic offensive, a strike that will alert the true Americans to the enemies within our own borders. However, we will need a few days' preparation before we can launch it, and we must keep the government's jackbooted minions unaware of our plans.''

''We're gonna need a diversion,'' the colonel said.

''Precisely, Colonel,'' said Douglas, gratified that Paris saw his train of thought. ''But what shall we give them?''

The Supreme Commander of Liberty's Torch reached down for one of the previously discarded newspaper. He held up the paper so the front page of the *Globe*, with its photo of Captain America and its scurrilous headline, faced Paris.

''First, we make them sweat a bit. Call all the branches and instruct them to delay all planned activities. Nothing more should happen until I give the order. Then, after we've had them waiting a bit, we'll act. We shall, with one bold strike, give the federal government their diversion *and* neutralize the threat of Captain America. When next we strike, Colonel, it shall be at the very symbol of the betrayers.

''Our target will be Captain America.''

9

ATTACK

teve Rogers stared at the Statue of Liberty as it grew large before him. Standing on the bow of the ferry, almost at attention, he barely noticed as the cold came off the water and beat against him. He couldn't take his eyes off the Lady, not even to pull his coat closed.

Although it was early summer, a strong wind from the Atlantic passed through the Verrazano Narrows and seemed to key on the ferryboat taking Rogers and others—mostly tourists—from Battery Park to the statue. Around him, those other passengers were scurrying into the ferry's large cabin seeking protection from the chilling gusts that whipped their faces. He remained; he would never turn his back on a lady, especially *this* lady.

That morning, Captain America had decided to visit the Statue of Liberty. If it was whim or need, he didn't know. He dressed in his civilian clothes so as not to attract attention, and rode the subway to Battery Park. He caught the nine A.M. ferry and took up his position at the bow, staring at the statue as the boat carried him to Liberty Island.

Although he had to squint against the bright morning sun, still hanging low in the eastern sky, Steve never took his eyes from the statue during the crossing. At one hundred and fifty-one feet high, standing on a one-hundred-and-fifty-six-foot pedestal, it was the tallest statue of modern times, an 1884 gift from the French government to commemorate the friendship that had formed between the two countries during America's War of Independence. It was magnificent.

Steve remembered the first time he had gone to the statue, one of the few excursions on which his parents had taken him before his father's death. He recalled straining his neck to look up at the copper-green giantess as his father recited from memory the inscription on the monument:

Give me your tired, your poor
Your huddled masses yearning to breathe free,
The wretched refuse of your teeming shore,
Send these, the homeless, tempest-tossed, to me:

I lift my lamp beside the golden door.

He could almost hear his father explaining to him what those words meant, how the United States was a land of opportunity for all people, from all lands, to come and try to build a better life for themselves. He felt again the awe he had felt as he looked at the Lady then and understood, even at a young age, what she stood for. And he remembered feeling proud and grateful that he had been born in such a country.

Though it was half a century later, Steve Rogers still felt that same pride and gratitude as he studied Lady Liberty from the ferry. His gaze traveled up her length, centering on the upraised torch in her right hand. He moved his head a few degrees, positioning the torch directly between himself and the morning sun. Now, as the sun's rays came around it, the torch seemed to burst into flame, blazing brightly as the beacon it was meant to be. The invitation. The symbol.

This grand lady standing watch over a nation's heart and soul, this was the *true* torch of liberty. Not the hate-filled terrorists who had taken the name for their own twisted ends.

When he got off the boat, Steve walked to the western end of Liberty Island. The Lady's reflection fell onto the water, stretching back toward Manhattan as if she were protecting it.

He followed the reflection until his gaze fell upon the city he loved as much as he loved his lady. It was far from perfect, but to his mind, there was no better city. He looked at the glass and steel and stone towers that shone and sparkled in the morning sun and he was renewed. He looked back at the statue, craning his neck so he could see all of her from where he stood at her base, and, if only for a moment, he was a boy again. But it was the man who found himself, in a voice low and determined, making a solemn promise to Lady Liberty.

"I will find them. I will bring them to justice. I will see them pay in full measure for the dream they have disgraced and the innocents they have harmed."

As he finished speaking, an errant gust of wind brushed his cheek like a kiss. It reminded him of his mother.

With the Captain's eyes, Steve looked across at the city. Things had been quiet there. For more than a day, nothing had happened: no beatings, robberies, or break-ins, no sign of Liberty's Torch at all. Not in New York, Chicago, San Francisco, San Antonio, nor any other city that had suffered one of the militia's vile attacks.

Although there was some solace to be taken from the surprising cease-fire, the Captain found the lull disquieting. He wasn't naïve enough to believe that capturing four of its foot soldiers had scared the Torch into abandoning its grand design, whatever that design might be. At best, it was regrouping; at worst . . . the worst wasn't something he wanted to think about. His instincts, honed in a thousand battles on the home front, across the seas, and even in distant galaxies, made him certain this calm would be followed by a storm of hurricane proportions.

Unless he could do something about it.

Taylor Douglas sat behind the massive desk in his study and looked out the large arched windows to the north. The second-story windows of the hilltop mansion were high enough that, on a clear day like today, he could see across the upper tip of Lake George all the way to Fort Ticonderoga. Indeed, he had chosen this room as his study precisely for that view.

The taking of Ticonderoga in May of 1775 was perhaps the first decisive victory the colonists had against the British, and it became a symbol that they could defeat what was, at the time, the most powerful army in the world. Now the fort, despite its conversion to a tourist attraction for the diversion of the mindless masses who failed to see the treacheries heaped upon them by the federal government, was the same to Douglas: a symbol of what was to come. Just as an unorganized and untrained army of ragtag settlers had, against all odds, won their freedom from the government that oppressed them in 1776, so too would he and his followers win their freedom from their oppressors, however strong those oppressors might seem. He would win, because right was on his side.

Douglas's study was dark—he had left the lights off so that he could see the fort better. He sat there, staring at the honored stones and thinking.

A small part of his Revolutionary War memorabilia collection was displayed around the study. Nearly one-third of the war's battles had been fought in New York State, and Douglas had made it his goal to collect as much from them as he could.

Busts of the war's heroes looked out from niches built into the study's cherry-wood panelling. Muskets and sabers used in the war hung on the walls. Maps in heavy, protective frames, some of them the actual ones used in the war, others painstaking reproductions, also adorned the walls. And, in a far corner of the room, a diorama re-created what Douglas considered the war's turning point, the battle of Saratoga.

Douglas's most prized possession hung next to the large arched window: the flag that had been carried into the battle at White Plains by George Washington's army.

"What do you think of it?" Douglas had asked Norman Paris, when he first showed the flag to his second-in-command.

"You want my honest opinion?" Paris had waited until his general had silently nodded his assent and then continued. "You ask me, it's a mite ratty. You should have it restored, like they do with paintings."

Douglas had shaken his head.

"I think not, Colonel. Oh, I agree it is much worse for wear, but that's as it should be. This is a symbol of America, my friend: what it was—proud and strong—and what it has become after the ravages of time and misuse from those who have been entrusted to keep her—ragged and worn. No, this relic of our country's past should stay as it is until we can restore America to *its* previous splendor. And when we have accomplished that, we shall also restore this flag.''

Douglas turned from Fort Ticonderoga and looked down on the waters of Lake George, at the dozens of boats dotting its surface. Rowboats, fishermen, water skiers, scuba divers, and, somewhere among them, the watchers.

He had picked them up two days ago. Three rotating teams of federal agents. Their black cars followed him, going wherever he went but always at a discreet distance. They were so obviously out of place among the fun-seekers in this vacationer's paradise it was almost painful to watch them attempting to blend in with the crowds. And, as the agents watched him, his men watched them, at a far *more* discreet distance and through the crosshairs of their targeting scopes. Just in case.

Douglas wondered if the agents could see him now. Did they have the house under the most basic observation, or were they looking through the windows with their high-powered spy equipment to discover what went on within? It hardly mattered one way or the other; there were no windows in the bathroom.

Once he shut the door behind him, Douglas felt secure. Even if his watchers were using highly sensitive parabolic microphones, they would not hear a thing through the heavily soundproofed walls of this chamber.

Douglas realized that, if they were watching him this closely, they had likely tapped his phones, or, to be more accurate, those phones they knew about. He smiled as he turned on what appeared to be a television, just another of the extravagant luxuries found in homes such as this.

When the screen flared into life, he saw Jerry Springer being knocked to the floor by a Roman Catholic nun. He rolled his eyes in disgust, barely wondering what possible theme the vulgar talk show host could be exploring today.

He pressed a concealed sensor beneath the shelf on which the television sat. Springer's pained expression vanished in a flurry of static, fleeing into the vast broadcast wasteland to be replaced by the solemn face of Norman Paris.

One of the advantages of designing weapons and defense systems for the government, thought Douglas, is that one then knew how they worked and how to get around them. Like all the televisions in his house, this one was connected to a huge satellite dish in the backyard and was capable of picking up over three hundred channels of whatever garbage cluttered the bandwidth. But *this* television also emitted and received a special signal, one piggybacked quite undetectably along the regular signals that travelled in and out of the dish, a signal linked directly to the secret base of Liberty's Torch.

"Sir," Paris said, snapping to attention when he saw Douglas's face on his screen.

"It's time to proceed, Colonel. Are all of the preparations complete?"

"Everything is set, sir. Exactly as you ordered it."

"You look troubled. Is there a problem?"

"Permission to speak freely, sir?"

"Granted."

"Then, begging the general's pardon, is it smart to jack the same clinic where our men were slammed last week?"

"Inordinately so, Colonel. *They* will think that *we* think we are being clever, patting themselves on the back for having figured out our plan and never realizing, until it is far too late, that they have deduced only what we *wished* them to deduce. Instruct our operatives in New York to proceed at 1315 hours tomorrow."

"Yes, sir."

"One more thing, Colonel."

"Sir?"

"Make certain our man in the street keeps to the script. He must be discreet in his indiscretion."

The word spread as intended. Following Douglas's plan, one of the Torch's operatives made an apparent slip of the tongue to a person who could be trusted *not* to keep the "secret." That person told another person, who told another, who also told another. Sometimes money changed hands with the information, sometimes the word was passed for no reason other than the desire of the teller to prove to someone else how in the know he was. Whatever the reason, it was passed from mouth to ear, from person to person, from seedy bar to dimly lit street corner until the word finally reached its ultimate destination: Avengers Mansion.

"You think the info was on the up and up?" the Falcon asked as he and Captain America rushed to their destination.

The Captain ran the tip he and the Falcon had received only minutes earlier through his mind, processing it through his years of experience. One of Sam's contacts had called him at Avengers Mansion with news. The word on the street was that there would be a second raid at the clinic where they had captured the militiamen just days earlier. And the raid was going down in a matter of minutes.

The two heroes had leapt into action. The only way they could reach the clinic in time was for the Falcon to fly and carry the Captain, so they did exactly that, without hesitation.

"We can't be certain," the Captain answered, "but we have to proceed as if it is."

"The *same* clinic? Isn't that awfully . . ."

"Arrogant?" the Captain finished his partner's thought. "Yes. And that's one of the reasons I think the tip is for real. They're assuming we wouldn't suspect them of hitting the same place twice. They're counting on the element of surprise."

"And the other reason?"

"We made them look bad the other night. They figure they can pull this off under our noses and make *us* look bad, get back some of their own. Anyway, we'll know soon enough if this tip was good. And, if it turns out to be bogus, well, at least we got some relatively fresh air checking it out."

The tip *was* good. As Captain America and the Falcon flew over the free clinic on Westchester Avenue, they spotted several armed men running from the building carrying bags and firing their weapons in every direction.

Dropping the Captain onto the fleeing men as if the Avenger were a human bomb, the Falcon's eyes were on the clinic. If they followed their usual M.O., there would be a bomb somewhere inside and he could reach it faster alone.

The Falcon flew into the clinic, looking over his shoulder only briefly to see Cap plowing into the militiamen, a red-white-and-blue whirlwind in a field of military fatigues. He smiled as he saw his partner knock one "patriot" clear over a parked car with a powerful uppercut.

Inside the clinic, the gas cloud that had knocked out everyone there was starting to dissipate. Before entering, the Falcon had sucked in as much of that "relatively fresh air" Cap had mentioned as his lungs could hold. It wasn't hard to find the bomb—they had left it in the lobby, confident no one would regain consciousness before the bomb exploded.

Scooping up the bomb, the Falcon soared from the clinic and up into the air. Below him, he saw Captain America knocking out the last of the militiamen. Four armed men in maybe thirty or forty seconds—that was fast work even for Cap.

The Falcon flew west toward the Harlem River. He heard the screech of tires moving much too fast and turned his head to look back. A car driven by another man, probably the getaway car, was hightailing it out of the area, without any concern for where it was going—and where it was going was toward a group of children playing on the street.

Much as he wanted to, the Falcon couldn't turn around. He had to dispose of the bomb or even more people could be killed in the ensuing explosion. But, even as he raced toward the River, he knew Cap would be moving to intercept the speeding car.

The Captain had heard the screeching tires at the same moment as the Falcon and had instantly realized what was happening. He turned from his defeated foes without a thought, running toward the sound. He saw the getaway car was a convertible with the top down, probably chosen so the men fleeing from the clinic could jump into it quickly. Instantly, he formed a plan.

He jumped on the hood of a parked car and leapt into the air, performing a perfect flip to land in the seat next to the startled driver. Before the driver could recover, the Captain pulled on the steering wheel, directing the vehicle away from the kids and into a lamppost. The car struck the post with enough force to knock out the driver. A second before the impact, the Avenger sprang out of the car, grabbing and swinging around the post to slow his own momentum.

As the Captain landed on the ground, a second car roared down the street bearing directly down on him. He had time only to put his shield between himself and the car. The vibranium-adamantium alloy of the shield absorbed most of the brunt of the car, but the impact still knocked the shield's owner backwards and into a very solid brick wall.

The Captain hit the wall hard, unable to get his shield all the way in front of him. The chain-mail of his tunic cushioned the crash but slightly. He fell to the pavement, dazed and groggy and with a sharp pain in the shoulder where he'd hit.

Before he could recover, the men from the second car were on him. They shot gas into his face, rendering him unconscious in seconds, then dragged him into the waiting car.

A team from a third vehicle—a van—were pulling their fallen and unconscious companions from the street and into the van. They carried out the operation with military precision. Within seconds, both teams were on the move again, with their men safe and Captain America as their prisoner.

As the Falcon flew, he could hear the muffled explosion of the bomb detonating from several feet under the Harlem River. But any satisfaction he might have felt faded quickly as he reached the free clinic to see several militiamen loading the unconscious form of Captain America into a car.

The militia vehicles raced away in opposite directions.

The Falcon immediately started after the one carrying his partner. He would have caught up with them within seconds, if it weren't for the bomb that had been left behind in the getaway car. The bomb detonated with enough explosive force to scatter bits and pieces of the car the length of the block. His eyes were still ringing when he heard the first cries of pain and terror.

For a moment, the Falcon was torn by the choices before him. People had been hurt back there; they needed his help. But if he turned away from his pursuit, those murderous slimewads would get away with Cap.

Swearing under his breath, the Falcon veered back toward the clinic, even as the car carrying the Captain careened out of sight. It was the most difficult thing he had ever done, but the Falcon knew it was what Cap would have wanted.

The street outside the clinic looked like the aftermath of a war. Doctors were tending to those injured by the explosion or gunshots.

As soon as the Falcon made sure no one was at further risk, he activated his Avengers communication card. Cap's own card would be emitting a powerful tracer signal the Falcon could follow anywhere in the tri-state area. Unfortunately, the signal came from inside the clinic. The Falcon cursed; the kidnappers must have known about Cap's card and how it could be used to track the Avenger. They had thrown it into the clinic before fleeing with him.

Undaunted, he flew after the car that had fled with the unconscious Captain America. He found it easily enough— empty and parked on a side street four blocks away. They had switched cars.

The Falcon had no idea what kind of car he was looking for. He flew in widening circles, hoping to catch sight of something. He found the van, also parked and empty. By now, the kidnappers and their prisoner were probably miles away, heading only they knew where.

Realizing it was a lost cause, the Falcon flew back to the

clinic, using his comm card to brief Jarvis, then remained to offer whatever assistance he could and to give his statement to the police. Detectives Briscoe and Logan showed up to tell him that both abandoned cars had been reported stolen earlier that day and couldn't be traced back to the Torch.

There was rage burning deep within the Falcon's soul, but he pushed it down even deeper as he tended to the injured. The finest man he had ever known was in the hands of a vicious enemy and no amount of rage could change that.

But, he knew that capturing Captain America was not at all the same thing as *defeating* Captain America, nor was it the same as beating his partner. The militiamen had won a battle, but the war was just beginning.

10

THIS JUST IN . . .

AMERICA
ON TRIAL

The BOLO went out almost immediately and with almost no hope of success. Police cars across the state, as well as in New Jersey and Connecticut, were told to, "Be on the lookout for . . ."

And that's where the problem lay: be on the lookout for what? The authorities didn't know what kind of car was being used. They didn't know, and in any case thought it unlikely, that the drivers would still be wearing the "uniforms"—black, sleeveless T-shirts and fatigue pants—they wore at the clinic. They simply didn't know who or what they were looking for.

The police believed Captain America was being transported in a panel van or a truck, one where no one could peep through the rear windows and catch a glimpse of an unconscious figure stretched out on the floor and wearing red, white, and blue chain-mail. And, even if the police theory were correct, they couldn't stop and search every panel van and delivery truck in the tri-state area. There weren't enough hours in the day or enough police officers in the entire country to do that.

Moreover, the van theory hinged on the kidnappers still carrying the Captain in a car or van. They could as easily have driven to the Hudson, Harlem, or East River, and transferred the Avenger to a boat. Or, for that matter, gone to some fellow "patriot's" secluded farm and surreptitiously boarded a helicopter or private plane.

The police asked the federal government for information on who Captain America was behind the mask: his name, a photograph, or, at the very least, a description. That way, if the kidnappers removed the Captain's costume while they were transporting him, the police would still be able to recognize him. The request was denied for national security reasons.

Ultimately, all that could be done was to send a bulletin to all contiguous police agencies explaining the situation and urging them to be on the lookout for Captain America. The search went on, but without much hope. No one embraced the chance that they would be lucky enough to stumble upon *the* disabled car or out-of-gas boat or downed airplane that just happened to have a bound-and-gagged Captain America sitting in the back seat.

The search lived up to their lack of expectations.

Taylor Douglas had anticipated the increased surveillance on his house. A figure as important as Captain America wasn't taken without repercussions. Still, without proof, the authorities could do little more than watch him even more closely than they usually did.

Good, he thought, *let them. Their surveillance will "prove" I've done nothing. Nothing out of the ordinary. Nothing that could possibly connect me with this afternoon's unfortunate business in any way.*

That was all well and good for him, but, as Douglas also realized, it would not be enough that *he* do nothing which could attract the watchful eye of the government. *Everyone* in his organization had to do the same.

He went to his bathroom, closing the door behind him. He switched on the television screen com-link. When Colonel Paris's face appeared, Douglas snapped, "Report."

"The target was acquired precisely on schedule, General. We anticipate rapid delivery of the package in three hours."

"No. Speed is not of importance here. If that means it takes them four or five hours, then it will take them four or five hours. We've waited this long to make our first statement, we can afford to wait a bit longer. When the teams arrive, take our guest to the compound's cell block. And, until I say otherwise, make sure he remains *completely* sedated."

"Yes, sir."

"Colonel, I have further and equally crucial orders. For the foreseeable future, we will cease *all* other activities. There are to be no maneuvers, no training, and especially no further raids. Except in the compound itself, no one is to wear their uniform. Only civilian clothes. These orders will remain in effect until I, personally, give the countermanding orders. Any deviation from these orders will be regarded as treason, Colonel. Am I understood?''

"Yes, sir.''

"Leon, you are *not* looking at the big picture.''

Actually, despite what the Falcon had said, Leon *was* looking at the big picture. His eyes were, in fact, open so wide he could see *all* of the big picture. The picture didn't get much bigger than looking at the entirety of Manhattan as seen from two thousand feet up and while hanging upside down by one leg.

"Man, I done told you I don't know nothin'!''

"Bzzt,'' the Falcon said, imitating the sound of a buzzer. "Oh, sorry, Leon. That was the wrong answer.''

The Falcon looked around him at the magnificent spectacle that was Manhattan at night and gestured over it with his left hand, a bit of drama lost on Leon, who was now shutting his eyes as tightly as he could.

"Me, I love it up here at night. Quiet, peaceful, nobody watching us. Wind whipping through my hair. The lights of that big old city twinklin' below us like thousands of stars. I could stay up here all night. But you . . .''

The Falcon looked down at Leon Cooper, a thoroughly frightened little bug of a man. Leon wore a bright green suit which, because he was so skinny, used so little material he should have gotten a discount. Although his right leg was held firmly by the Falcon, his other leg and two arms all flew out at odd angles and looked like the thin, gangly legs of an insect. His hair, normally slicked back with a thick pomade, was, because of the pull of gravity and the wind that cut through it, starting to hang down below him.

"While you're enjoying the view, Leon,'' the Falcon continued, "there are two things you should know. The first of those two things is that I don't believe you. See, one of my homes told me about a deal going down at the free clinic, a deal that was actually a trap to capture Captain America. My homey told me he got it from a guy, who told me he got it from another guy, who got it from another guy, who got it from another guy, who—wait for it—got it from *you*. The way I figure it, the people who set the trap had to be sure Cap would be there when it went down. So they came to you and told you to spread it around so that I would find out about it just *before* it went down. That being a new and, by the way, butt-ugly suit, I figure they paid you pretty well. Don't worry about the pigeons. I'm sure it'll wash out.

"Now *I* want to know who talked to you to get this whole chain of communication going."

"Wha . . . what's the *second* thing?" Leon asked.

"The what?"

"You said that there was *two* things I gotta know. What's the second thing?"

"Oh, *that*? Just that my arm's gettin' tired."

Leon didn't know as much as the Falcon had hoped he might. Two white men paid him to spread the news about the planned raid on the free clinic so, just as the Falcon suspected, it would get back to Captain America. Unfortunately, that was really all the scared little man knew. He didn't know who the men were, had never seen them before, didn't ask their names. The best he was able to do was give their descriptions to a police sketch artist, two more sketches added to the ones Captain America had drawn after the hotel bombing. The sketches were circulated to every police department in the country. It wasn't much to go on, but it was better than they had at the start of the day.

The story was covered in every paper in the country, from the very detached story in the *New York Times* to the lurid one in the *Globe* that appeared under a headline some idiot must have thought was oh-so-clever: CAP-NAP.

The story was picked up by every wire service and was the lead on every news broadcast in the country, both local and national. WNN devoted ten minutes out of every thirty-minute broadcast to the kidnapping.

Across the country, the same question was on everyone's lips: Where was Captain America?

The answer came the next day.

It came by way of a tape—sent not to any of the reputable news programs or networks, but to *Coast to Coast*, a syndicated news program known equally well for its emphasis on scandal and shock and its lack of journalistic standards. A tape first played on that program, but swiftly picked up and replayed on every news program on every channel across the country and around the world. A single audio tape, altered and filtered so the voice of the speaker was unrecognizable and untraceable.

"Fellow citizens of the United States," the voice on the tape said, "for too long, we have been duped by a government that has refused to serve our needs and would force us to serve its needs. For too long, have the poor and the foreign born ruled our nation at the expense of God-fearing, hardworking, honest Americans. For too long have we, the people, been downtrodden, oppressed, and ultimately betrayed by those very officials whose duty it was to protect and nurture our interests. Our government, my fellow Americans, has betrayed us. Has committed treason against us, treason most foul. We know these are most serious charges. Yet, over these next days, we will prove the truth of them to you.

"You have heard of the capture of Captain America. Captain America, the very symbol of the government that has betrayed you and me. The media has called it a kidnapping. It was not. It was a lawful arrest. As the symbol of the government, Captain America is as guilty of that corrupt government's crimes and treason as any of the other functionaries who have committed these acts against the American people. Like the traitors who presently infest Washington, he is a criminal. And, like any criminal, he will come before a jury to account for his crimes.

"We have Captain America, my fellow Americans. And

tomorrow, we shall put him on trial for treason. We will provide tapes of each day's proceedings to this program, so that you can witness the trial for yourself, so that you can see the evidence for yourself. And, most of all, so that you can judge the government's guilt for yourself. The evidence against Captain America is overwhelming. There can be no doubt of his guilt. And, once you have heard it, you, too, shall have no doubts. You will judge Captain America *and* the American government and you will judge them both guilty. Guilty of treason against the people of America. Treason of the worst kind.

"And, in this country, the punishment for treason is death by firing squad."

Taylor Douglas could receive over three hundred channels on the enormous satellite dish behind his house. That night, he taped and watched every news broadcast on every one of the channels that had a news broadcast, no matter how modest.

He taped and watched the shows dedicated to analyzing the day's events. He even taped and watched the late-night talk shows. He found the situation perhaps best summed up in the opening monologue from one of those shows.

"You know this 'Captain America on trial' thing is going to create a whole new area of legal practice. New crimes and new defenses. I mean, it's not like you can use the 'Twinkie defense' when the judge and jury trying you are already a bunch of Twinkies themselves. I mean, Captain America? Captain 'I've Saved The World More Times Than Dennis Rodman Changes His Hair Color' America? I mean, if you've got *that* much of a death wish, you might as well shoot yourself into space and visit Galactus wearing a sign that says, 'Eat me! Eat me!' I mean, why do you think the Red Skull is red? It's 'cause he's *embarrassed* that Cap has kicked his butt every other week for the past fifty years! What next? Are they going to marry O.J. Simpson?"

As the rimshots and raucous laughter following the so-called jokes died down, Douglas smiled. For the most part, it appeared, no one was taking this seriously. Oh, they would, soon enough. After the trial started and America saw the plain, simple, unrefutable proof of Captain America's crimes. Yes, soon America would know.

But, for now, the laughter and the rimshots were exactly how Taylor Douglas wanted it.

11

THE LAW IS A ASS

They drove up Interstate Route 87, the New York State Thruway, called by some the most beautiful drive in the world. They didn't bother looking at the scenery. They had, in the first place, already seen it any number of times, including on the drive down that morning. And, in the second place, they were far more concerned with the figure lying in the back of their van.

"Have you checked him recently?" asked the driver.

"What, you didn't see me go back there?" the passenger said with more than a little exasperation in his voice. "You didn't see me get up out of my seat and walk to the back of the van? You *know* when the last time I checked him was."

"Check him again."

"No."

"I said, check him again."

"Or what? You gonna turn this van around and go home, Daddy? *You* drive, I'll worry about him."

The driver did just that. He drove, looking straight ahead, gripping the steering wheel much too hard. Occasionally, he would remove one of his hands and flex it quickly, spasmodically, to restore the feeling to it. He would then resume his white-knuckle grip until the other hand cramped up and repeat the nervous pantomime.

It was just the two of them in the van, three if you counted their cargo. They had left the others off at a service plaza along the thruway, figuring the police might be looking for a vehicle with several people in it. If they broke up into smaller groups, they wouldn't be noticed.

The others got a nice, pleasant, sit-down breakfast, before they would split up and go to the cars they had parked in the lot on the trip down. He got a large coffee in a styrofoam cup, which he wouldn't—couldn't—drink for fear he might spill it and get them into an accident.

As he had been instructed, he drove in a leisurely manner, the cruise control set at exactly sixty miles per hour—five over the posted speed limit. That way they wouldn't be pulled over for speeding or for going too slowly and impeding traffic. That was important to him, not being pulled over by a state trooper. He didn't think he would be able to explain to Barney Fife, let alone a real police officer, why Captain America lay drugged, manacled, and unconscious in the back of the van.

"How is his breathing?"

The passenger rolled his eyes up, sighed, and turned his head toward their cargo.

"Still heavy."

"You sure he's not comin' out of it?"

"Positive."

"Because we could always give him another dose."

"We don't have to give him another dose. He's had plenty. He'll be out for hours."

"You sure? I don't need even a groggy Captain America comin' after me."

"I'm sure. He don't need another dose."

"Would it hurt to be sure?"

"Look, you wanna kill him with an OD? That would be a real holiday, wouldn't it, if we killed Captain America? Then we'd have both the general *and* the Avengers gunning for us. He's fine. You're fine. We're *all* fine. Just drive."

He drove. He watched each mile marker as it went past, so he would know exactly how much longer the trip would last. Every now and then, he'd sneak a peek into the rearview mirror. It was a paneled van with no rear windows—chosen so no one would be able to see into the van and catch a glimpse of their prisoner—so the mirror didn't offer a view of the outside. But he had repositioned the mirror so he could see Captain America in it. The Captain lay very still in the back of the van, not moving, breathing slowly, barely enough to signify that the Avenger was alive.

He drove. Watching each mile marker, one after another after another after another, occasionally sneaking a peek at the Captain or flexing the cramping fingers on his hands.

"So, have you checked him recently?"

• • •

It was late afternoon when the van arrived at the Liberty's Torch compound. Under the watchful eye of Norman Paris, it pulled into the delivery garage.

Once inside, the driver and his companion tried to drag the unconscious Captain America from the van, with only partial success. There was solid muscle under the Captain's legendary costume and in his present state, that added up to two hundred and forty pounds of dead weight.

"You two girls through dancin' with him?" Paris asked them with a sneer.

"He's heavy, Norm."

"It's *Colonel* now, you numbnuts, and you'd better get used to it. Maybe I should run your butts around the obstacle course a few times to improve your memory." He called to another man. "Johnson!"

"Sir?"

"Get over here and help the Bally's dropouts. I'm gonna be ready for retirement before they get him out."

Johnson and the others lifted Captain America out of the van and placed him in the rear of a golf cart. Then, with the three men running along beside him, Paris drove the cart through a tunnel and down into the underground compound.

Years ago, Paris had gone on a vacation to Disney World with his family, back when he still had a family. Along with riding all the rides, eating the same lousy food in different restaurants, and dropping a month's worth of his salary, they took a backstage tour of the Magic Kingdom.

The tour included a trip along the *Utilidors*, a series of underground tunnels, passageways, and roadways running beneath the park, which employees used to get from one point to another without being seen by the tourists and spoiling the magic. The Liberty's Torch complex was very similar, a weblike network of underground roadways and tunnels that connected the various locales within the compound.

Paris motored along the corridors until he reached the cell blocks, twenty concrete, windowless jail cells in the north wing. When the revolution finally came and the enemies of real Americans were put on trial, the defendants would be housed here first. Some of them would never leave the compound again.

Paris supervised as the three men lifted Captain America off the golf cart and dragged him toward a cell. The enemies of America were still enjoying their undeserved liberty, so all but one of the cells were empty. When the occupant of that cell saw the men drag the Captain past him, he yelled out to them.

"What's going on?" he demanded. "Who are you people? Why am I being held here?" And, then, in disbelief, he added, "Is that Captain America?"

The militiamen dragged the Captain to an empty cell at the other end of the block and, struggling, heaved him onto the cell's cot. Paris entered the cell behind them, verified their prisoner would remain unconscious for quite some time, then went back to his golf cart.

The colonel stopped in front of the shouting man's cell and drew his firearm. The man's eyes went wide and he retreated to his cot. With his free hand, Paris raised a single finger to his lips, and, chuckling, said, "Shhh, he needs his rest."

The Captain's shield was lying in the golf cart. Paris picked it up and placed his left arm through the shield's loops as he got back into the cart.

"The general's gonna love this."

Looking back toward his men, he asked, "Are you coming with me or you fixing to stay here and play with the rats?"

Johnson got into the shotgun seat and the other men sat over the rear tires. They drove from the cell block and up the corridor toward the Central Command area.

When they arrived, Paris called Douglas on the secured satellite carrier line to tell him their package had arrived.

"Was the package damaged in transport, Colonel?"

"Nope. It's pretty sturdy."

"Excellent. Please insure our guest remains asleep for the next several hours. I want to be ready when he wakes up, but I have a few matters to attend to first."

Captain America awoke in the cell to find himself manacled. It wasn't the first time he had found himself in such circumstances, and, he suspected, it wouldn't be the last.

He was without his shield. It had been like a part of him for so long that he was as instantly aware of its absence as if one of his legs was missing.

He felt the pouch sewn into his uniform shorts. His Avengers comm card was also gone. His captors had obviously found it and left it somewhere, likely somewhere very far from this place so it couldn't be used to trace him. No matter. He hadn't expected this to be easy. He never did.

The Captain looked at the manacles. There was a set around his wrists and another around his ankles, three-foot-long chains connected to shackles on each end. They were designed more to hinder one's movement than to immobilize a prisoner completely. He pulled his arms as far apart as they would go, testing the strength of the manacles. He wouldn't be able to break them.

The Captain looked around at the cell. It was a small room, a four-by-six-foot rectangle, solid concrete walls, no windows. To one side, a small metal sink and toilet were attached to one of the walls.

On the back wall was the bed on which he had been lying when he awoke. It was a solid metal frame attached to the wall. It had a thin mattress, a thin sheet, a blanket, and a pillow. Functional but unimaginative. The Captain expected little more from Liberty's Torch.

He walked over to one wall and ran his hand over it. It was poured concrete, which he judged to be at least a foot thick. If he were Thor or the Hulk, or even Spider-Man, he would have been able to break through the wall easily. But, though his strength had been increased by the Super-Solider

Serum that coursed through his veins, such a feat was beyond him.

He turned his attention to the cell door, a simple rectangle of bars attached to hinges. They had not been bolted in after the wall has been set, but inserted into wet concrete which had then hardened over them. No chance there.

The Captain felt the bars. Two-inch thick rods of solid iron. He wouldn't be bending them with his bare hands.

Having satisfied himself as to the strength of his cell, the Captain turned his attention to what he could see of the corridor outside his cell. Its walls were constructed of the same poured concrete as his cell. He could see several similar cells across the corridor from his own, obviously anticipating a time when they would hold many enemies of Liberty's Torch. But, for now, they all appeared to be empty.

The Captain looked and saw there was a video camera on the wall directly across from his cell. The camera was mounted on a swivel, so it could move back and forth to take in the corridor.

By learning against the cell door, the Captain could see down the corridor. He determined that he was at one end of a row of twenty cells. He saw two more video cameras, similar to the one near his cell, mounted on the walls at the far end of the cell block.

Completing his explorations as well as he could from his cell, the Captain returned to the cot. Since he wasn't going anywhere at present, he would conserve his strength until his unseen captors came for him.

It was perhaps twenty minutes later that the Captain heard the echo of footsteps coming down the corridor toward him. He listened to the two men talking as they approached.

"I don't see why we haven't taken his mask off yet," he heard one of them say peevishly.

"General's orders. He says it doesn't matter who's under the mask. What's important is the mask itself and what it stands for."

"Still sounds screwy to me."

"Yeah, well, why don't you let the general hear you say that? Besides, whadda you care? Once this is over, we're gonna ice him anyway. Who cares if we see his face *before* we kill him? He'll still be just as dead."

One of the two men, whom the Captain could now see was dressed in the fatigues and T-shirt uniform of Liberty's Torch, appeared in front of his cell.

"Hey, lookee here, he's awake."

Captain America rose to his feet and walked toward the man. Although the militiaman was tall and probably considered himself to be in top condition, the Captain was taller still and more massive. The man's eyes widened and, even though there were steel bars between them, he took a step back as the Avenger drew closer.

"Who are you? Why have you brought me here?" the Captain demanded, fixing a cold, grim stare on his guard. The militiaman jerked back involuntarily from the forceful power of the words, but recovered quickly.

"That's none'a your business!" The guard straightened his back stiffly to add a fraction of an inch to his height. He motioned for the second guard to join him, then turned back to the Captain.

"You're comin' with us. After all, you gotta meet your lawyer before the trial starts."

Lawyer? Trial? Although the Captain was puzzled, he didn't let it show. Showing confusion empowered one's opponents, and he wouldn't willingly surrender any advantage to this foe.

The second guard stood far away from the cell door. He assumed a practiced two-handed stance—legs set shoulder length apart, knees slightly flexed, his right hand holding onto the gun, his left placed underneath the right to steady the aim—and pointed his pistol directly at the Captain's head. Cap recognized the weapon: a Heckler & Koch P7-M13, a serious nine-millimeter semiautomatic handgun with a thirteen-round capacity, capable of dropping him with any one of those thirteen shots. The man handled himself and his gun in an efficient manner; the Captain had no doubts that the man would be able to fire the weapon with equal efficiency. At this range, the human head was not a particularly small target.

While the second guard aimed his weapon directly at the Captain, the first unlocked the cell door.

"Get out," he said.

Captain America stepped out into the corridor with a grace belying the manacles around his ankles. The gunman moved behind him, still aiming his weapon at the Captain's head. Then, when the gunman had fully repositioned himself, the first guard pushed their prisoner roughly toward the other end of the corridor.

"Get moving!" the man said, his brusque voice revealing a bit more confidence and command than previously.

They walked down the corridor, the first man frequently pushing the Captain forward to establish exactly who was in control here. At the corridor's end, the guard slid open a barred door and they went into an adjoining corridor.

They passed a checkpoint. There were three more militiamen there, two armed, one wiring a console.

"It's gonna start soon," the guard said to them. "You should finish up here and get ready."

The others nodded their acknowledgement.

The Captain was led down the corridor to a small room. The first guard opened the door and shoved the Captain inside. It was a small, windowless room containing only a single table and two chairs, at which sat a man. From the looks of him—five foot eight, skinny, thinning hair pulled back into a ponytail, bushy moustache, and an inexpensive suit that looked as if he'd been sleeping in it for several days—he did not appear to be a member of Liberty's Torch.

The Captain's appraisal was confirmed when the guard said, "Your lawyer. You have fifteen minutes before the proceedings start—and that's more than you deserve."

The steel door of the room slammed shut.

The lawyer rose and stared at the Captain, a look of incredulity on his face.

"Are you *really*—"

"Yes."

The Captain held out his manacled hand and the lawyer shook it, pumping the Captain's arm as if he were trying to draw water from a long-dry well.

"Man, am I glad to see you."

"And you are?" the Captain asked.

"Oh, right" the lawyer blushed. "My name is Marcus Gruenwald, sir. 'Mark' to my friends."

"My friends call me 'Cap,' Mark. Can you fill me in on what's going on here?"

Cap raised his manacles to indicate the chairs. The two men sat at the table across from each other.

"I'm afraid I don't know that much myself. I'm a lawyer in Albany. I run the Legal Aid Society there. We provide free legal services to—"

"To the indigent. Yes, that would be very much in keeping with the Torch's M.O."

"The *who*?"

The Captain quickly explained the who and what of Liberty's Torch. Gruenwald nodded his understanding.

"That explains it," he said, when the Captain had finished. "A couple of days ago, these . . . uh . . . 'gentlemen' broke into my house and kidnapped me. Brought me up here so I could represent someone in a trial."

"A citizen's court," the Captain verified.

"Do you have any idea on what charges I'm supposed to be representing you?"

"My guess would be treason."

Gruenwald looked at Captain America, stunned into silence for a moment. After a beat, the lawyer recovered.

"They're going to kill us, aren't they?"

"I won't let them."

It was a simple declaration, but the Captain said it with all the confidence his years of experience had given him. He looked directly at Gruenwald. He saw the obvious nervousness in the man's eyes, but no fear. He saw a fire, an unshakable spirit that matched his own.

"Are you good?" Captain America asked.

"I think, given the circumstances, I'd better be *very* good. As much as these people will allow, Cap, I'll give you the best defense possible."

Captain America smiled. Gruenwald's voice carried the same fire the Captain had seen in his eyes.

"Then I'm not worried," the Captain said with a confidence that reinforced Gruenwald's own spirit. "Liberty's Torch may not believe in the American system, but *I* do. Justice will prevail in this trial, Mark. We *will* win."

The first thing Captain America noticed upon entering the courtroom was his shield, which hung on the wall directly behind the judge's bench. *I will get you back, old friend*, he thought as his eyes fell upon it.

The Captain looked at the judge, recognizing Taylor Douglas, who sat behind the dais of the bench wearing a judicial robe. A banner displaying the same Liberty's Torch emblem the Captain had seen on their web page hung on the front of the bench.

The Captain quickly looked around, taking in the whole room. It was a large and quite elaborate courtroom: wood paneling and wainscoting on the walls, a wooden judge's bench and jury box with wainscoting in the same pattern as the walls, wooden tables for the prosecution and defense teams, and even a spectator's gallery with several rows of wooden bench seats. With grim humor, the Captain thought that this place would be a fire marshal's nightmare.

This was not some makeshift room hastily cobbled together for the purpose of one trial. It had been built with the intention of using it for many such citizen's courts in the future. The Captain made a silent vow: when his trial was over, this courtroom would never be used again.

The Captain noticed the jury box to the right of the

judge's bench was filled with twelve men, all of them wearing suits instead of their uniforms, but all obviously members of Liberty's Torch. As he looked at the jurors, the Captain realized with a start, that he recognized one of them. The balding man sitting in fifth seat of the front row matched the sketch he had drawn from Ordell's description of the hotel firebombers.

The Captain noted the man's confident bearing as he sat in the jury box, sneering at the Avenger. If it were possible for a man to swagger while sitting, this juror was doing so. The Captain figured him for one of Taylor Douglas's chief aides, quite probably his second-in-command. He assumed the man would serve as foreman of this jury and thus insure a guilty verdict.

The Captain continued to look over the courtroom. Another man sat at the prosecutor's table, glaring as the defendant was led into the room. At the far end of the courtroom and to the left of the bench stood another man who wore what appeared to be a rented security guard uniform and carried a semiautomatic handgun in a holster strapped to his leg. He was this vile court's version of a bailiff.

Next to the bench near the bailiff, a man carrying a portable video camera taped the proceedings. At the back of the courtroom, on either side of the rear doors, two more men in rented uniforms stood. These men carried AK-47s, which the Captain suspected had been modified to be fully automatic.

There were several people in the spectator's gallery. The Captain recognized the man sitting directly behind the defense table as the other firebomber he had sketched. From the man's strategic positioning in the courtroom and the obvious bulge of a shoulder holster under his suit coat, the Captain pegged him as another high-ranking killer in the Torch hierarchy, likely charged with keeping things under control if the Captain tried anything. *Control* doubtless meant shooting the defendant and his lawyer at the first sign of trouble.

All told, there were twenty-three people in the courtroom, not counting him and Gruenwald. The Captain hadn't seen anyone in the corridors as the pair of them were led to the courtroom; perhaps everyone in the compound was here to watch the proceedings. As the Captain and Gruenwald walked down the center aisle to sit at their table, the room came alive with the buzzing of whispered comments, the electrified militiamen voicing their excited approval to each other.

Taylor Douglas glared down at Captain America and banged his gavel to quiet the courtroom. The bailiff stood up and commanded, "All rise," with a booming voice. The Captain almost chuckled as everyone in the room stood; this man was obviously chosen because he had the deepest voice in the compound.

"Hear ye, hear ye, this honorable court is now open pursuant to adjournment. The honorable Taylor Douglas presiding."

Douglas banged his gavel again and said, "Be seated." The scuffle of people sitting down filled the courtroom. "The prisoner will approach the bench."

Captain America stood and walked to a spot directly in front of the bench. "Captain America, the grand jury of this great state has returned an indictment against you and charged you with fifteen counts of treason," Douglas said, picking up a pile of papers and reading from them. "Count one specifies that you, as the duly-sanctioned representative of the federal government, did commit acts of treason against the inalienable rights of all citizens by enacting the so-called 'Brady Bill' in violation of the God-given right to bear arms."

"I object," Gruenwald said bolting out of his chair. "The charge is preposterous. My client did not personally enact the Brady Bill and, even if he had, there is nothing illegal about the legislation."

"Objection overruled," Douglas said.

"Yeah, siddown," one of the jurors said. As Gruenwald

had spoken, this juror had ripped a sheet of paper from the legal pad he kept for notes and balled it up. He stood up and threw the ball at Gruenwald to emphasize his point. Some of the spectators also got to their feet, muttering under their breath insults about lawyers, and making it clear they wouldn't hesitate to use force to insure the trial proceed as they wished.

Without a word, Captain America rose, moving between Gruenwald and the jury box. He stood and looked straight at the juror, his body language making it clear that, manacles or no, he would not tolerate any further abuse of his attorney. The juror sat down meekly. Out of the corner of his eye, the Captain could see the spectators also sit down.

Douglas banged his gavel angrily. "Order. Counsel is instructed not to provoke this court."

"Yeah!" the juror who had stood said, trying to regain what he could of his lost stature.

"Captain America, how do you plead to the charge?"

"As my lawyer said, the charge is nonsense. Obviously, I plead not guilty."

"The defendant's remark will be stricken from the record," Douglas said, facing the cameraman. "Enter a plea of not guilty for the record. In count two, the grand jury has indicted you with treason in that you, as the representative of the federal government . . ."

The arraignment progressed, with each of the fifteen charges of treason being read to the Captain—each for some imagined wrong committed by the government on the people—and the Captain entered his plea of not guilty to each.

When the Captain had entered his pleas to all fifteen counts, Douglas banged his gavel again.

"Be advised, Captain, that this country is at war. It may not realize it, but it *is* at war. And, in times of war, treason is a capital offense."

Douglas looked down at the prosecutor. "Mr. Prosecutor, does the State seek the death penalty in this case?"

"We do, Your Honor."

"Court is adjourned," Douglas said, banging a third and final time. "We will resume proceedings tomorrow morning at precisely 0600 hours."

Douglas watched the Captain and Gruenwald being let out of the courtroom, pleased with how well the day's proceedings had gone. Still, there was considerable work to be done on the tapes before they could be sent to *Coast to Coast*, the syndicated news show he'd chosen to broadcast the trial.

They would need to be compressed into twenty minutes of air time, so the program could show them with the usual commercials. Captain America's inflammatory remarks would have to be edited out. If the camera caught the Liberty's Torch banner that hung from the bench, that would have to be digitally removed. And Douglas's face, as well as the face of every milita member who might appear, would have to be electronically altered, replaced by a digital masking process so that, instead of features, all that showed would be a mottled and unrecognizable pattern of pixels. At the moment, the FBI only suspected, however strongly, the Liberty's Torch members of various crimes; he could not allow their actual faces to be revealed and confirm those suspicions.

At least not yet.

Douglas had deliberately kept the day's proceedings short. His plans required he preside over the trial during the hours of his usual morning exercise regimen. If he disappeared for those same few hours each day, those watching him from the lake wouldn't be unduly suspicious. But, if he were to be noticeably absent from the mansion for longer periods, it might attract undue attention at a time when it would be injurious to his designs.

Beside which, Douglas knew to keep the events brief, so as not to try the patience of viewers with even the shortest of attention spans. One summer, when he was a boy, he had worked in a travelling carnival. The ringmaster had taught him to always leave the rubes wanting more, a skill Douglas had mastered. He needed America's attention, even its outrage, focused on this trial.

He had learned the art of misdirection from another teacher, the carnival's magician. Distract the marks with the left hand and they won't see what's happening in the right hand until the trick is over and done. Give the American people the dramatic spectacle of a trial and they wouldn't consider what else Liberty's Torch was planning until it was far too late.

12

CALL OF THE WILD

Captain America had been missing for two days now, and, though rationally he knew it was not true, the Falcon still felt like it was his fault. If he had stayed with Cap—ordered Redwing to drop the bomb in the river—and stayed with his partner at the free clinic, Cap would now be a free man. Sure, his head told him that was a crock, that he couldn't have let the bomb explode in the clinic, that Redwing wasn't as fast as him and couldn't have gotten the bomb to the river in time, that he couldn't have stayed with Cap; but, in his heart, he felt—

He felt lousy.

No one blamed him for what had happened. No one thought there was anything else he could have done. The unanimity of opinion only made him feel worse.

Captain America—his partner, best friend, and mentor—was the prisoner of those murdering lunatics. Whether it was Sam Wilson's fault or not, it still added up to lousy.

The Falcon didn't think he could feel worse, until *Coast to Coast* aired what was billed as the first in a series of broadcasts covering Captain America's trial. The tape of the arraignment was preceded by a taped speech proclaiming that the citizen's court had chosen *CTC* as the forum for broadcasting their proceedings, because it was the only news program courageous enough to broadcast the real truth.

As the Falcon viewed the tape—watched Cap stand courageously up to his accusers, cowardly concealing their faces behind digital mixing—he could easily discern the actual truth. Liberty's Torch hadn't chosen *CTC* for its courage or journalistic integrity. *Coast to Coast* had been chosen because it was the only show irresponsible enough to broadcast this garbage.

Still, the program wasn't completely lacking in merit. As the Falcon watched, his anger and his determination grew. He would not allow these men to escape the consequences of their vile actions. He would find and free Captain America. And then, he and Cap would show Liberty's Torch why they were called Avengers.

That resolve came, not merely from his friendship with Captain America, but his realization of how much he owed the man. His life had not been the easiest in the past. He could easily have become exactly the type of criminal he and the Captain opposed. That he hadn't was due, in no small measure, to his first chance encounter with Captain America.

At first, Sam had been lucky as a child. Too many kids in the neighborhood did not have a role model while growing up. Sam had his father. The Reverend Paul Wilson was a dedicated and influential minister, striving to end the hopeless despair of his impoverished community. He organized drug and alcohol treatment programs, spearheaded gun buyback drives, taught in Project Head Start, counselled, advised, and, through his words, deeds, and actions, fought against those who would diminish his world.

Despite his youth, Sam tried to be like his father, joining in many of the reverend's community programs. He tried to see the world with his father's eyes. The world, not as it was, but as it could be, would be, should be.

Sam had few friends growing up. His peers were tight-lipped and secretive around him for fear that whatever they said to the son would be repeated to the father. And, in emulating his father, Sam had developed a straightlaced attitude that caused most of his boyhood friends to drift away from him, even as they drifted toward the pseudocamaraderie of the neighborhood gangs.

Sam tried not to care. His father's work was too important. He found other outlets for the companionship he could no longer get from his friends. There was, of course, his family: his father, his mother Darlene, his sister Sarah. They offered unswerving love and support to a boy growing up on unforgiving ghetto streets that swallowed boys whole. And, when the last of his old friends turned away from him, Sam turned to racing pigeons.

It started as a hobby, the reverend insisting that sometimes a fellow had to have some fun. Together, they built a rooftop coop, then scouted the best pigeons in Harlem. The birds thrived under Sam's care. They responded to his love and training—a talent for which he possessed a natural affinity—until both he and they were being noticed and admired in the competitive circuit.

Unfortunately, Sam was also noticed by others. Recognizing the Reverend Wilson as a threat, some of the street gang targeted Sam; attacking the boy to warn off the father who challenged them on their turf. The elder Wilson did not approve of fighting, but neither could he allow his only son to remain helpless before their enemies. That night, the reverend asked Sam to promise him that he would never *start* a fight. The next morning, he enrolled his son in the Golden Gloves program.

It was not an ideal existence, but it was bearable. Until the terrible night when the police came to the Wilson apartment. The officers' words came out haltingly. These were seasoned cops; they had carried such information before. But this was different. This was about someone they had loved, too.

The Reverend Paul Wilson was dead, caught in the crossfire of a gang fight he had tried to defuse.

The next thing Sam knew he was running; moving through the city streets as fast as one of his pigeons could fly, looking for his father. When he finally found the scene of the gang fight, the police had already cordoned off the area and would not let him approach. He could only stand behind the yellow police tape and watch as his father's body, covered from head to foot with a blood-red sheet, was loaded into an ambulance and taken away into the night.

Times got hard for the Wilson family. Their church tried to help, but it had never been a wealthy congregation. What little its members could spare didn't last them long. Sam's mother took odd jobs at first, then found work as a maid in a local hotel. It wasn't much, but it kept a roof over their heads and, most nights, food on the table.

Sam looked for work, but there was none to be found. When his mother took ill and missed a week of work, he sold his pigeons to pay the rent. It was like selling a piece of his father—but he had little choice.

It was almost two years to the day when the police next came to his door. Detectives, this time; he didn't know them and they didn't know him. His mother was on her way home from work when she was pushed into an alley at knifepoint. Maybe she didn't give up her purse fast enough, maybe she resisted—the detectives didn't know for sure—but Darlene Wilson's attacker stabbed her, took the money, and left her dying in the alley. The detectives told Sam they were sorry for the boy's loss and told him where he could claim his mother's body.

Sam and his sister were placed with separate foster families, the county unable to find a single home willing to take them both. Sam's placement was not a happy one. His new "family" wanted him more for the foster-care check than out of any true desire to help him. They got their money and left him alone. He was left to fend for himself. It wasn't very long before he took to the streets, hanging out with gang kids much like the ones who had murdered his father. On one of the rare occasions when he and Sarah saw each other, his sister commented that he had changed. Even then, Sam knew she was right.

Riddled with guilt that he hadn't been able to earn enough to keep his mom safe at home, refusing to acknowledge the loneliness that ate at his soul, unable to deal with his anger and grief, Sam grew increasingly moody and bitter. His father's community service and his mother's self-sacrifice had only resulted in their deaths. The new Sam had finally figured it out: there was only one person worth looking out for and that was Sam Wilson.

Sam ran away when he was fifteen, travelling around the country and perfecting his hard, cynical philosophy. He even left his name behind. Now he was "Snap" Wilson, a self-serving, petty criminal. By the time he hit Los Angeles, he didn't think twice about joining a local racketeer's mob.

Snap started small, running numbers and making money drops. As he proved his worth, he was given bigger, more important jobs. One such assignment was to have taken him to Rio de Janeiro, but he never made it there. His plane crashed, stranding the young man on a small Caribbean island with a large secret.

Sam was not alone on the island. The local natives took him in, eager to have another strong body to help with the fishing that made up their lives, eager because so many of their tribe had been taken. They had been taken to serve the Exiles, German war criminals hiding on the island and exploiting its natives.

A turf war was something Snap could understand. He tried to organize the natives to fight back, but he met with little success. These villagers were fishers, farmers, craftsmen; they had never been warriors.

But Snap would not submit. When the islanders would not join him, he fought for them on his own. He made daring guerrilla raids on the slave compounds, freeing as many as he could and returning them to their people. He scouted the island, finding snares and traps set by the Exiles, and springing them before any could fall prey to them. He hindered the raiding parties so that the villagers would be able to flee rather than be captured. And, as he did, the castaway came to care more about these people than he did himself. The selfless idealism of the father was reborn in the son. He was Sam again.

It was on one of his scouting missions that Sam found a large, red-winged falcon; he adopted the bird and named it Redwing. His natural affinity with birds allowed him to train the falcon and gave him an ally in his fight against the Exiles. He didn't count on fate providing additional allies: one false and one who proved to be the best friend an impromptu freedom fighter could have ever hoped for.

• • •

Thousands of miles away, the Red Skull, the most feared man on the planet since the days of World War II, had acquired the Cosmic Cube. The Cube transformed thought into reality and the Skull gleefully used it against Captain America, switching their bodies so he inhabited the form of his hated enemy and the Captain was trapped in the Skull's body. The seemingly omnipotent villain sent the altered Captain to the island of the Exiles, who hated the Skull, delighting in the irony of them disposing of Captain America for him. When they failed miserably, the Skull took a more direct hand.

The Red Skull knew of Sam Wilson from his surveillance of the island. He used the Cube to probe Sam's background, going back no further than Snap Wilson, for, after all, it was Snap who best suited the Skull's needs. He teleported to the island and began to mold Sam into his secret weapon.

The Skull ordered the Cube to bury Snap Wilson and turn the castaway into someone who would be readily befriended by the likes of Captain America. He believed he'd implanted a new personality into his human weapon, but he was wrong. Sam had himself purged Snap from his soul, replacing his dark grief with an idealism born and nurtured by the memory of his parents. The Skull's supposedly implanted personality was Sam's own.

In probing Sam, the Skull had found a latent mutant ability, a telepathic rapport with birds. Using the Cosmic Cube, the Skull enhanced the ability until Sam could make Redwing obey verbal and mental commands. He wanted to give his pawn a power that would make him worthy of being Captain America's partner. And, having, he thought, created the kind of person who would attract the good Captain's attention, the Skull placed a final order deep within Sam's subconscious, then sent him to the side of the man who was, in reality, Captain America.

Sam leapt to the aid of the man being attacked by the Exiles. Together, they sent the killers running. When the man learned of Sam's futile efforts to organize the villagers into a fighting force, he suggested Sam turn himself into a symbol, someone who would unnerve the Exiles and inspire the natives. With the stranger's help, a costume was made and a hero was born.

The Falcon trained with his new friend, honing his fighting abilities to levels he had never dreamed possible. They easily defeated the Exiles and even fought the Red Skull on his base. It was there Sam learned the true identity of his ally. Now Sam understood how the man had been able to train him so easily and thoroughly, how they had become such an effective team so quickly. Together, they even defeated the Skull.

Captain America and the Falcon remained partners, vanquishing many foes, and always fighting under the credo of King Arthur: might for right. It wasn't until years later that they again faced the Red Skull and learned the true complexity of the Red Skull's plan—when the Skull triggered the secret command he had planted in the Falcon. Partner became pawn as the Falcon struck down Captain America from behind.

The Skull had thought it his most brilliant plan, the creation of the ultimate sleeper agent, a criminal-turned-hero programmed to betray Captain America. He believed it would shatter the accursed Avenger to learn that his friend and partner was no different from those the Captain fought and then to have that partner betray him to his worst enemy.

The Skull was wrong.

Captain America defeated the Skull, then turned his attention to the Falcon. He would not accept Snap as the reality. He had worked too closely with the Falcon, seen too deeply into the man's soul, to believe Sam was nothing more than a façade, a mere patina artificially implanted then sloughed away like an old snake skin. There may have been something of Snap in the Falcon, but there was far more of Sam and *that* man was worth fighting for.

The reclamation of Sam Wilson's soul had begun on that

distant island. It continued with the best counselling the vast resources of the Avengers could provide, as well as the unwavering friendship and support of Captain America. It wasn't easy, but Sam reconciled his two lives. He couldn't change the past, but that didn't mean he had to allow Snap to define his future.

The Falcon owed so very much to Captain America, far more than even the partnership or friendship the Captain had given without hesitation. As far as he was concerned, he owed the man for more than his life: he owed him for his soul. Saving the Captain from the hate-crazed creeps of Liberty's Torch was only a down payment on a debt the Falcon knew he could never fully repay.

The Falcon flew to Avengers Mansion hoping the heroes were back from Olympus and ready to join in the search for their missing comrade. Jarvis gave him the bad news.

"No, Master Falcon, the Avengers have not yet returned from the other realm. Sadly, I have no idea when they might do so. Master Hercules once explained that time works rather differently in whatever dimension Olympus occupies; it's quite a common matter for someone there to lose track of how time is passing on Earth. As I understand it, they could be gone for weeks and believe it to be no more than a few days. However—"

Before Jarvis could continue, the phone rang. "Avengers Mansion," Jarvis said into the receiver, "How may I direct your call? . . . I'm sorry, sir. I'm afraid the Avengers are out of town on business at present. . . . Why, yes, the Falcon is here. . . . At once, sir. I shall put you on the speaker phone."

Jarvis pressed a button and they heard, small and tinny, the voice of Special Agent Mack.

"Falcon? Are you there, Falcon? I really hate these things. It always sounds like I'm talking in a sewer and *that* brings back memories you don't *want* to hear about."

"I'm here, Agent Mack."

"Good. Look, I'm calling with an official communication

from the Bureau. The government strongly requests that the Avengers lay off this whole Captain America thing.''

"Excuse me?''

"Yeah. We've got it completely under control and don't need a bunch of steroid cases in skintight zoot suits flying around queering the deal.''

Zoot suits? the Falcon thought. *Mack can't be that much older than me. It's not the kind of phrase he'd use. Unless...*

"I think I understand, Agent Mack.''

"That's good. The Bureau doesn't have any proof Liberty's Torch is behind any of this and, until we do, we gotta proceed by the book. The last thing we need is for a bunch of you mask-types to go barging in and turning the whole thing into some sort of Spandex version of Waco.''

"Well, it's like Jarvis said, Mack. The Avengers aren't here right now, so you don't have to worry about them.''

"Okay, as long as *you* understand that, if the Avengers do come back, we don't want them heading up there and getting in the way. We're on the same page here, right?''

"I think I can assure you on that score, Mack.''

"Great! I gotta go now, Wilson. People to see, places to go, you know the drill. Man, I really hate talking on these things. Catch you later.''

Mack hung up.

"A most unusual and frustrating conversation,'' Jarvis said. "Do they really expect us to do nothing while those— people have Master Cap?''

"Not exactly. Not if you listened to everything our friend in the Bureau said just now.''

"I'm afraid I don't understand, sir''

"Mack called the Avengers 'steroid cases in skin-tight zoot suits.' Zoot suits date back to when Cap was a boy. When was the last time you heard anyone use that phrase?''

"Now that you mention it, I haven't heard that expression in a good many years.''

"It wasn't Agent Mack's phrase. He was repeating what

someone a lot older had told him. It was his way of telling us he was just following orders and relaying a message. But he also gave us another message. He let it slip that the FBI believes Liberty's Torch has Cap and that the Torch compound is 'up there,' which I figure means the northern part of the state. He told us the Bureau doesn't want a 'whole bunch' of us going up there to find Cap and, that if the Avengers come back, they should stay out of it.''

"I see what you mean, sir. It is certain Agent Mack would be conversant enough of our present roster to know you are no longer an active Avenger and haven't been one for years. When he said the FBI did not wish a group of Avengers, plural, to attempt a rescue, he was hinting that a single individual might escape notice, were that individual to attempt some sort of intercession.''

"That's the way I read it, Jarvis. Mack knows I wouldn't stay out of this. Not only was Cap taken on my watch, but the Torch has been targeting a lot of my people. No, I'm in this one for the long haul.''

"I am delighted to hear you say that, sir. As I was about to say before we were interrupted by the phone, a Lieutenant Vincent Billinghurst of the Twenty-fifth Precinct called earlier today. He said he knew you, and he believes he knows someone who could assist in any rescue effort we might attempt.''

The Falcon had made Billinghurst's acquaintance shortly after the career policeman had transferred to the two-five from Midtown. The transfer had been somewhat forced. Billinghurst had, at his captain's request, involved the powerful alien known as the Silver Surfer in a sting operation the lieutenant had been spearheading to make sure some stolen M-16s never hit the streets and that no one was hurt when the arrests were made. Because the Surfer had no understanding of the American legal system, he chose to accomplish both objectives in the most efficient manner possible: he destroyed all of the weapons with a controlled blast of his Power Cosmic. He didn't know it was as important for the weapons to be recovered and used as evidence as it was that they never hit the streets. Captain Grobé caught major flack from all sides, and the lieutenant inherited the flack from Grobé with interest.

When Billinghurst learned of an opening in the Harlem precinct, he transferred there as quick as he could. It got him out from under the elephantine memory of Grobé and it was even closer to the Bronx apartment where he and his family lived.

Shortly after his transfer, Billinghurst learned the Falcon operated in the precinct. Although he had every reason to be wary of super-powered civilians, the lieutenant went out of his way to work with the Falcon. He understood the value of such a man as both a role model to the community and a friend to the police. He wanted to encourage both.

Billinghurst and the Falcon became good friends. They were even called the African-American Mutt and Jeff by some of the older officers in the two-five—the Falcon being tall and well-muscled, the lieutenant shorter and showing signs of middle-aged bulge around the waist. As they worked together, Sam had come to trust and depend on the policeman's judgment. So, if Vince Billinghurst had a militia expert whom he thought could help the Falcon, then the Falcon most definitely wanted to meet that man.

After doing so, the Falcon found himself questioning Billinghurst's judgment for the first time since he met him. Phillip Barry was not at all what he had expected.

The Falcon had assumed that, if Barry wanted to help against Liberty's Torch, he was probably a fellow liberal, someone who thought the militias represented a real threat to America. In his mind, Sam had pictured a bookish man, pale and thin, who spent much of his time quietly researching the militias and any other related subjects. Barry was none of these things.

As tall as the Falcon and equally physically fit, Barry looked like Grizzly Adams gone yuppie. He was obviously fastidious about his appearance. While he wore outdoorsman clothing, it was the stylish and well-tailored kind to be found at LL Bean. He had a thick head of bright, fiery red hair that showed no sign of thinning, as well as a full beard and moustache.

After Billinghurst introduced them, Barry shook the Falcon's hand and smiled broadly, revealing a mouth of white and perfectly maintained teeth. The man positively beamed, looking for all the world like what Santa Claus must have looked liked before he went prematurely white. Sam wanted to like him, but . . .

Barry was a card-carrying member of the NRA and earned his living from the highly successful gun shop he owned. Barry was a state's rights activist. Barry was a staunch conservative who despised affirmative action and thought the welfare system, while perhaps necessary when it was first created back during the Great Depression, had long outlived its usefulness.

Barry was not, in short, a kindred spirit.

When the Falcon expressed surprise that Barry wanted to help them against Liberty's Torch, the man let loose with a full, rich laugh from deep within him and which roared like the rushing rivers he obviously loved.

"Don't tell me, let me guess," Barry said. " '*You* want to help us? You look like you belong to a militia, not someone who wants to fight one.' Am I right, wings?"

Before the embarrassed Falcon could admit Barry was completely accurate in his assessment, the man added another surprise. "Maybe that's because I do belong to a militia. More than one of them, to be exact."

"*What?*"

"Let's get real. How did you *think* I became such a hotshot expert on the militias? Surfing the web? Not me. I'm more of a hands-on kind of guy. Look, there's nothing wrong with rational militia groups. First of all, there's a little matter of freedom of assembly and of speech. I assume you've heard of them, but let me know if I'm covering new ground for you here. Second, rational militia groups serve a viable purpose. Most of them are really just social clubs, you know, kind of like Augusta, except we play paintball and not golf. And, by pointing out where we think our government is wrong, maybe even abusing its power, we can help keep those abuses in check. But that doesn't mean we think the Social Security system is actually a plot to create a nation-wide identity card system which will allow the government to keep track of us.''

''And what about the irrational groups?'' the Falcon asked.

Barry turned toward Billinghurst and smiled. ''Vince, I like him. He picks up on the subtext.'' Turning back to the Falcon, Barry said, ''The other kind of militia aren't any kin to me and mine. It's not just because they give the rest of us bad names, although they certainly do manage to do that. I can live with a bad name. Hell, I suppose I've done enough things to give myself a bad name all by my lonesome. No, it's because I believe they are every bit as vile as you believe they are. Bigoted, extremist, paranoid, conspiracy-theory mongers who think nothing is out of bounds—not murder, not massacre, not even terrorism—if it allows them to ac-complish their ends. What's not to hate about them? And, of all the bad militias, Liberty's Torch is the worst. So, if you want my help rescuing Captain America or, even better, bringing down the Torch, it's all yours. You need help know-ing how the Torch does things. I figure I can do that and, for extra credit, teach you a few other things about militias.''

This time, it was the Falcon who held out his hand and smiled broadly. ''My friend, you already have.''

Within the hour, they were driving up the New York State Thruway. Barry knew the general vicinity of the Liberty's Torch main compound and suggested they begin their hunt there. It was a pretty good bet that's where they had Captain America. The Falcon agreed. Before they left, Barry loaded his truck with provisions for what could well be several days of camping and searching in the virgin woods upstate.

At first, the Falcon wasn't comfortable with their driving to the area. He had wanted to fly up and start their search at once. Barry convinced him otherwise.

"And how am I supposed to get up there? Does this rig look like it has eight tiny reindeer under the hood? No, better we drive, give me time to fill you in on a few things."

"Fine, start now," the Falcon said. "What did that tape mean? About their trying Cap for treason?"

"Some militia groups think the feds are guilty of all sorts of crimes against the people and personify the government's evils into people. To them, if you work for the feds, you *are* the feds. And Captain America is like waving a red flag in front of them, no pun intended. He personifies everything they hate. Lots of militias also think they have the right to conduct trials under procedures dating back to the start of this country. Y'know, when we still operated under common law."

"Common law?" The Falcon knew the phrase, but wasn't sure how it applied to the period shortly after the Revolutionary War.

"Back then," Barry explained, "except in the big cities, the prosecutors weren't elected, full-time officials. In the more remote areas, private citizens were appointed as prosecutors. The procedures still exist today; that's how we get special prosecutors. A lot of militia groups believe that's the way it should *still* be, so they take it on themselves to bring criminals to trial. They claim they can use the procedures to appoint themselves prosecutors and try individuals for imagined crimes committed by the government. It's called a Citizen's Court. There have been reported cases of militias kidnapping people and subjecting them to these courts."

The Falcon shook his head. It was sheer lunacy, but no less frightening for it. He asked the obvious question. "Do you think they'll really execute Cap?"

"If they find him guilty."

"Is there a chance they'll find him not guilty?"

"No," Barry said grimly, gripping the steering wheel a

little harder as he increased their speed, "not a one."

They drove in silence for several minutes, Barry still looking at the road, while the Falcon moved around on the car seat trying, without little success, to get comfortable. Finally, Barry broke the silence.

"Look, wings, we may not be going up against the costumed super-villains you're used to, but that doesn't mean this will be any kind of easy. Check out that case behind you. You'll find a few things in there."

The Falcon turned around awkwardly and opened the case. He was shocked at the array he saw within.

"Those are guns," he said, both surprised and annoyed.

"You got a great grasp of the obvious, wings. That there's the pick of the litter from my shop. Take your pick. If you're not used to firearms, I recommend the Glock. It has a laser sight in the handle. Just aim and shoot."

"You're kidding, right?"

Barry shook his head. "I can't promise this won't turn into a deadly mission, wings. And, despite what you may have read, guns don't kill people. *I* do."

The Falcon looked at Barry, the color draining from his face. Barry noted the Falcon's anger and discomfort and added, "But only when there's just no other choice."

Barry's grin, confident without being prideful, reminded the Falcon of Captain America's own smile. He wondered if Cap and Barry might not have more in common that either of them realized. He shuddered at the thought.

13

OPENING STATEMENTS

"**A**h . . . gentlemen of the jury."

Hugh Semper's high-pitched voice filled the courtroom. The prosecutor spoke loudly hoping to project it through the courtroom and out the rear doors. It remained a loud squeak.

Although Semper was an associate in a Glens Falls law firm, he was a tax attorney and had never tried a case in a real courtroom in his life. When Taylor Douglas told him what would be expected of him, he had to ask the firm's litigation partner how to speak in a trial and was now doing his best to follow the advice.

He stood straight and puffed out his chest, attempting to look taller than his five-foot-seven frame would permit. He squinted slightly, thinking the touch would give his eyes a more determined, glaring look, and hoping the jurors could see it through the thick lenses of his glasses. He also found himself wishing his hair were any color other than its natural nondescript shade of not-quite-blond-and-not-quite-brown.

"How many of you have lost your job?" he continued.

"Objection," Gruenwald said, virtually leaping to his feet. "The prosecutor is attempting to appeal to the bias of the jury on completely collateral matters."

"Objection overruled. You may proceed, Mr. Prosecutor."

"Yes, ah, I was saying, how many of you have lost your jobs? Lost them because our Ford plant shut down when the Toyotas invaded our country?"

"Objection."

"Overruled."

"Lost it because affirmative action laws required the company employ a less-qualified minority person over you?"

"Objection."

"Overruled."

"Lost it because the usuriously high taxes required to pay for welfare deadbe—"

"Objection."

Semper whirled and stared at Gruenwald angrily. "Would you be so kind as to allow me to finish just one paragraph?"

Douglas banged his gavel. "The objection is overruled. Counsel for the defense is cautioned not to further disrupt these proceedings."

"Thank you, Your Honor," Semper said as he turned back to the jury. He took a deep breath and paused a second moment to regain his composure. "Lost it because the usuriously high taxes required to pay the welfare deadbeats made it economically impossible for your boss to stay in business? Gentlemen, I know most of you, most of you know me. And one thing *all* of us know too well is that the answers to my questions is, too many, far too many of you."

Semper walked up to the jury box and leaned forward, placing his left hand on the rail and sweeping his right hand backward in a gesture that singled out Captain America.

"And it's *his* fault!"

Gruenwald started to rise to object again, but the Captain placed his hand on the lawyer's arm. He turned his head almost imperceptibly toward Gruenwald and said under his breath, so softly that only Gruenwald could hear him, "Let him go."

Gruenwald turned toward his client and whispered, "Let him go? But this isn't a proper opening statement at all."

"I realize that. But, objections won't accomplish anything right now. We have to let it go."

The prosecutor continued. "Oh, he didn't bring the imports to our shores or create the quota system. And, although he was himself a creation of President Roosevelt, he didn't even create the welfare system. All the same, Captain America is still to blame for all those things. You may ask yourselves, how? How is this man responsible for so many crimes against the American people?"

Gruenwald whispered, "This ought to be good," and Captain America smiled in response.

"The defendant—Captain America—is responsible for all these crimes simply by being. Who permitted Toyotas into this country instead of recognizing the danger inherent in allowing foreigners to usurp what had been America's strongest industry? It was the federal government. And when we, the American people, complained, that government responded with absurd lies about reciprocal trade requirements. Fancy words, to be sure, but what they really mean is that the federal government is more concerned about getting along with foreign countries than about protecting the interests of its own people.

"Who established the affirmative action quotas that demanded less-qualified minorities get the education and the jobs that you needed to survive, that you were entitled to? Once again, it was the federal government. And, when we, the people, asked the federal government why it was keeping us from those jobs, why it was making sure they went to those not qualified to do them, the government answered that it was reparation for years of mistreatment. Whose mistreatment? Yours? Did you ever own a slave? Did you ever keep women from getting the vote? Did you exploit migrant workers at starvation wages? Do I even have to ask? The answers are no, no, and again, no! Did these things happen, gentlemen of the jury? Regrettably, they did. But *you* are not to blame for them! *You* should not be punished for them! The *Holy Bible* teaches us that the sins of the father should not be visited on the son. Yet the government chose not to hear the words of God, but to hear instead the whining of those allegedly mistreated people. It chose to punish you and to mistreat you for things you never did."

Semper turned again to face Captain America, anxious to see the worried expression on the Avenger's face as he realized how eloquently the prosecutor had put his case. He found the Captain sitting calmly, looking ahead with no trace of emotion on his face. Thrown by the Captain's stolid, unperturbed manner, Semper had to pull a collection of three-by-five note cards from his pocket and fumble through them to find his place.

"Ah, yes, as I was, ah, saying, gentlemen of the jury,

who created the welfare system that forces the hard-working and honest citizens of this land to pay exorbitant taxes on our wages—taxes that threaten to bankrupt us—to support the moral and economic equivalent of sponges, those who do nothing but suck in whatever they can get without giving anything back in return? Who created a system of so-called entitlements that allow the lazy and unwilling to believe they are entitled to do nothing and get paid for it—paid with your money and mine? It was, again, the federal government. And, when we complained that the government was taking too much, that we couldn't live on what they left us while it assured a high standard of living for every shiftless creature who found his or her way to our country, the federal government *tsked* at us. Actually *tsked* at us as if we were wrong for wanting to keep what we had rightfully earned.

"Gentlemen of the jury, I give to charities. I do my part and I know you do, too. You and I give what we can *afford* to give and we give to the charities we choose to support, not the ones forced on us by the government. How dare the federal government treat me that way? How dare it treat *you* that way?

"How did it happen? How did we, the people, let it happen? How did we let the government become the servant of the foreign and the lazy instead of our servant? Sad to say, it was because we let it happen. We let the government treat us shabbily and we did not complain."

Gruenwald could not believe what he was hearing. The argument was illogical and filled with contradictions. It made no more sense than letters floating in a bowl of alphabet soup. It was the worst opening argument he had ever heard in his sixteen years as an attorney. None of which mattered to its audience.

Gruenwald allowed his eyes to move over the jury, scanning their faces. They were nodding, smiling. Every one of them believed it. To a man, they *believed* this drivel.

Semper's voice grew even squeakier—which Gruenwald

wouldn't have believed possible five minutes earlier—as he continued.

"But, you may ask, why *didn't* we complain?" Semper pounded his fist on the jury box rail and then again swept his right arm back toward the Captain. "Why? Because of this man. Because of the defendant. Look at him, gentlemen. He dares to sit here. Dares to wear our flag. He dares to call himself Captain *America*. And we took him as exactly that. In the great war, he fought our enemies. He fought for us. Never forget that, he fought *for* us. And so we came to believe in him, to believe that he would *always* fight for us. We came to believe that if Captain America said it was all right, then it must be all right. That if Captain America did not fight against it, then it could not be bad. We took him at his word that he would *always* fight for us. But, he stopped, gentlemen of the jury. He stopped fighting for us. He did not oppose the tyranny that took our jobs and sold them to foreigners. He did not oppose the demagogues who said we couldn't be hired, so that the less deserving *could* be hired to right alleged wrongs we never committed. He did not stand against the government-sanctioned thieves who took our money, took the food from our mouths, so that it could be handed to the indolent and the unworthy. Where was Captain America when the federal traitors did this? Where was he when they tried to rob us of our sacred right to bear arms? Or our right to meet together? Or our freedom of speech? Where was this defender, this symbol of America? He was in the pocket of the tyrants, that's where he was. He was bought and paid for by the government that gave him his regal costume and his pretty shield and his mighty powers. He was serving the demagogues who gave him a grand mansion to live in, who gave him his own manservant, who gave him his very identity. That's where Captain America was.

"He was in league with the traitors, gentlemen of the jury. He was doing their bidding and not speaking out against the wrongs they did to us. And because he didn't speak out, because he, the heroic Captain America, didn't fight for us, we thought there was nothing wrong and we did not fight for ourselves. Did not fight for ourselves until it was almost too late. Until the traitors had almost destroyed us.

"Thank God, it's not too late. We can start fighting for ourselves. We can start fighting back against the traitors in the government. And we can start fighting back by telling them we are, at last, fully aware of their deceptions and their lies, fully aware of their evil. We start with him, with this so-called Captain America. We start by convicting him for the crimes of his masters, the federal government. The crimes he did not oppose and, by not opposing them, allowed to take place. *That* is how we start. We start by finding Captain America guilty of treason. Thank you."

When Semper sat down, applause broke out in the courtroom. Taylor Douglas tapped his gavel gently in a half-hearted effort to restore some semblance of order. He let the applause play itself out, then said, "Thank you, Mr. Prosecutor."

Turning his head toward Gruenwald and his client, Douglas asked, "Is the defense ready to proceed?"

Gruenwald stood up and faced the jury. They were on the edge of their seats, ready to show their displeasure at anything the attorney might say, anything but what he *did* say.

"Gentlemen of the jury, I hardly know where to start. In the face of such eloquence, I don't know what to say. Except—he didn't do it. None of it. Not one charge. My client, Captain America, didn't do any of the things of which the eloquent prosecutor has accused him. And when you've heard the evidence, you will agree Captain America didn't do any of it and, as jurors, honest and true, return the only possible verdict: Not guilty."

Gruenwald didn't say thank you. He simply sat down, catching the courtroom, Semper in particular, unprepared. The prosecutor had expected a long argument and, instead, got something so short it didn't even allow him time to object.

"Thank you, Mr. Gruenwald," Douglas said, after he'd recovered from his own surprise. He brought his gavel down on the bench with a loud bang. "Court is adjourned until tomorrow morning, when we shall proceed with the prosecution's case."

A short time later, when the lawyer and his client were back in their respective cells, Gruenwald called down the long corridor to Captain America. "How you doing, Cap?"

"Fine, Mark. How are you?"

"Okay, I think, all things considered. I realized something when I stood up to give my opening statement: this was a first for me. In my sixteen years practicing law, I've faced hostile judges, hostile witnesses, hostile opposing counsel, even hostile jurors. But, I've never faced a *completely* hostile courtroom before. Never had a proceeding where everyone— every participant and even every spectator—was against me. It rattled me. I'm sorry my opening statement wasn't longer."

"It was perfect, Mark. Anything more would just have played into their hands."

"It's nice to hear you say that, but I'm still not sure I'm up to defending you in this crazy thing. There wasn't a procedure in there that was by the book."

"That's our strength, Mark. Who says we have to follow their rules? They might be able to force us to play on their ballfield, but they can't force us to play their game. We'll make our case with the real laws of the land, not their insane corruption of them. The American justice system may not be perfect, but it's a heck of a lot better than what we saw in there. And this is our chance to prove it."

Gruenwald listened to the words, each one spoken with honesty and strength. As the confidence in Captain America's words washed over him like an ocean wave, he realized he could not let this man down. All the Captain had ever asked of anyone was that they try their best. Gruenwald would not disappoint him.

Maybe they couldn't win, but they would certainly go down fighting.

14

LOOKING FOR AMERICA

P hillip Barry's contacts had given them the general vicinity of the Liberty's Torch compound, but did not know the exact location of the hidden militia base. After only a short time, the Falcon had decided that, all things considered, *general vicinity* was a somewhat optimistic view.

They were in the middle of thousands of acres of virgin woodland that revealed few signs of construction, human activity, or even life. Trees, they saw enough to satisfy one hundred and one *thousand* dalmatians. Clues to the whereabouts of Liberty's Torch, however, seemed nonexistent.

The Falcon and Barry had arrived late in the afternoon, then hiked into the woods. They didn't want the sound of the truck to alert any Torch outposts that might be scattered about the area. They looked for signs of Torch activity, but saw nothing except one hell of a lot of trees.

When it grew dark, Barry advised they make camp for the night. They could resume their search when the sun rose. But wandering around these woods at night would accomplish little except for their getting lost and conceivably becoming a meal for the various night predators who inhabited these woodlands. They would be safer near a campfire.

The Falcon agreed reluctantly. He understood everything Barry said and, on an intellectual level, he knew the man was right. On a emotional level, he didn't want to stop. If they were close to Cap now, he wanted to keep going until they found him.

He considered debating the point until he realized how dark the forest was becoming. It was a new moon; there was no light in the sky at all. Barry *was* right, it was too dark to be wandering these woods. They could only get lost or worse, and the Falcon had little desire to find out what worse was.

"Think you can pitch this tent, while I build us a fire?" Barry asked.

"Tell you what," the Falcon said. "You're more familiar

with the tent, you should pitch it. I'll build the fire."

Barry shrugged. "Suit yourself," he said, offering the Falcon his lighter. Sam waved at the lighter, giving it a disdainful glance.

"No thanks," the Falcon said, "I prefer to start my fires the old-fashioned way."

Barry shot him a look, and the Falcon had to hide a smile. Obviously, Barry had pegged Sam Wilson as a child of New York City who had no idea how to start a fire that didn't involve charcoal.

Barry set up the small, two-man tent he had brought with him. As the Falcon had suspected, it was his own tent and he was obviously very familiar with how to set it up. Meanwhile, the Falcon collected the right type of kindling and dried leaves to start a fire, assembled them into a perfect formation, and then proceeded to start the fire by efficiently rubbing two sticks together.

"You know," Barry said as he watched the Falcon turn the small fire into a larger one, "even with the circus costume and all, I hadn't really pegged you for such a showoff."

The Falcon smiled up at Barry, the lights and shadows of the flames moving across his face as the fire crackled. "So, you want to break out the coffee pot, or shall I?" the Falcon asked. "And please don't tell me you only brought decaf."

"You're pretty handy for a city boy," Barry said.

The Falcon thought back to the long months he had spent living in a primitive fishing village on the remote island of the Exiles. "I've been around a bit. Learned a few things. You want to see me catch a fish?"

"You planning on turning a tree branch and some stripped bark into a spear-and-rope tackle?"

"Nope," the Falcon said. "I hid a Popeil Pocket Fisherman in one of the backpacks."

The two men laughed as they cooked their dinner over the fire. The Falcon told Barry about his months on the island and Barry told the Falcon about his experiences in the military. By the time they had finished their dinners and the tales of their lives, it was nearing ten and Barry suggested they turn in for the night. If they were going to rise with the sun to continue their search, they had best get their sleep while they could.

"What? No ghost stories and S'mores?" the Falcon asked and faked a pout.

"Hey, I saw what passed for coffee in your cup. No more sugar for you. Seriously, wings, you want to flip for first watch? And I *don't* mean judo."

"You drove all the way up, I'll take first watch."

"Okay," Barry said, as he climbed into his bedroll, "but don't go sneaking off searching for clues. I don't wanna be looking for two lost super heroes tomorrow."

The night passed slowly and restlessly for the Falcon. When he was on watch, he could do little more than stoke the fire so it wouldn't go out, that and sneak off into the bushes when nature called. When it was his turn to sleep, he found that difficult as well. That he was sleeping on the ground for the first time in many years was only a small part of his problem. He was still concerned for Cap.

Although everyone from Mack to Jarvis to Billinghurst to Barry had assured him that Cap was all right, that Liberty's Torch wouldn't want to risk anything happening to the main attraction of its media circus, the Falcon kept thinking, *What if they're wrong?*

So, for the most part, the Falcon lay awake staring up at the stars above him. On those infrequent occasions when he slept, he tossed and turned, disquieting dreams of the Captain assaulting his sleep. When morning finally came, it was a relief.

After they struck camp—Barry making sure no easily visible trace of their presence remained behind—the two men continued their search.

The still-rising sun peeked down through the leaves of the forest, casting thick, varying patterns of shadows in the treetops, which the Falcon took advantage of as camouflage. As he flew, he kept to the shadows as best he could. At six-foot-two and wearing his bright red-and-white costume, he knew he wouldn't be mistaken for a bird by anyone who saw him clearly. What worked so well for him as a symbol in Harlem worked against him here in the New York woodlands. He found himself wishing for his old green costume—at least it made him look more like the bird of prey from which he took his name.

The Falcon flew in and out of the treetops, always searching for any signs of human beings. At the same time, Barry pounded the ground using the tracking methods taught him by his Sioux friends, or so he had said last night. If there were any of Taylor Douglas's little soldiers nearby, Barry seemed confident in his ability to find their trail. This far into the woods, the weekend warriors of Liberty's Torch were probably not being careful about leaving no trail.

At regular intervals, the Falcon would fly back along their search patterns and check in with Barry. They didn't want to risk using radios; the frequencies might be monitored by unfriendlies. As he flew around and continued to see nothing, the Falcon grew frustrated.

He knew Taylor Douglas's house was not far away. As his frustration grew, it was all Sam could do to resist soaring off and paying Douglas a visit. Just burst right in and have a nice little chat with the man, from, oh, a thousand or so feet above the elegant mansion. But, while that method was fine for a Harlem street hustler like Leon, that approach could have nasty consequences with someone as prominent and well defended as Douglas.

It was at the fifth check-in that things changed. For the previous two hours, they had searched the woodlands and found nothing. Now Sam swooped out of the sky for his rendezvous with Barry, and he could see the man's broad grin from half a mile away.

"Please don't tell that smile is because you found a pizzeria that delivers out here," he said as he landed.

"This smile," Barry said as his smile got even broader

and he pointed toward the ground, "is for that broken branch. Broken, I might add, by a rather clumsy human foot. I've already examined it fully, so you don't get the pleasure of watching me crawling around or putting my ear to the ground to listen. From what I saw, we should look that way," Barry said, indicating a northerly direction. "I suggest we fly low to the ground. Your jets are quiet; there won't be any chance of them hearing us rustling through the brush."

The Falcon picked up Barry and started to fly in the direction indicated. "Let me know if you get tired," Barry said after they had flown several minutes.

"Tired? Not when we're this close." A few minutes into their flight, the Falcon spoke again. "Tell me something. Did you really put your ear to the ground?"

"Yup."

"One of the tracking tricks you were taught by your Native American friends?"

"Yup."

"They *really* did that?"

"Who do you think invented Q-tips? It was the Sioux during the rainy season."

They didn't fly much longer before Barry instructed the Falcon to land. "Smell that?" he asked.

The Falcon sniffed the air and detected the odor of cooking bacon.

"Late risers," Barry said, a trace of contempt in his voice. "Up for a little breakfast, wings? It *is* the most important meal of the day."

They moved carefully through the woods, not making any noise, until they came upon a mobile camp. The three men there had been assigned to what was probably the outermost perimeter of the Liberty's Torch compound. Two of the men were next to a tent, packing it up. The third was cooking breakfast over a portable propane stove. A shiny jeep the men used to drive around on their patrols was parked near the stove.

"Rugged individualists," Barry whispered to the Falcon.

"I count three of them, each armed with an AK-47—probably converted to full auto—handguns—probably nine millimeter—and knives. Three of them, two of us. What's the plan?"

The Falcon smiled. It was a simple-but-effective plan: separate the men from their weapons as quickly as possible. They attacked from two fronts. The Falcon flew in from one side, plowing into the two men by the tent as fast as his wings could take him. Barry leapt from the underbrush onto the man cooking breakfast. It almost worked. But when the Falcon hit his men, both of them dropped their rifles. One of the rifles discharged upon hitting the ground.

The Falcon immediately turned and flew toward Barry to make sure the man was unharmed. It was a lesson—protect the innocent—that had been drummed into Sam by Captain America many times, so many times it had become instinctive.

As the Falcon jetted away from his two men, one of them drew his handgun and fired. Although the militiaman missed the flying hero, an errant shot punctured the propane tank of the stove. It blew in a fiery discharge that ignited the gas tank of the jeep. For the merest second, the jeep burned. Then it, too, exploded in a violent blast that turned the camp into a fireball.

When the smoke cleared, the camp was a smoldering ruin and the three men lay dead on the ground.

The Falcon and Phillip Barry were luckier. As soon as he saw the stove explode and catapult its flames onto the jeep, the Falcon had grabbed Barry by the arm and lifted them straight up into the air, as fast and as high as he could go.

The main force of the explosion missed them by a few feet. As it was, the shockwave washed over the Falcon causing second-degree burns on his arms and a pronounced ringing in his ear.

Even with that ringing, the Falcon could hear Barry cry out in pain. He looked down and saw that a piece of shrapnel had ripped a gash in Barry's left leg. The dripping blood sizzled as it hit the still-steaming ground below.

After the Falcon put out the fire, he tended to Barry's wound. "You know, wings," Barry said as the Falcon dressed the gash on his left calf, "I saw you come to protect me when things got hairy. You didn't even think about it. You just did it, like it was some kind of knee-jerk reflex." Even as he grimaced in pain, Barry grinned that wide grin of his. "I never figured I'd be so happy to be hanging around with a knee-jerk liberal."

The Falcon laughed in spite of himself and continued to tend the wound.

Barry looked at the smoky remains of the camp. Anger crept over his face as he noticed the weapons. "Will you look at that?" he said.

Following his gaze, the Falcon asked, "What?"

"The morons left their safeties off," he said, shaking his head in disbelief. "Amateurs."

Turning back to Barry's leg, the Falcon finished bandaging the wound. "Look, you have to stay off that leg for a while, but we can't afford to sit around and do nothing. We must be close to something worth guarding. Unfortunately, we can't ask them," he said bitterly, inclining his head toward the camp, "what it is. You rest your leg for a bit while I do a little scouting, see if I can spot any more camps in the area."

At Barry's reluctant-looking nod, the Falcon flew off.

15

WITNESS FOR THE PROSECUTION

"**Y**our Honor, before the trial begins, I would like to move for a separation of the witnesses."

The courtroom buzzed as several of the spectators murmured in confusion. Captain America heard the whispers of the man sitting behind him. "What's he trying to do? Keep us from watching the show?" the man asked of another sitting next to him.

Taylor Douglas stared down at Marcus Gruenwald and drew his lips back into a slight snarl. Douglas had never watched a trial before—other than on *Perry Mason* or *Matlock*—and had no idea what *separation of witnesses* meant. Regardless, if defense counsel was asking for this motion, he wasn't disposed toward granting it. But, he still had to know what the motion meant, so he could offer an explanation for denying it.

"And your reason for this extraordinary request, counselor?" Douglas asked.

"It's a standard motion."

Semper stood and said, "Defense counsel is asking that anyone who is going to be a witness be removed from the courtroom, so no one who will be testifying can hear what other witnesses are saying and modify their testimony accordingly."

"The motion is denied," Douglas said and slammed his gavel down with an angry bang. "That may be necessary with your clients, Mr. Gruenwald, who, no doubt, lie with as much ease as they draw breath, but it serves no purpose here. We do not have to lie or modify our testimony. We only have to tell the truth here. That will be more than enough to convict your client." He turned to Semper. "Mr. Prosecutor, call your first witness."

"Your Honor, I call—"

Semper was interrupted by the sound of Douglas pretending to clear his throat, a not-so-subtle reminder of the instructions Douglas had given him earlier: *No names.*

"I call this man," Semper said pointing to a spectator in the first row.

The witness approached the stand. He was a short, sad-faced man who looked to be forty-five going on seventy. Lines and crevasses were etched so deeply in his face that they looked as if they had been sandblasted there. What little there was of his hair was combed futilely over the shinier parts of his head. His eyes were dull, gray rainclouds. He looked like a man beaten down by life and then kicked when he asked it for mercy.

The man wore a dark blue suit with a white shirt and a striped maroon tie. The conservatively cut and very proper attire would not have been out of place in a bank boardroom. Douglas had, in fact, purchased the suit for the witness. Since his face wouldn't be visible on camera, Douglas wanted his clothes to be as respectable as possible.

As the man walked up to the witness stand, the bailiff stepped forward with a Bible in hand. The witness placed his right hand on the book and raised his left.

"Do you solemnly swear to tell the truth, the whole truth and nothing but the truth, so help you God?" the bailiff asked, giving the phrase the same breathless, hurried-up intonation Douglas had heard so often, if only on television.

"I do," the witness said nervously and then sat down.

"Are you familiar with Captain America?" Semper asked.

"Begging Your Honor's indulgence," Gruenwald said, rising to his feet behind the defense table, "but might we at least have the name of this witness?

"For what purpose, Counselor?" Douglas asked.

"Why, so I know to whom I'm directing my questions," Gruenwald said, his tone indicating it was a ridiculously obvious response. "As well as what his biases might be, and whether or not he has any criminal record."

"That's insulting, Mr. Gruenwald. I don't call witnesses with criminal records," Semper said, snapping his response as if it was a bullwhip. "He's an American. A *real* American. You don't need to know anything more than that.''

"Quite correct," Douglas said, striking the gavel against the bench. "Objection is overruled."

"To repeat," Semper said, "are you familiar with Captain America?"

There was a microphone next to the witness stand and the man leaned directly into it. "Y-y-yes," he said, but the answer was lost in a squeal of feedback that flowed from the loudspeakers and filled the room. The witness glanced up at Douglas and looked for the world like a little boy whose mother had just caught him in the cookie jar. Douglas glowered at the witness and motioned for him to sit back, away from the microphone. The witness leaned back and said, "Sorry," in a soft, sheepish tone.

"What was your answer again?" Semper asked.

"I—I said, yes."

"Yes, you are familiar with Captain America?"

"Yeah."

"Do you see him in this courtroom?"

"Sure," the witness said pointing. "That guy sitting there in the costume. Who else could he be?"

"Let the record reflect the witness has correctly identified the defendant," said the prosecutor. "Now, *how* are you familiar with Captain America?"

"I dunno. I seen him on TV."

"And what was he doing when you saw?"

"He was fighting."

"Who was he fighting?"

"A whole bunch of folks. I seen him fightin' Dr. Doom and the Scorpion and the Red Skull and—uuh, what's his name? You know. The French guy that jumps around and tries to kick him."

"You're referring to super-villains, correct?"

"Yeah, that's it."

"How did it make you feel watching Captain America fight these super-villains? Did it make you feel proud?"

"Yeah."

"Secure?"

Gruenwald rose again from the defense table.

"Objection, Your Honor. If the prosecutor is himself going to be testifying, he should be sitting in the witness stand."

"Overruled. Proceed."

Semper looked at the witness waiting for him to answer the question. The witness sat dumbly in his chair.

"I said, did it make you feel *secure* to see Captain America fighting those super-villains?"

"Oh, yeah."

"Like he was fighting *for* you?"

"Yeah."

"Like, as long as he was there, you didn't have to worry about anything? Like he would take *care* of it?"

"Yeah."

"Do you presently have a job?"

"Hell, you know I was laid off three years ago."

"What did you do?"

"Sold cars down in Schenectady."

"What happened?"

"The dealership shut down when the Honda place moved in and everybody started buying them foreign cars."

"Did you try to find another job?"

"Sure. Lots of times. Didn't get squat. They wasn't hiring, least not white guys. I saw the blacks gettin' jobs. Some Puerto Ricans, some Orientals, a bunch of women. But me? Not a damn thing. Hell, even had one lady who ran a fast food joint flat out tell me she was *only* hiring women."

"What happened?"

"My wife had to get a job to support the family. That didn't sit well with me and—well, we're divorced now."

"Answer this. If the government hadn't opened our country's doors to Japanese cars, would you have lost your job?"

"Not in a hundred years!"

"I have one final question. Did you ever hear Captain

America speak out against this deplorable foreign car situation or the way it ruined your life?"

"Nope, not a peep."

"Your witness," Semper said and sat down.

Gruenwald didn't even stand up, which Douglas found annoying. "How did you feel when Captain America answered your letter?" Gruenwald asked, a question Douglas found equally annoying and baffling.

"I never wrote him no letter."

"Oh? Then you spoke with him on the phone."

"No," the witness said as if it were the most ridiculous thing in the world.

"You never talked to him?"

"No."

"You never wrote to him?"

"I already said I didn't!"

"Ah, then you must pray to him, because, otherwise I don't see how he could have *known* about your situation."

"Objection!" Semper sprang to his feet so fast he knocked his chair over. Douglas had to wait for the laughter to subside before he could slam his gavel and sustain the objection.

"To the best of your knowledge, did Captain America authorize importing foreign cars into this country?"

"Not that I know of."

"In fact, didn't that happen while Captain America was still in a state of suspended animation, missing somewhere in the North Atlantic? Didn't it?"

"Objection sustained," Douglas shouted, banging his gavel once again, not even waiting for Semper to raise the objection. Semper, like an idiot, objected after the fact. Douglas made a note to fix that in the editing room.

"Well, you're not saying it was Captain America who opened the Honda dealership, are you?" Gruenwald asked.

"Wha— No!"

"Or that Captain America fired you?"

"No!"

"You never heard him tell those other places not to hire you, did you?"

"No!"

"What exactly *did* he do to make your life so bad?"

"He coulda done something for me, but he didn't!"

"So, what you're saying is, Captain America didn't really do anything, aren't you?"

Before Semper get another objection out, Gruenwald announced that he had no further questions.

The prosecutor called two more witness, both looking weathered by life, but immaculate in their suits. The first witness accused the federal government of selling out its citizens to an international conspiracy, while the second directed similar rancor at welfare crooks and "unproductive moochers."

Gruenwald's cross-examination of the witnesses went the same way as it did with the first: they were unable to identify the Captain as an actual participant in any of them. When he finished, the attorney allowed himself a quick smile at his client.

Douglas, who was definitely not smiling, caught that. He decided he had best break up this rhythm the defense had created for itself. He ordered a brief recess and summoned Semper to his chambers.

While they waited in the deliberation room, most of the jurors talked about how well the trial was going. Norman Paris was the lead singer in this particular choir.

"Norm, I don't think we're supposed to be talking about the trial now," said John Richards, the juror whose seat was directly behind Paris' in the box. "I think we're supposed to wait until we hear all the evidence."

Paris shot Richards a look that could have withered weeds. Richards was ten years younger than Paris, which alone was enough to make Paris resent him. When you added the facts that Richards was thin—the gift of a metabolism that allowed him to eat heartily without gaining weight—and possessed a thick crop of reddish hair, it was sufficient to make Paris want to reach out and sock his fellow juror with a baseball bat.

"And how, exactly, would you would know this, Richards? I mean, did I somehow overlook the law school diploma hanging on the wall of your barber shop?"

"Come on, Norm. Didn't you watch the O.J. trial? Judge Ito was always telling the jury not to discuss the case until they got all the evidence."

"Oh, right, like I'm gonna put my faith in the legal stylings of Lance freaking Ito, the kamikaze judge. Besides, what's there to discuss? That star-spangled Skeezix is guilty as hell; ain't no evidence gonna change that. Am I right, boys?"

Around the room, most of the other jurors nodded—most, but not all. Paris noticed that one man, Sherman Fairchild, wasn't exactly singing on key.

Fairchild was something of a puzzle to Paris. At sixty years, Fairchild was old enough to be someone's grandfather; hell, he *was* someone's grandfather. He was short, gray-haired, wrinkled with a kind of knowing, fatherly look. He reminded Paris of George Burns. But, despite his age, Fairchild was able to keep up with the younger members of the Torch on the training field and in his duties. Paris had to admit, the old guy had gumption, which was exactly what Paris didn't need at the moment.

Fairchild was respected and well liked. A lot of the younger men looked up to him. His voice would carry a lot of weight in the deliberations and Paris wanted to be sure that voice was going to say the right things.

"Hey, Sherm, you're awful quiet. You got a problem?"

"Only trying to figure out exactly what it was Captain America has done to make him guilty of treason."

Yup, Paris thought, *gumption*.

"What he's done, Sherm, is betray all of us, sell us out like he's the judas goat in the slaughterhouse and we're all nothing but prime sirloin-to-be."

Paris nodded to another juror, then walked behind Fairchild. The juror Paris had signaled stood in front of the older man and jabbed a finger inches away from Sherm's face.

"You don't doubt the government is selling us up the river, do you?" the man asked.

When Fairchild agreed, Paris spoke from behind him in a loud and booming voice. He hoped to intimidate the man without being *too* obvious about it.

"That flag-wearin' freak *is* the government. They paid for him out of our taxes. He does whatever they tell him to do and says whatever they want him to say. If they order him to jump, he don't just ask 'how high,' he gets out a tape measure to make sure he don't short them any. You go all over the world and ask people what they think of when they think of the U.S. Well, it ain't the Grand Canyon or the Statue of Liberty, it's Captain freakin' America.

"Well, if he wants the title, he's gotta be prepared to defend it, especially when the crooks he fronts for grab us by the short and curly ones and sell us to the first oil sheik or slant-eye who ponies up a thousand-buck campaign contribution. He works for the government. He's their symbol. That makes him guilty of the government's crimes."

Paris brought his hand down on Fairchild's shoulder. It could have passed for a friendly gesture, if it hadn't come down hard enough to make its true intent apparent.

"That clear things up for you, Sherm?"

Fairchild mumbled a few fast words of agreement. Paris smiled, glad that he'd gotten through to the old man.

After things quieted down, Paris walked over to Donnie, who sat to his immediate right in the jury box.

"Donnie, when they call us back in there, you go ahead and sit in Sherm's seat. He should sit next to me, just in case he starts getting confused again."

"Sure thing, Norm."

When the trial resumed, Fairchild saw Donnie in his chair and, seeing no other available seats, meekly took the one next to Norman Paris.

• • •

The next prosecution witness was the second firebomber Captain America had sketched—Ray Marks. As before, the bailiff used the whole-truth-and-nothing-but-the-truth routine, which once again prompted a barely suppressed chuckle from Gruenwald. No one, the lawyer had explained in a whisper, used that oath anymore.

If the previous witnesses had offered strange testimony, Marks outdid them, making statements that would have fit very comfortably into the Wonderland courtroom of the Red Queen.

After Semper led Marks through the same introductory questions as his other witnesses—the questions designed to identify Captain America and then elicit the witness's former feelings of pride and security at seeing the Captain fighting for him—the prosecutor asked Marks how he felt about Captain America now.

"Ashamed," he answered.

"How so?"

"My grandpa used to tell me stories about how Captain America fought in World War II, how the man made him feel proud to be an American and share the same name. But, the thing is, he ain't fighting for world peace these days. He's fighting against it."

"Please explain."

"Okay, what's the biggest threat to world peace today?" the witness started by way of explanation. "It's the United Nations. The world would be a pretty good place, if America could do what it *should* be doing, which is kicking the crap outta little, pissant, third-world countries what needs it. But, we can't do that because the UN—which we mostly pay for, by the way—tells us we can't. You got all them ambassadors sitting around and yelling and looking out for their own country's interests instead of looking at the big picture. So America sits on its hands doing nothing, instead of doing what needs to be done, because the feds don't want to piss off their buddies in the UN. And does Captain America, the guy my grandfather counted on, speak out against this crock of manure? Hell, no, he supports it! He's fought alongside UN troops and even saved their big New York palace from being blown up. Meantime, because America keeps sitting on its rear, the world's going all to hell. How's *that* for selling us short? But I don't know why we should expect anything else from this flag-waving phony. It's not like he cares about us Americans. Not really, anyway.''

''I see,'' Semper said, stopping the testimony for a second. He looked at the jury, to emphasize the witness's point, then faced Captain America. ''And why,'' the prosecutor asked, still looking at the Captain, ''do you say that the defendant doesn't care about Americans?''

''He's supposed to be this defender of the common man, right? Only who does he hang around with? Not ordinary guys like you and me. All of his pals are muties, ex-cons, water-breathing freaks, Vietnamese—which is consorting with the enemy—African royalty, robots, and guys who think they're gods. Sure, they've saved the world once or twice, but that's only because they live here, too! Hell, the only normal guy in the Avengers is their butler. Their servant. What does that tell you?''

When Douglas asked Gruenwald if he had any questions for this witness, the lawyer dismissed Marks with a brusk wave of his hand and a contemptuous, ''Not on *this* planet, Your Honor.''

That evening, just as Taylor Douglas was preparing to view the day's proceedings on *Coast to Coast*, Norman Paris came to him. The colonel, back in his Liberty's Torch uniform, looked disturbed and didn't mind showing it. That was one of the reasons the man was so useful to Douglas. His other officers were reluctant to deliver bad news to their general. Paris simply considered it another part of the job.

''Something troubling you, Colonel?''

''We got intruders, General.''

''Intruders?''

"Yeah, Captain America's Negro partner and some local guide, name of Phillip Barry. They found one of our outposts yesterday and—well, it ain't good. Our guys managed to blow themselves up in between wettin' their pants. Since then, they been wanderin' around the perimeter looking for a way in. We've been lucky; they ain't found one yet. A couple of our troops took some shots at 'em, but they're still out there."

Douglas did not say anything at first. He sat in his chair and stared at Paris, his face going red. When he finally spoke, it was an explosion.

"This is *unacceptable*! I want you to round up our best men and find them. Their condition doesn't matter. *Just get them!*"

"Yes, sir."

Paris was halfway out the door when Douglas called him back. When the colonel turned to face his commander, he saw a much calmer man sitting in the chair.

"A thought occurs to me, Colonel," Douglas said. He smiled and was obviously quite pleased with himself. All too often, he would react to bad news with a jolt of anger, only to realize later what he should have done. Sometimes that realization came too late to do any good. This time, he had managed to suppress his initial anger almost as soon as it happened and, once out of its control, could think more clearly.

"These intruders might well be in communication with the local authorities, possibly even the FBI. For now, said authorities seem content to allow their agents to tramp around the woodlands in the hope that they will stumble upon our headquarters. If they were to suddenly disappear, or even fail to report in, their masters might well intensify the effort to find us. I think it better if we let them continue to search in vain. As long as they do that, our cautious government may be content to let that be the extent of their interference with our plans. Those two cretins could be as much a diversion as the trial. Tomorrow, once our objectives are met, we can arrange for the Falcon and his friend to meet the same fate that awaits Captain America. But, for now, Colonel, let them be.''

"Understood, sir."

Douglas turned his attention to his computer. He keyed in the password that kept all but him from using it, then called up his journal to enter his decision about the intruders. He knew that, in the decades to come, his story would inspire the nation to new heights of glory. He wanted to capture each moment as it happened and while it was still fresh in his mind.

Yes, he thought, *far better to let them wander about aimlessly and deflect the government's attention. In fact, I should devise some other way to use them as a diversion, as well. It would be a shame to let such resources go to waste.*

As he finished writing, Douglas noticed *Coast to Coast* was about to start and clicked on his television. He was particularly proud of this aspect of his plan, how he had arranged to deliver the trial tapes to a nationally syndicated television show under the very noses of his enemies and without them ever succeeding in tracing the tapes back to him.

Every day, after the tape of the day's proceedings had been edited, Douglas had one of his men drive it to New York City and then hire a messenger service to deliver it to *CTC*'s Manhattan offices. Every day, he used a different driver and a different messenger service, so the tapes could not be easily traced back to Liberty's Torch. Not even the FBI had the staff to track every package accepted and delivered in the Big Apple.

The show started with the usual trumpeted teaser promising the latest on *"the trial of Captain America!"* after the usual commercial messages. Douglas poured a brandy from a cut crystal decanter into a fine crystal glass. He swirled the brandy, marveling at its rich color. He inhaled the bouquet.

It was an excellent vintage. Not a Napoleon brandy, at least not yet. The time for that would come later.

When *Coast to Coast* returned, its anchor mechanically informed the viewers that the program was not responsible for the content of the tape; it arrived to them already edited.

"Today's tape," the anchor continued, *"was edited more heavily that the previous tapes, which leads us to wonder what exactly was being left out and if we should broadcast these tapes. We at* Coast to Coast *feel these cannot be our concerns. We cannot say what was edited—that is for you to decide. As for broadcasting the tapes, we believe we have a journalistic responsibility to report whatever information we receive, no matter how offensive it may be. If we didn't broadcast these tapes, it would be a betrayal of that sacred responsibility."*

A wry smile spread across Douglas's face. *A responsibility that lasts just as long as the tapes continue to bring in the big ratings*, he thought. He had a kind of unofficial partnership with the program; he supplied it with what he wanted the people to know and *CTC* made sure it got to them.

He leaned back in his chair and considered tomorrow's trial and tomorrow's tapes. *Maybe*, he thought and took a long sip of the most excellent brandy, *I should find a way to make tomorrow's tape even* more *offensive.*

16

SOMETHING'S BURNING

By the second day of their search, the Falcon had decided to ground himself as a precaution. A near miss from a sniper's bullet was a key factor in this decision.

During the first day of the search, he did fly for much of the time. He would take to the skies, darting in and out of treetops, hoping to glimpse something that might lead him and Phillip Barry to Liberty's Torch. His lack of success in these airborne excursions had been spectacularly disheartening.

He found no trace of the main compound he and Barry believed to be near; *near* being a relative term considering the immensity of the woodlands they searched. Their progress had been slowed by Barry's wound. Although Barry still moved at a remarkable pace, he simply couldn't walk as fast as before.

Given the circumstances, the Falcon didn't want to stray too far from the man. He continued to search from the air, but never more than a mile or two from where Barry scouted.

Barry covered his ground as best he could. Although his best was, even now, better than most people would have been capable of, he still cursed his leg wound. He knew what he was capable of. On a good day, he could have traveled as efficiently on foot as the Falcon could in the air. This was far from a good day. He knew how much he was slowed by his wound, not to mention how much he was slowing their search for Captain America, and he hated it.

At the end of that first day, they had nothing further to show for their efforts. Save for the base camp where three men had died senselessly, they had found no trace of their foe.

The second day started much the same as the first. The Falcon and Barry rose early, ate quickly, and again began to search. By midafternoon, just as Sam Wilson was starting to believe Barry's information had been wrong, that they were nowhere near the Torch's headquarters, a bullet whizzed past his head.

Reacting immediately, the Falcon began flying in the zig-zag patterns he and Captain America had devised, the flip-flopping, stomach-churning evasive maneuvers the Captain had made him repeat over and over during their training. So many times, in fact, that Sam had once told Cap he was buying a lifetime supply of Dramamine. Those drills were certainly paying off for him now.

The Falcon flew the darting and random patterns—cutting left and then right, down and then circling, changing course in ever-more unexpected directions—with no more conscious thought than he would expend walking. His muscles knew what to do. The sniper fired twice more. The shots didn't even come close.

Even as he darted this way and that, the Falcon tried and failed to spot the man shooting at him. Sam didn't think it wise to spend too much time looking. The sniper may have missed with his first shots, but, the Falcon's evasive maneuvers notwithstanding, the shooter might get lucky with his fourth or fifth.

The Falcon jetted back to Barry's position. Phillip advised that, for the time being, the Falcon confine himself to the ground. They would be harder to spot if they remained on foot. Though he knew it would slow their search considerably, the Falcon agreed.

They walked for hours, still finding nothing. As they made their way through the woods, Barry studied the ground, bending low on occasion to examine it more carefully. When he did, the Falcon could see his companion move cautiously, making sure he didn't bend his wounded leg the wrong way. The man was clearly in pain, but he would never complain or suggest they slow their pace.

Once, they found an extinguished campfire. Barry knelt next to it, studied it, then announced it was several days old. Someone *had* been here, but it was impossible to say exactly when. But it did seem they were getting closer.

By nightfall on the second day of their search, the Falcon and Barry had found no more signs of Torch activity. They decided to set up camp and get some rest. It was as they were cooking dinner that the shot rang out.

Two things happened almost simultaneously: the two men heard the rifle shot and the pot the Falcon was holding jumped from his hand. As one, he and Barry dove for cover, trying to get as far from the light of their fire as they could and into the cover of the surrounding woods.

The Falcon lay in the brush, trying to look two ways at once. He looked in the direction of the shot to see if he could detect the man or men who had fired on them and saw nothing. He also looked toward Barry, trying to determine if his companion was unharmed. He couldn't see Phillip either.

Barry was his biggest concern. He wanted to make sure the man was safe and decided the best way to do so was to draw any gunfire that might follow toward him.

Moving quickly, the Falcon darted back to the camp and grabbed a flashlight. He thumbed the button and flew up into the trees, darting around the night sky like a bat. He held the flashlight at arm's length to mislead the sniper and shined its bright beam down onto the ground. He hoped to catch their attackers in its beam. Failing that, he hoped the flashlight would draw their fire away from the campground where Barry lay hidden.

There were no more shots. When the Falcon satisfied himself that the area was clear, that the snipers had retreated, he flew back to his camp. He found Barry had already extinguished the fire and was backing up their gear.

"The good news," Barry said, as he finished what he was doing, "is that we're getting close. The bad news is, I think we've lost the element of surprise—if we ever had it. It's not safe to stay here anymore. They'll go back and report our position."

"Why didn't they finish the job?"

"You," Barry answered. "Face it, you're an Avenger. For most people, that's pretty intimidating. Those toy soldiers didn't want to mix it up with one of you costumed types. When that first shot missed, they probably hightailed it out of here. But they will report that we're in the neighborhood.''

''What do we do now?''

''You're not going to like it, wings. We can't stay here. And I don't think it's safe to set up a camp or start a fire anywhere in the vicinity. That would just draw them back to us. Our best bet is there,'' Barry said, pointing up at the treetops.

They dug a hole, not too deep, but big enough to conceal most of their gear from any new visitors. They uprooted some underbrush to cover the hole. When they had finished stowing all the gear except for some blankets and a length of rope, the Falcon flew them into the trees.

It wasn't easy in the dark, but, eventually, they found a tree suitable for their needs. It was tall and full of large leaves to conceal them from the hunters below. It had thick branches which would not only support their weight, but formed into large V-shapes where those branches met. The Vs were large enough that they could sit in them, somewhat comfortably, and not be overly concerned that they might slip from their new perch.

After they found a suitable spot in the trees, Barry cut a six-foot length of rope and handed it to the Falcon. Then he cut a second length. Barry wrapped one of the blankets around himself. He then took the rope, passed it around his torso underneath his arms, and wrapped it around the tree branch he was leaning against, repeating the process, and securing the rope loosely. He instructed the Falcon to do the same, cautioning the Avenger to tie the rope tight enough to keep him from slipping out of the tree, but not so tight as to cut off his circulation.

When they finished, the Falcon asked, ''Now what?''

''Now we sleep?''

''Sleep?''

''As best you can. Things are going to get a bit more hairy tomorrow and—''

''And we need our beauty sleep?'' the Falcon interrupted.

Barry rubbed his beard with his right hand. "I'm afraid that ship has sailed." He looked at the Falcon and found the Avenger staring down at the ground. "You know, wings, for a guy who spends as much time as you do flying around, you seem awfully scared of heights."

"It isn't that. I was just wondering, first I fly, now I'm sleeping in trees. What comes next?"

"Get some sleep. Tomorrow, for breakfast, I'll cook us up a nice purée of nightcrawler."

The Falcon didn't think he could have spent a less-restful night than he had the night before. He was wrong. If this was what sleeping in trees was like, Darwin had been wrong—humans and apes did not spring from common stock. Eventually, however, he did fall into an uneasy sleep.

He awoke to the sight of a campfire in the distance. It was early morning, the sky that strange shade of off-blue it becomes shortly before sunrise. However, it was still dark enough that the campfire was very bright by contrast and had easily attracted the Falcon's attention.

He turned to nudge Barry, but found that the man was already awake and also looking at the fire.

"What do you make of it?"

"I don't know. It could be another Liberty's Torch base camp, but it doesn't feel right."

"What do you mean?"

"They know we're out here and looking for them. It doesn't make sense they'd attract our attention this way."

Even as Barry spoke, the fire suddenly went out.

The Falcon looked at Barry. Barry looked back at the Falcon. They both shrugged their shoulders, then proceeded to climb out of their blankets.

They approached the campfire warily. They moved slowly and silently, alert for any militiamen that might be nearby. But, when they got to the fire, they found no one.

The fire itself was in a clearing. They made sure no one was around, then entered the clearing to examine the fire.

"Look at the logs," Barry said, directing the Falcon's eye to the wood in the fire. "They're barely burned at all. Whoever set this put it out almost as soon as they started it. It couldn't have been burning more than a few minutes."

"Did they break camp in a hurry?"

"Look around us. I don't think there ever was a camp here. There's nothing here *except* this. Someone set this fire, made sure we saw it, and then made sure it was completely extinguished before they left. They didn't want its ashes to reignite and maybe spread to the surrounding trees."

"I'm going to head topside, see if I can't catch some sign of them," the Falcon said and activated his wings to lift him. He rose slowly until he reached a height of approximately a hundred feet above the clearing. Then, he slowly glided around the tall trees looking for any signs of their mysterious neighbors or that this was some sort of trap.

There was no one anywhere in his field of vision, save for his companion in the clearing. There was no indications of any kind of trap. There was, however, something below that caught his eye and made him shake his head in astonishment.

Rocks. They were rocks so light in color that they stood out even in the moonlit dawn and they were in the clearing. From the ground, they would have appeared to be nothing more than rocks, but from his vantage point, the Falcon could see they formed an arrow and that the arrow was pointing to a large tree on the far side of the clearing.

The Falcon marked the location of the tree, then landed to tell Barry what he had spotted. This was a matter that definitely cried out for further investigation.

They approached on foot. Instead of going across the openness of the clearing, they took a circular path through the trees. It took them a few moments to find the tree again, but they did find it. They also found another mystery.

Hanging from the tree, covered by soot from the campfire so it would be invisible to anyone not practically standing in front of it, was a nine-by-twelve manila envelope.

"I'll be—" Barry said, as the Falcon took the envelope from the tree and wiped its surface free of the soot.

"Look," the Falcon said, holding the envelope out so that Barry could see it more clearly. In the upper left corner was the printed logo and return address—just a distant post office box—of Liberty's Torch. But, the real surprise, the surprise that made Barry gasp audibly, was what was hand-scrawled on the center of the envelope.

SAM WILSON & PHILIP BARRY.

Their names.

The envelope was addressed to them.

17
WITNESS FOR THE DEFENSE

Taylor Douglas sat in his office in the Liberty's Torch compound with Norman Paris and Hugh Semper. The militia chieftain had stayed up much of the night refining this or that nagging detail of his various preparations and now wanted to review how matters stood.

"Gentlemen, the trial of Captain America concludes today," he said, attaching an air of regal proclamation to the matter-of-fact statement. He leaned forward in his chair, looming over the desk and looking directly at Semper. His eyes locked onto those of the nervous prosecutor with a firm and cold expression that made it clear Douglas would tolerate no discussion or deviation. "If you were planning on any more witnesses," he said, "*don't* call them. We have made whatever points we were going to make with the unenlightened public."

Douglas leaned back in his chair. Having made his main point in such a forceful manner, he felt he could adopt a more cordial demeanor for the remainder of the review.

"If we prolong the trial, we risk losing the attention of our fickle audience. They might become bored with our presentation and even start to resent us."

Douglas looked around his office in the underground compound. It was from here he would run the matters of Liberty's Torch for the foreseeable future, until a time when events in this land were more conducive to an open approach. Although this office was not as opulent as the one in his home, he had managed to duplicate, albeit on a smaller scale, some of its grandeur. Simulated wood paneling substituted for the cherry wood of his house. His desk, although big, was not as huge or as ornately carved as the one from the mansion. His chair was vinyl instead of leather. Still, there had been some things that he insisted had to be the same here as in his previous command post.

Several days ago, Douglas had ordered his computer moved from the mansion to this office. Not trusting to any backup system, he thought it more prudent to transport the actual equipment rather than leave it unsecured in the house.

At the same time, under the guise of moving it into the historical museum, he had announced his diorama of the Battle of Saratoga was broken down, transported, and reassembled in the room's center. There, always in his view, it would remind Douglas of his destiny and inspire him to see it through.

Most important, the tattered flag that George Washington had carried into the battle of White Plains now hung in a place of honor on the far wall of this office. He could see it whenever he sat at his desk, a fitting symbol of how he, too, would lead his troops to victory.

Douglas's eyes fell upon that flag and he smiled.

"Yes, it is clearly time to end this trial and wipe that smug expression off the masked traitor's face. He has become tiresome, extremely tiresome. And, truth be told, I must turn my attentions to other matters." Douglas turned to Paris. "Colonel, how is the jury?"

"I'd be lying if I said we weren't ready for this thing to end, too. There's been more than a little, well, I guess you could call it, *antsiness*."

Douglas glowered at the colonel. He was not a man who enjoyed surprises of any kind, and this was the first he was hearing of any problems with the jury.

"Oh? Do you have something to report, Colonel?"

"Nah, not really. Sherman Fairchild was getting restless a while back, but I arranged for him to sit next to me. I can remind him of his civic duty better that way. I think the old man understands what he's supposed to do."

Paris grinned at Douglas. It was meant as a friendly gesture, but, coming from Paris, the effect was lost. His smiles tended to pull the corners of his mouth back across the jowls of his cheeks, making it look like he was a dog baring his teeth than a human smiling.

"See that he does," Douglas said. He also smiled, but it was a cold, hard smile. It was not a sign of friendship, but rather a reminder to Paris of their respective places.

"Make sure Fairchild understands the importance jurors play in our system of jurisprudence. We wouldn't want *any-one* shirking his duty, would we?"

"No, sir. I can personally guarantee old Sherman will deliver on all of his obligations."

Douglas leaned back in his chair, steepled his fingers, then tapped his fingertips together rhythmically. He stared at Paris, his eyes still cold and now partially closed for emphasis. He said nothing, just stared until Paris felt uncomfortable and shifted his position in his own chair. It was only then that Douglas finally spoke again.

"Very good, Colonel. Inform the guards that we want them positioned closer to the defense table today and not back by the door. After the verdict comes in, I expect things will have to move quickly if we wish to avoid any outbursts. The closer they are to the defendant, the better. You should also instruct them to be in their actual uniforms. When we carry out the court's sentence on the defendant, it must be done properly, with full uniforms and military ceremony. Captain America may be a traitor, but he was once a soldier who served our country proudly and honorably. As such, he shall be treated with respect in his final moments."

"Yes, sir."

Douglas looked at Semper and dismissed him with the advisory that the proceedings would resume shortly. The prosecutor left to make his preparations. After Semper had gone, Douglas looked back at his second-in-command.

"And the other matters, Colonel?"

"Both taken care of, sir. That poor sap you selected?" Paris brought his hands up, imitating the motion of a stick being snapped between them. "Hell, they say most serious accidents happen around the home, if you know what I mean."

"And you left him *where*, Colonel?"

"Where you said. In the armory."

"And the dental records?"

"You know, General, I think you ought to know by now

that you can trust me to do the job right. I switched your records for those of our boy, just like you wanted. When the bomb goes off, it's gonna look like you was workin' on something that blew up in your face and took you out like last week's garbage. No fuss, but one hell of a lot of muss.''

Satisfied, Douglas nodded. He had been planning this step for several months, knowing it would be necessary for him to disappear without a trace. He had found a member of Liberty's Torch who was his equal in size and build, an expendable member who would play the role of Taylor Douglas's corpse. This afternoon, when he triggered the bomb in his mansion, the world would assume him dead.

He would live in the underground complex where no one would find him, until such time as more of his ultimate plans had come to fruition. It was unfortunate, perhaps, that a loyal member of Liberty's Torch would have to die, but they were in a war and, in a war, there are always casualties.

He *would* miss the mansion, though.

He had ensured that he would have enough to live on and Liberty's Torch would have sufficient operating funds. He had changed the beneficiary on his insurance policies—both personal and on the house—to a trust fund he had established to cover the militia's expenses. When he died, when his house was a smoldering ruin, the trust would receive millions in insurance benefits.

Over the past several months, Douglas had also sold off most of his remaining assets, converting them to cash and gold so that his holdings were extremely liquid. He especially enjoyed this part: he would have plenty of operating capital while having made certain that very little remained for his ex-wife to claim or which the government could attach for estate taxes. Oh, his wife could still make her claim, the government could still attempt to attach, but they would be fighting over next to nothing.

Douglas stood and donned his judge's robe. ''Excellent,'' he said, almost hissing out the word, as he slipped the shroud-like garment of executioner's-black cloth over his head.

"General, not everyone is gonna be convinced you're dead. It ain't like coming back from the dead is unheard of. How many times *is* it for Dr. Doom now, fifty-seven and counting? My point being, sooner or later, someone's gonna come lookin' for you. You sure no one will be able to find this base?"

Douglas adjusted the lie of his judicial robe, so it was flat and wouldn't bunch up on him. "Colonel, after Tony Stark stopped manufacturing weapons systems, *I* became one of the chief suppliers to the government and to S.H.I.E.L.D. It was one of my companies that designed the very detection devices they would use against us, as well as the shielding mechanisms the government employs to protect itself from screening by enemy powers. I know what they'll be using against us and I know *exactly* how to counter it. No one will ever find this base. Now, shall we resume the trial?" he asked, waiting impatiently for the colonel to open the door for him.

"Your Honor, the prosecution has no further witnesses," Hugh Semper said on cue.

Douglas looked down at Gruenwald. "Does counsel for the defense wish to call any witnesses?"

"Will the court grant a continuance so that I can secure the testimony of such witnesses?" Gruenwald asked flatly. He already knew what Douglas's answer would be; he was simply going through the motions as per his and Cap's plan.

"This court does not see how the testimony of any defense witness could nullify the overwhelming evidence presented by the prosecution. That being the case, this court sees no reason to further delay these proceedings."

"I figured you would say that," Gruenwald responded, as flatly as he had spoken before. Then he smiled broadly; time to throw the complacent Taylor Douglas a significant curve. "In that case, the defense calls Captain America."

The courtroom quickly filled with whispers, as the people in the gallery exclaimed their surprise. Even Taylor Douglas audibly gasped. The judge recovered quickly, however, and banged his gavel for silence.

"I confess I am pleasantly surprised your client will testify, counselor," Douglas said. "Although I am pleased the jury will be able to hear Captain America's guilt from his own lips, I had been led to believe he did not recognize this court's jurisdiction over him."

"*Habeas corpus*, Your Honor," Gruenwald said matter-of-factly, an ear-to-ear grin on his face. Seeing the tightly controlled Douglas lose himself that way had been one of too few satisfying moments in this kangaroo court. "He who holds the body obviously has some jurisdiction over it, no matter how much that jurisdiction might be disputed. As for my client admitting his guilt, I believe we may just be able to surprise you a second time this morning."

As Gruenwald stood to begin his direct examination, he heard someone behind him mutter, "That lawyer thinks he's so smart."

"Don't worry," came a muffled reply. "He ain't in a courtroom with the rest of his kind. Now he's facing *real* Americans. We'll see how smart he is."

How enlightening, Gruenwald thought. *I thought Neanderthal man died out millennia ago.*

Gruenwald turned his attention to the front of the courtroom. While he had been listening to the two men behind him, the bailiff had administered the outmoded oath to Captain America and Cap had moved into the witness box.

The Captain stood straight and tall in the box.

"You may take your seat," Douglas said looking down at Captain America with undisguised malignity.

"I prefer to stand, thank you."

"Very well. Counselor, you may proceed."

"Please state your name for the record."

"Captain America."

"Objection," Semper said, rising to his feet. "The witness should give his real name."

Before Douglas could say anything, Gruenwald responded to his opponent's barb. "I believe this trial is supposed to determine the 'real name' of my client. It would seem that, for the purposes of these proceedings, 'Captain America' would be all the name you would need. Or want," he added under his breath.

"The objection is overruled," Douglas said. "In the future, counselor, it is not necessary for you to speak before I rule on an objection. Unless, of course, you are attempting to show contempt for this court."

God save me from the easy ones, Gruenwald thought.

Norman Paris had watched attentively as Captain America was sworn in. He had expected Captain America to testify—was, in fact, looking forward to it. *Here's where those two get some of what they deserve*, he thought. He wanted to enjoy the proceedings, but knew he couldn't simply sit back and watch. He had to keep an eye on Sherman Fairchild next to him, had to make sure none of Captain America's lies struck a nerve with the old geezer.

"You have been charged with treason, Captain. How do you feel about these charges?" Gruenwald asked.

"They're laughable," the Captain said, even as Semper vaulted to his feet to voice his objection.

"Sustained."

That's one, Paris thought, a smug look of satisfaction on his face. He turned toward Fairchild and saw with equal satisfaction that the exchange hadn't appeared to have any effect on the elderly militiaman.

Good for you, Semper. Keep them lies comin' from Flag-Boy and I won't have to worry whether Sherm is buying into them. Still, a little positive reinforcement couldn't hurt none.

"See that, Sherm," Paris whispered to the older man. "He's gonna try to lie, but our boy Semper is gonna catch him in it every time."

Paris placed his beefy hand on the man's shoulder and pressed down just hard enough to make Fairchild wince. It was a reminder of where they were and what was expected of them.

"Do you think of yourself as some sort of a national symbol, as someone who is supposed to fight America's battles for her?" Gruenwald asked his client.

"Objection."

"Sustained."

"Are you saying I can't answer the question?" Captain America asked Douglas.

"The objection has been sustained. The answer is irrelevant," Douglas snapped. "Move on."

"Do you believe the government acts through you?"

"Objection. Irrelevant."

"Sustained."

"Do you approve of everything the government does?"

"The objection is sustained," Douglas said before Semper could even voice the objection.

With each word Semper and Douglas said, Paris smiled and said, "Good," in a voice just loud enough for Fairchild to hear. He emphasized each utterance by hitting his fist against his own leg, the leg next to Fairchild. He didn't hit his leg hard enough for it to hurt, but in an obvious enough manner for Fairchild to see him do it and understand the intent behind the action.

Behind them, John Richards had also watched Captain America closely. Unlike Douglas and Paris, he *wanted* to hear the Captain's answers. He was interested in what the man might say, certain he could see through any lies in the man's answers. Why, he wondered, didn't they just let him answer the questions?

He also wished Colonel Paris would leave Fairchild alone. He knew, when it came to it, that Fairchild would do the right thing. But Sherm was an old guy who looked more and more ashen with every reminder. If Paris wasn't careful, he'd give Fairchild a heart attack right there in the jury box.

"Sir, do you consider yourself a traitor?" Gruenwald asked. He didn't even get to finish the word *traitor* before Semper gave his expected reply.

"Objection. Objection! *Objection!*" Semper was screaming by the time he voiced his third objection and flecks of spittle actually flew from his mouth.

"Sustained," Douglas barked from the bench. "Counselor, your repeated attempts to inject irrelevancies into these proceedings have grown tiresome. Either move on or take your seat!"

"Very well," Gruenwald said. He looked at Captain America and the Captain smiled back in return. Not a question he had asked had been allowed, not an answer had been permitted. Both Gruenwald and the Captain felt they had made their point.

"If it pleases the bench," Gruenwald said, "and I'm sure it does," he added, the sarcasm in his tone unmistakable, "I have no further questions for my client."

Semper sprang to his feet. Captain America, in response, sat down in the witness box for the first time, as if to show his utter lack of regard for the prosecutor. Semper fumed at the gesture. He turned his back on the Captain and fiddled with the buttons on his suit coat. Gruenwald tried not to grin, as that was the first thing law school taught you not to do in a courtroom. Then, Semper looked at the spectators sitting behind him. Without turning, he swept his arm back and pointed at the costumed figure in the witness stand.

"Watch this," he whispered contemptuously and was rewarded by the hyena-like grins of his audience.

"Go get him, boy," one of the men said. Gruenwald rolled his eyes.

Semper walked slowly toward the witness stand, still saying nothing. Before him was everything he despised—the complacent, self-satisfied federal government all rolled up into this one man. He would face this traitor and challenge him, his pointed questions devastating the hated foe on this, Semper's chosen battlefield. And, in doing so, Semper would raise his own stake in the future of the new America that Liberty's Torch would build.

Semper strode determinedly toward the seated Captain America, a dream of glory manifesting itself on his face with a contemptuous sneer for the defendant. He opened his mouth to ask his first withering question.

And said nothing.

From behind his mask, the Captain's eyes burned. They seemed to stare not at Semper, but through him, boring twin holes in the back of the man's head. In that moment, it seemed as if every vile thought within the prosecutor's mind was escaping, like air hissing from a punctured balloon. The steel-blue eyes of Captain America blazed with the fire of Liberty herself and burned Semper to the very core of his soul.

Semper felt his knees buckle, turn to water beneath him. He whirled from the stand and shuffled timidly back to his table. He never raised his eyes from the courtroom floor and he never looked back at the witness.

"I have no questions," he said.

"*What?*" Norman Paris screamed and jumped to his feet.

Semper did not stop at his table but continued walking, a little faster now, up the center aisle toward the rear doors.

Without waiting for permission from the bench, Captain America rose from the witness stand and walked back to the defense table. Semper could hear the sound of the heavy shackles around his ankles dragging against the hardwood floor even above the tumult exploding in the courtroom around him.

Semper also heard Taylor Douglas smash his gavel down onto the bench. "Court is adjourned for twenty minutes. Mr. Prosecutor," he added in the deadliest tone Semper had ever heard him use. The prosecutor froze in his tracks, inches away from the rear doors. "I will see you in my chambers immediately!" Then he turned to the armed guards and shouted, "I want this court cleared during the recess. Cleared!"

Douglas stormed out of the rear doors, brushing past Semper and heading down the corridor to his office. The heavy sounds of his footfalls echoed loudly off the walls of the empty hallway and drowned out the chaos in his courtroom.

He entered his office, sat behind his desk, and looked up at the tattered flag hanging on the wall before him—drinking in its power. He waited with only his breathing piercing the silence of his chambers.

The knock on his door was timorous. "Enter," he said in as formal as tone as his rage would allow

Hugh Semper pushed open the door slowly and obeyed the order given him, still stooped and cowering, exactly as he had in the courtroom. Douglas watched him enter and did not motion toward the chair. Semper stood in front of the desk, his knees weak, his arms hanging limply at his sides. He did not look at Douglas, could not raise his head. It was as if the muscles in his neck and spine had disappeared.

"What was *that*?" Douglas asked slowly, deliberately, drawing out every word so that each was spoken as if it were, in itself, a separate sentence.

"I, ah, that is, er, I didn't feel that I, ah—needed to cross-examine him," Semper said in a whispered stammer that sounded for all the world like the helpless tone of a child caught with his hand in the cookie jar. "Our case against him was strong and you, uh, you did say you wanted the trial over soon. So, I decided not to cross-examine him."

Douglas said nothing. He leaned forward in his chair, his elbows on the arm rests and his fingers steepled, and said nothing. He looked at Semper without blinking, communicating every iota of the loathing he felt for the weak thing that cowered before him. Douglas stared at Semper until the prosecutor finally lifted his head to look at Douglas.

As soon as their eyes met, Douglas locked his gaze on Semper. The prosecutor could not look away.

"You would add lies to your cowardice?" Douglas asked. Semper did not answer.

"Cowardice in battle is a court-martial offense, Mr. Semper. There is no doubt of your guilt and this court finds you guilty. Sentence to be carried out immediately."

Douglas raised a military-issue forty-five-caliber automatic equipped with a silencer and shot Semper one time, directly in the forehead.

Semper fell to the floor, dead instantly.

Douglas did not so much as glance at the body in front of him. As he removed his judge's robe and placed the weapon in a shoulder holster under his suit coat, he studied George Washington's flag. After a moment, he activated a hidden door in the paneling behind him to reveal an elevator.

He rode the elevator to the surface of the compound, where he stood and looked in the direction of his house. He pulled a remote detonator from his pocket and activated it even as he cursed Captain America with his every thought.

A bright orange-red fireball launched itself into the heavens with a roar. Douglas, still shaking with rage, watched it and knew it signaled that the last tie to his old life was gone. He could do nothing from this point but go forward.

He rode the elevator back down to his office. He walked to the outer door, taking care to step *over* Semper's body instead of going around it. As he walked down the empty corridor and back to the courtroom, he readied himself for the battle.

It starts now, Captain America, he thought to himself, *the destruction of your masters and my rise to power. And it starts with your death.*

18

THE LIGHT OF DAY

Taylor Douglas made one brief stop on his way back to the courtroom, a fast visit to the Liberty's Torch communications room. Although the room itself was large, with both equipment and space enough for three men, there was only one man on duty there.

"Corporal, are the intruders still out there?" Douglas asked the man. The corporal sat up straight, coming to attention in his chair, and put his hand to his radio earphone, as if to hear it better.

"We haven't received any recent reports, sir. The last report was that they were being allowed to explore our perimeter as per your order."

"How about our usual watchers? Has there been any activity from the FBI?"

"No, sir. As the general predicted, the enemy observers appear to be waiting to hear from the Falcon and are not taking any initiatives of their own."

"Excellent," Douglas said and resumed his walk back to the courtroom. With Captain America's trial distracting the people on one hand and the Falcon diverting the authorities on the other, no one suspected the Torch's true objective. All was going exactly as Douglas planned. Captain America would continue doing exactly what Douglas wanted. The Falcon and this Barry person would continue doing exactly what Douglas wanted. If he had any complaint, it was that everything was almost too easy.

Still, that was to be expected. In the face of his superior planning, how else could it be?

"I don't like it," Phillip Barry growled.

He looked one more time at the papers that had spilled from the manila envelope addressed to him and the Falcon. Page after page of printouts that purported to be from the Liberty's Torch computer and which detailed many of the militia group's secrets: the entrance to its hidden base; the number of guards patrolling the base; an actual map of the underground Torch compound. All they were missing, Barry mused, was the Torch secret handshake and their dinner menu. All this with nary a word of explanation as to who the papers were from or how their mysterious benefactor had gotten them into their hands.

Barry didn't have to believe in a third gunman or the grassy knoll to suspect the veracity of these documents. He considered the possibility that they were bait for a trap to be very high. And, if the maps leading them right to the Torch's front and back doors weren't enough to make him suspicious, the rest of the package put the whole thing way over the top.

The Falcon had told Barry how everyone involved in this case had agreed with Captain America's assessment that the Torch raids were a front designed to raise money to finance the militia's true objective. The second set of papers in the envelope revealed what that objective was.

According to those papers, which appeared to be printouts from the personal journal of Taylor Douglas, there were military games being held later today in some woodlands one hundred miles to the south. These weren't ordinary war games, however, but part of a planned series of United Nations training exercises.

The world, to be sure, was an unsettled place: political hot spots, border wars, human rights violations, and more. Already, while diplomats worked on negotiations, UN peacekeeping forces patrolled many of these areas in the hope of keeping bad situations from becoming worse. At the same time, growing troubles in several South American nations and in Eastern Europe threatened to increase dramatically the need for such forces.

The UN found it necessary to train its troops for the dual purposes of patrolling to preserve the peace and fighting, should hostilities break out around them. The United States government had offered its country for this training. Virtually any type of ecological environment, from deserts to mountains to tropical rain forest, could be found on American soil.

No matter what conditions were required, those conditions could be found here.

One such training mission was taking place in the forests of upstate New York. It was to be a series of mock encounters between armies made up of soldiers from virtually every member nation of the UN.

Liberty's Torch had learned of the exercises. The words Taylor Douglas wrote about the UN peace-keeping forces were filled with hate. These forces were exactly what he and his followers feared, seeing them as the first step toward the formation of the one world government Douglas was sure was coming. A global domination plan in which the United States would play but a subservient part, instead of the lead. Nothing could be a more tempting target. It was, as Douglas phrased it, where they would draw the line—in the blood of their enemies.

The journal entries detailed a plan by which the Torch would launch a strike at the convoy of trucks transporting the troops and their commanders to the games. The instrument of their wrath would be a Cobra assault helicopter, armed with a full compliment of TOW air-to-ground missiles. Many of these foreign invaders would die and, in the aftermath, fingers would be pointed, accusations made, and confidences shattered. Ultimately, no nation would fully trust any of the other nations, and all of them would be wary of future offers of American aid.

"This reeks of divide-and-conquer, wings," was Barry's quick assessment of the information. "They get you zooming off to stop this supposed helicopter attack, while I infiltrate their compound on my own. That way neither one of us has any backup and it's that much easier for them to pick us off."

"You think I don't realize that?" the Falcon replied. "Hey, I don't like the smell of this any better than you do. Especially that part about the Torch having a Cobra."

"Actually, that's one of the few things in these papers that rings true. There's about two dozen privately owned Cobras in the U.S. alone—that I know of—and that's not counting the ones Uncle Sammy has sold to our pals around the world. Douglas was a weapons tycoon. If anybody would be able to get their hands on a Cobra, it would be him."

"You're full of happy thoughts today, aren't you?" the Falcon muttered, then continued: "Okay, this could be a trap. I know that. But, something inside me tells me it isn't. I can't explain it. I just have a gut feeling this is for real. And even if I didn't have this feeling, the bottom line is, real or not, I can't ignore it. If this *is* straight up, then I'm probably the only chance those solders have got. I can't stand by and let them get slaughtered."

"I don't care about any of that," Barry protested. "I don't care about might-bes and what-ifs. Our mission is to rescue Captain America and get out alive. And— Ah, hell." Barry spat out the curse in sheer exasperation. He knew that the Falcon was right. Hell, if he was the ones with the wings, he'd be doing the same thing himself. He watched his friend take to the skies and shouted up to him.

"Be careful, wings. You're heading for mean skies."

The Falcon called back, "You, too, big guy. You won't exactly be meeting the welcome wagon yourself."

Barry craned his neck up, watching the Falcon disappear into the early morning sky. Then he collected the papers and carefully checked his rifle. "Big Roger on that, wings," he said to the now-empty sky above.

Because he would need his hands free to carry the maps, he slung the rifle over his shoulder. As he did, he patted its stock almost affectionately and said, "Come on, Betsy, let's go make us some new friends."

Barry picked up the maps and started limping in the direction that would take him to the Liberty's Torch compound and its first guard outpost. He muttered under his breath as he walked, berating himself for actually being fool enough to follow the maps. Still, even as the Falcon had to do what the papers required of him, so did he. A good man was being held somewhere in that compound—a man worth two of him and at least a hundred of the guys holding him. Barry was going to get that man out. No might-bes or what-ifs about it.

He moved carefully through the woods, taking great pains not to rustle the underbrush or make any noise. Still, his injured leg dragged ever so slightly behind him, leaving a trail-like line in the ground. Every few minutes, a drop of blood from his unhealed wound would break the line. He kept going.

The attack was set to go down in minutes. There was no time for the Falcon to contact anyone about the strike. The signal of his Avengers comm card wasn't strong enough to carry all the way to Agents Mack and Hattori; he couldn't warn the FBI. He had no idea what frequency the convoy of trucks was using and didn't have time to try all the possibilities before death rained on them from the skies; he couldn't warn the troops.

So he flew.

As fast as the turbines on his wings would carry him without him passing out, he flew. He flew above the treetops so he could fly in a straight line toward the convoy, hoping he was high enough that he would be able to see either the convoy or any ambush that he was being led into.

The minutes stretched out like hours as he scanned the ground below him looking for any trace of the convoy. He saw none. The sun was beginning to appear over the treetops, which would, he hoped, make his task easier. At least now he wouldn't have to be searching in the dark. He still saw nothing.

Sam felt a headache forming in the tense muscles at the base of his neck and was almost ready to agree that Barry's pessimism had been dead on, when he saw it.

The helicopter was coming in from the opposite direction. It was keeping the sun at its back, but it was heading toward the same coordinates as the Falcon. Even as far away as he was, the Falcon recognized the chopper's silhouette as that of an AH-1S Cobra.

He took a deep breath and increased his speed. Although his wings could reach a top speed of one hundred and forty miles per hour, he rarely pushed the limit. Any quicker and he risked moving faster than he could breathe. Prolonged travel at top speed could actually cause him to black out. But he had no other choice.

The Cobra was closer to its target then he was. He knew the helicopter's top speed was one hundred and twenty-three knots per second when loaded with a full complement of TOW missiles, about half of his own ultimate capability. But the Cobra didn't have to reach its goal. It could fire and guide its deadly cargo from as many as two and a half miles away, with the missiles hitting only twenty-two seconds later. The only chance he had of intercepting the Cobra before it came within range of the troop convoy was for him to pour it on.

He altered his course, now moving on a diagonal calculated to intercept the Cobra as it traveled on its flight path toward the convoy. As he flew, he kept an eye out for the convoy, all the while feeling the cold morning air beat against his face and arms, giving him wind burn.

Thirty seconds passed. The Cobra was larger now, but still so far away. Forty-five seconds. To his right and below, the Falcon could see dust rising. He suspected it was the troop convoy. At fifty-five seconds, he was close enough to confirm his suspicion. The trucks were moving along an unpaved road in a clearing that snaked between the trees below him.

At sixty seconds, he was close enough to the helicopter that he could see, underneath its stubby wings, the tubes from which the missiles would be launched. He pressed on. At eighty seconds, he felt his lungs start to pound within his chest, complaining they were empty. He ignored them and continued toward the interception point.

He flew as the pounding of his lungs became more insistent. He felt the muscles of his neck start to contract spasmodically, the body's method of forcing him to open his mouth and breathe.

He flew.

And was too late.

Even as he reached the interception point, the Cobra launched the first of its payload. The Falcon opened his mouth and didn't even have enough air to scream as the TOW's flight motor kicked in and propelled it at more than four hundred miles per hour. He would never be able to intercept the missile before it shredded the convoy below.

19

CLOSING
ARGUMENTS

The heavy iron manacles around Captain America's ankles dragged noisily against the floor as he and Gruenwald were pushed down the corridor to the courtroom. The guards—there were now four of them—didn't care that they were forcing the Captain to move faster than someone dragging so much weight could be expected to move. If anything, the sound of the chains encouraged them to push the Captain harder.

The Avenger shuffled along the corridor, encouraged at every step by the AK-47 barrel one of guards continually shoved into his back. The Captain kept as far ahead of the guard as he could. He had heard the guard take the safety off the powerful rifle and Cap didn't want it to discharge accidentally. He had also noticed all the guards had changed into the sleeveless T-shirt and fatigues uniform of Liberty's Torch. He knew why.

As he and Gruenwald were herded into the courtroom, the Captain saw that the guards on duty within the room were wearing their uniforms as well. He noted they now stood on the far side of the railing separating the spectator gallery from the front of the courtroom. The safeties of their rifles were likewise disengaged.

The Captain and Gruenwald sat down. Two guards positioned themselves on either side of the defense table. It seemed justice, or what passed for it in this mad place, was to be served quickly this day.

Swiveling his head slightly, the Captain took in the entire courtroom. Everyone had returned from the recess, save for Taylor Douglas and the prosecutor. It did not escape the Captain's notice that, when the bailiff commanded the courtroom rise, the prosecutor was still nowhere to be seen.

Taylor Douglas entered the courtroom, no longer wearing his judge's robe. He did not take his place behind the bench, but instead walked to the jury box. "Gentlemen of the jury," he said, "I'm afraid our prosecutor is a bit under the weather."

The small red spot on Douglas's otherwise pristine trousers leg and the lump that spoiled the otherwise impeccable cut of his suit also did not escape the sharp eyes of Captain America. He knew at once that the prosecutor's actual condition was more severe than Douglas was revealing.

"We have reached that portion of the trial known as closing arguments. As our prosecutor is unable to carry out his duties, I will give his closing argument for him. And don't even *think* about objecting," Douglas added, not even deigning to look at Gruenwald.

"Object? Me? Now why would I do anything so demeaning to the dignity of this honorable court?" Gruenwald stage-whispered to the Captain.

If the militia leader heard the comment, he did not react to it. Douglas instead stood before the jury box and, at first, said nothing. The jurors leaned slightly forward in their chairs, as if they were having problems with their hearing. Only then did Douglas start to speak.

"My friends, you have heard all the evidence. Witness after witness relating sad history after sad history. It leaves us with one inescapable conclusion: our own government has betrayed us. It has betrayed the citizens of this great land, the very citizens it was privileged to serve. And it has sought to strip us of our God-given rights. The right to bear arms. The right to assemble. The right to voice our protests against even our own government's tyranny. It oppresses us with an illegal income tax and then spends the money, not for the betterment of its citizens, but to support legions of lazy, slack-jawed, slope-browed, inner-city parasites. Slackards, who contribute nothing to our society, but who take everything that is handed to them. The government calls it 'entitlements,' my friends. And that is, perhaps, the problem: it teaches the parasites to believe they are *entitled* to the money, *entitled* to do nothing, *entitled* to steal from hardworking, honest Americans like us. And we find ourselves taxed to the point of poverty ourselves, just so the government can continue these so-called entitlements. The government uses the money it extorts from us to send foreign aid to governments who openly dispatch murderous terrorists into our country. The government forces trade agreements on us that drive this nation deeper into debt and rip desperately needed jobs from our shores, sending them to the cheap labor camps of our enemies.

"The government does little to stop the flow of illegal aliens into our country. Indeed, it has a vested interest in seeing them continue to flood America. Their campaign contributors line their pockets with the money they save by hiring these wetback laborers for pennies on the dollar. The government permits these illegals to steal our jobs. It indulges the lazy welfare cheats who drain our resources. It looks the other way at the oppressive trade regulations enacted by the Japanese and other foreign businessmen. It bows to the oil sheiks who rob us at the pumps and use their blood-stained profits to send terrorist assassins into our cities. It suckles at the breast of the international Zionist conspiracy that tries to shape how we think through its nigh-complete control of the newspapers we read and the television programs we watch. It funds, then submits to the United Nations when that body tells our government it must put the needs of the American people below the concerns of third-world dictators, demagogues, and all those others who actively seek to destroy our way of life.

"Our government does all these things, my friends, in direct violation of its founding principles, the principles of serving we, the people. It does all that *to* us, but it does nothing *for* us. It does *nothing* for the American people!"

As Douglas spoke, Norman Paris kept a watchful eye on Sherman Fairchild, making sure the older man was paying attention to their leader's words and, more important, accepting them. Whenever he felt Douglas had made a particularly compelling point, Paris would pat Fairchild's leg in what appeared to be a show of friendship, but with far more than friendly force. The pats were hard enough to remind

Fairchild that there was more behind the gesture than friendship. Occasionally, Paris would lean over to Fairchild and whisper, "You got that, Sherm?" or, "The man's makin' sense." He did and said other things as well, all calculated to keep Fairchild mindful of exactly what was expected of him.

Behind the colonel, John Richards could not help but notice Paris's orchestrated campaign or feel a little uncomfortable at it. *Geez, leave the old guy alone, Norm,* he thought. *He'll do the right thing by us.*

"*For* the American people," Douglas repeated, "the government does nothing. *To* the American people, well, that's very different. It oppresses us. It betrays us. It sells us out to whichever backwater mudhole happens to be this month's most favored nation. Every day, day in and day out, it betrays us."

Gruenwald looked around the room as Douglas spoke. It was the same thing over and over. The same nebulous charges the trial's witnesses had levelled now spilled from Taylor Douglas, charges for which there had been no proof. Still, everyone in the courtroom, not just the jurors, but everyone, listened as if Douglas were delivering the Sermon on the Mount instead of this paranoid drivel. They followed their leader with their eyes. Their heads moved as he moved. They nodded when he made a point and repeated what he said in whispered tones. They even seemed to breathe only when he breathed.

Turning to his client, Gruenwald realized he was wrong. Not every eye was on Douglas. Captain America was not looking at the militia leader. He was, in fact, not looking at any person in the courtroom. Instead, the Captain stared, without moving, without even blinking, at the American flag that stood to one side of the courtroom. No matter how Liberty's Torch had defiled it by displaying it in this kangaroo court, that flag represented America—and the Captain did not take his eyes off of it.

Gruenwald suddenly realized the courtroom had gone silent. He looked up, wondering if Douglas had finished his argument. No such luck. Douglas was only pausing for effect.

"My friends," Douglas said, "this has not been easy for me." He walked to the defense table and stood next to Captain America, holding out his hand near the Captain's shoulder without actually touching it. "This defendant had been a loyal soldier to this country. His heroism and deeds in World War II are unquestioned and every one of us in this courtroom owes him a great debt for his service then. None of us here are old enough to remember those exploits firsthand. We are all too young to have had our chests swell with pride as we read about how Captain America fought our fight against the Axis forces, to have felt a lump in our throats as we watched those battles on the newsreels. None of us can know what it was like, back then, to have Captain America fighting for us against the Nazi menace. Our fathers, our grandfathers, knew his deeds as we know the morning news. But for us, they can only be history. And that is an important fact to remember. Those heroic deeds were in the past—and they cannot redeem the crimes of the present.

"You ask, can a man who served his country nobly and proudly betray it? Can a once-great soldier turn quisling? Sadly, tragically, the answer is . . . yes. Benedict Arnold once served this country as a great soldier. In 1775, when hostilities broke out at Lexington, he volunteered for service in the Continental Army. He fought with Ethan Allen and helped take Fort Ticonderoga from the British. He commanded a flotilla on Lake Champlain that inflicted severe damage to an enemy fleet of superior numbers. In April of 1777, he repelled a British attack on Danbury, Connecticut. In August, he won the battle of Fort Stanwix. In September and October, the advance guard he led was instrumental in our country's great victory in the battle of Saratoga, the turning point of the war. He served well, my friends, and was promoted several times, attaining first the rank of brigadier general and, ultimately, that of major general.

"How many of you knew these historical facts? How many of you remember Benedict Arnold as a great soldier who fought nobly for the American cause? Few, if any. The only thing most Americans remember about Benedict Arnold is that he was a traitor. When the war didn't go as he wished, he conspired to sell West Point to the British for twenty thousand pounds. When his scheme was discovered, thankfully before he could carry it out, Benedict Arnold left his coconspirators behind to be hanged and he fled to England. In the closing days of the war, he fought for the British against the Continental Army and, when the war was finally over, he lived out the remainder of his wretched life in England, ostracized by the British and hated by the very Americans who had once honored him. To this day, Benedict Arnold is not remembered as a great general like George Washington. For us, the name Benedict Arnold is synonymous with traitor. It is an epithet of the foulest kind, reserved for the foulest kind. We did not let the past deeds of Benedict Arnold blind us to what he had become and prevent us from judging him a traitor.

"In the same way, we cannot let the past deeds of this defendant blind us to what *he* has become or prevent us from judging *him* a traitor, as well. You have heard how the federal government has betrayed the American people. Of that, there can be no doubt. But what *is* the federal government? Or, rather, *who*? It is a cadre of elected and appointed officials who unite to carry out their treasonous ends. The government is not a thing unto itself; it is made up of the people who set the policies and carry them out. So when I say the federal government is guilty of treason, it stands to reason that those who serve that government are traitors. People like the defendant.

"Captain America. His very name claims he represents America. He was created by the government for the war and served its ends then. He still serves its ends today. He serves as an operative for the government's intelligence forces. He leads the Avengers, a paramilitary force designed to keep us dependent on the federal government and its policies. He has come, through the years, to represent this country in the minds of nearly all its citizens. When you think of America, you think of Captain America. He is as much a part of the government as the President or Congress or any elected official and is, therefore, as guilty of treason as all of them.

"In truth, he is *more* guilty of treason. Governments are always looked upon with a degree of suspicion and mistrust. Captain America, on the other hand, was trusted by us all, loved by us all. So when he betrayed us by helping the government sell us out, when he did nothing to defend us from the government's tyrannies, his crime was even greater than those with whom he acted hand in hand. You have heard the evidence of the government's treason, my friends, and you know it to be true. You also know that Captain America, as that government's agent, as that government's symbol, is as guilty of treason as any member of that government.

"It is inescapable, my friends. If you believe the federal government is guilty of treason—and how could you not?—then the defendant, Captain America, is likewise guilty of treason against the American people. The evidence does not lie, my friends, even if the government does. And, as we draw close to the end of these proceedings, the evidence proves one simple and inescapable fact: Captain America is guilty of treason and you must find him so by returning a verdict of guilty."

Douglas abruptly turned on his heel and walked back to the bench. He did it so quickly that, at first, it caught Gruenwald off guard. It was only when Douglas climbed behind the bench that Gruenwald realized that the closing argument had reached its end.

As their leader resumed his judge's seat, a few spectators started a mild round of applause. Then, others joined in as well and the applause grew louder.

Douglas allowed the applause to swell to a moderate level—just enough to make its meaning clear without letting it grow too loud or obstructive. Gruenwald despite himself was impressed with Douglas's restraint. When the applause had grown too loud, he rapped his gavel on the bench and called for order.

As the room quieted, he looked down toward the defense table. "Mr. Gruenwald," Douglas said, "this court shall hear the defense's closing argument."

Gruenwald didn't move.

"Mr. Gruenwald," Douglas repeated, "does the defense intend to offer a closing argument?"

Gruenwald didn't answer. He had watched earlier, when Douglas had done nothing and got the undivided attention of everyone in the courtroom. He decided to use Douglas's own trick against the man. He did nothing until he was certain every eye in the courtroom was on him. Finally, when Douglas asked a third time, "Mr. Gruenwald?" this time with a hint of irritation in his voice, the attorney nodded slightly.

Then the sound of chair legs scraping against the floor filled the courtroom, followed immediately by the sound of Taylor Douglas's demanding voice—this time more noticeably irritated—as he spat out, "Mr. Gruenwald, what is *this*?"

Every head in the courtroom turned toward the defense table, but not toward Marcus Gruenwald. For it was Captain America who was standing to deliver the closing argument.

"Your Honor, Captain America stands accused by this court of treason. These are serious charges, capital offenses. I can think of no one better to refute those charges and let the truth be known than Captain America himself."

The room hummed with the electricity of whispered and outraged comments. Curses against the shyster and his tricks flew from one end of the court to the other. Taylor Douglas slammed his gavel down on the desk with a boom that echoed across the room like a thunderclap.

"Order! Order! There will be *order* in this court!"

It took a moment, but the courtroom did quiet. Then Douglas announced, "Mr. Gruenwald, you are out of order."

"Begging Your Honor's kind indulgence, but the case of *Faretta* v. *California* does grant defendants the right to waive counsel and represent themselves. Captain America wants nothing more than to exercise this right. For the closing argument, Captain America *will* represent himself."

Douglas was about to slam his gavel down onto the bench once more and deny the request, when Gruenwald hurriedly added, "Or are you afraid to let him speak? Here in your courtroom, deep within your compound. Here in your own backyard. What are you afraid of, Your Honor?"

Douglas stared down at Gruenwald. He looked like he was ready to pick up the bench and bludgeon the lawyer with it.

Every person in the court, including the cameraman, was looking at the Captain and knew the video camera was focused on the Avenger, recording every moment of this courtroom drama. And high drama it was.

"Mr. Gruenwald," Douglas finally said, "this court resents your impudent attempt at reverse psychology and it finds you in contempt, sentence to be passed later." The anger in Douglas's voice was obvious. He took in a deep breath and exhaled it slowly. "Nevertheless," he continued, more calmly, "you make a valid point. This court need fear nothing. It has the truth on its side and no legal maneuvers by you or your client will ever change that. Captain America, you may proceed."

"Thank you, Your Honor," Captain America said in a soft voice. There was an honest sincerity in the Avenger's tone, a deference, Gruenwald knew, that was to that American flag standing off to one side of the room, not to Taylor Douglas.

He said nothing more at first. He simply walked to the jury box and allowed the sound of his dragging manacles to carry through the now-silent courtroom. Then he stood before the jury, placed his chained hands on the railing, and smiled at the men seated there. Even coming behind his mask, the Captain's smile was powerful. It was as full as any Louis Armstrong had ever flashed and so bright it could have cut a San Francisco fog.

"My fellow Americans." The Captain paused for a moment, letting the phrase sink in. "I apologize for the clichéd salutation. Under the circumstances, none is better suited. I call you my fellow Americans because that is what we are. All of us. Not the government and the governed, but each others' fellow Americans. I note this court takes pains to refer to, not the *American* government, but the *federal* government, attempting to legitimize the court's assumed authority by characterizing that government as somehow removed from its people. I could speak to that, but it is not an argument that addresses the charges that have been made here over these past few days. You claim to have grievances with our government. I cannot address those grievances, either. As much as the prosecution would have it otherwise, I am *not* the government. Captain America was created in 1941 to be a soldier, the first recruit in what was hoped to be a battalion of similarly empowered soldiers. An assassin's bullet murdered that hope, leaving me the sole inheritor of a brilliant man's work. But, although Captain America was created to be a soldier, I have tried to make him far more than that.

"America is a country of great promise, not only for those you deem worthy of the promise, but for all. First and foremost, I am the guardian of that promise. To carry out my mission, I may work *with* our government, but I do *not* stand for it. I stand for the ideals that formed our government in 1776, the ideals that continue to be its foundation to this day. You have claimed I represent the government, that, somehow, I am that government. That is a falsehood. I *cannot* represent our government. That is the responsibility of our President and our elected and appointed officials, laid upon those men and women by their oaths of office.

"I represent the American *people*, but not in the same

manner that those men and women do. I swore no oath of office. What I represent is the *dream*. The freedom to become all you can imagine becoming. *That* is the core ideal of this country. *That* is the promise our land makes to the world. I am a soldier. I fight to preserve and defend the ideal and the promise.''

The Captain paused, turning to stare intently at the flag that stood in the corner of the courtroom. He continued to look at the flag until the eyes of all the jurors were also focused on it.

''The flag that you so proudly display in this courtroom is one symbol of the American dream. And, because that flag serves as the model for my own uniform, I have tried to be another. Every day, I strive to be the living embodiment of the dream, to do right so that the dream can live on in me, and through me, reach others. By my actions, by my example, I serve to remind the citizens of this great country that we must be ever vigilant if we are to keep our dream alive, that we must be ever on our guard to defend the dream against those who would destroy it. Being Captain America has been *my* American dream. It has allowed me the opportunity to be all I ever wanted to be. It has allowed me, even against the deadliest foes, the toughest odds, to defend the rights of all men and women and, I hope, to inspire others to have done the same.

''I did not commit these crimes, these alleged crimes, of our government. I cannot have committed them. I am not the government. I cannot be the government. I am and can *only* be a man. A man who lives by the American dream. Now I am asking *you* to live by the dream as well and do what is right, even against the toughest of odds. I am asking you to find me not guilty. Thank you.''

Before Captain America could walk back to the defense table—before he could even turn toward it—Taylor Douglas stood up behind his bench.

''You have heard the evidence,'' Douglas snarled. ''You

all know what you *must* do. Now is the time for you to discharge your duty to this court.''

Douglas looked at the armed guards flanking the defense table. The guards immediately leveled their rifles directly at Captain America, even as their fingers began to tighten nervously on the triggers.

''Gentlemen of the jury, what is your verdict?''

20

DRAWING THE LINE

The Falcon had twenty-two seconds. From the moment that the TOW missile left its launch tube, little more than a score of seconds would pass before it slammed into its target and detonated, less if the Cobra wasn't firing from its maximum range. Twenty-two seconds before the missile slaughtered a lot of innocent soldiers in the convoy below.

The Tube-launched, Optically-tracked, and Wire-guided missle did not have an internal guidance system. In the Cobra's cockpit, the two-person crew would actually direct its flight from the tube to the target.

A Telescopic Sight Unit fitted into a small box on the nose of the Cobra. A Forward Looking Infra-Red tracking system in the same housing sent images to the Heads Up Display in the gunner's helmet. Through the FLIR, the gunner saw what the helicopter's TSU saw. His HUD also contained the gun sight crosshairs. After a missile launched, he kept the crosshairs centered on the target with a simple joystick. The helicopter's computers did the rest.

The missile itself had a light source on its tail, which the TSU tracked. The helicopter's computers used the tracking light to coordinate its position with the target. The tracking system sent any course corrections to the missile along twin copper wires that trailed behind the missile and which were anchored to a spoon in the launch tube.

It almost seemed silly: guided missiles directed by wires. With all the computer technology available, surely a better method of guidance was available. But the Falcon knew the TOW's wire-guided system had been used in Vietnam and proved quite effective for sending signals to a missile in the smoky environment of a wooded battlefield.

The Falcon also knew what he had to do in the next twenty-two seconds. He angled his flight to take him up to the Cobra, using every erg of power his wings could provide. He fought against the propwash downdraft of the twin GE T700-GE-401 engines rotating the Cobra's blades at one thousand seven hundred seventy-five horsepower. It seemed to take forever, as he moved up through the molasses-like air beneath the helicopter's spinning blades.

Then he grasped the outside latch of the Cobra's canopy. He rotated it, pulled the canopy door up with his left arm, and used the jets behind his arm to push against the downdraft so that he could open the door. Even so, even with his wings doing most of the work against the powerful downdraft, the muscles of his left arm strained at the effort and the Falcon felt acute pain from his shoulder to his fingers.

With the door open, the Falcon leaned into the cockpit. "What the—?" the startled gunner yelled as he saw the Falcon, while the pilot screamed for the gunner to shoot the winged hero. The Falcon didn't hesitate—he reached into the cockpit, grabbed the joystick and pushed it hard.

The crosshairs in the targeting system moved off the convoy. Along the twin wires, the Cobra's computer sent what appeared to be a course correction to the TOW missile. The Falcon looked over his shoulder at the missile. He smiled widely as the missile veered up off its original course, missing the troop carriers and exploding harmlessly in the ground several dozen yards away.

The Falcon didn't have time to celebrate; he had to insure the Cobra's crew could not launch a second missile. Although he was leaning partway into the cockpit, the front of the helicopter was short. His feet hung down by the nose. The Falcon brought his left leg up and with a kick powered by the jet in his boot, kicked the TSU housed in the box on the Cobra's nose.

He cracked the casing of the TSU and broke two toes on his left foot in the process. The casing, made of sapphire, was harder than he'd expected. Ignoring the pain, he reared his leg back for a second attempt and revved up his wings. This time, the Falcon kicked with his heel, smashing the unit so hard it shattered into pieces. A hot jet of pain shot up his leg as the pieces dropped away toward the ground below. He had broken his heel as well.

The maneuver—how to deflect a TOW missile and take out its target system—was one that the Falcon had practiced many times at Captain America's insistence. In those first few months of their friendship and training, the exercise had seemed ludicrous. When, he had asked Cap, would he ever take on an assault helicopter at such close range?

"Sam," the Captain had patiently explained, "if you're going to fight in the air, you have to be ready for anything else that's up there with you."

Since then, his years of partnership with the Captain had also taught the Falcon the wisdom of Cap's words. And, just now, that wisdom had again proved useful.

The fight wasn't over by a long shot. The Cobra could still fly down and fire its remaining TOWs at close range; simple visual guidance could direct them to a target. Or the chopper could fire at the soldiers with the twenty-millimeter turret cannon mounted under its nose.

He pushed off the helicopter and allowed himself to fall away until he was free of its downdraft. He circled around in front of the Cobra, looping and taunting it. As he hoped, the gunner began to fire at him.

The Falcon was more agile than the Cobra and could fly faster than it. He could, in fact, fly literal rings around it. But the helicopter was armed to the teeth. The gunner couldn't use the TSU to aim the turret cannon any longer, but the gun could fire off its lethal charges at an alarming rate. All the pilot had to do was aim the Cobra's nose toward the Falcon while his gunner fired repeatedly. The smallest mistake in the hero's evasive maneuvers and he would be ripped apart by the bullets.

He had to think of a way to disable the copter permanently. And he was running out of time fast.

Phillip Barry had reached the first perimeter guard outpost indicated on the map. He hid in the bushes, studying it carefully. He saw only one guard; anyone else normally stationed here was probably in the compound. Barry had hoped the solitary guard would be careless, perhaps even nodding off to sleep after a long night's watch. No such luck. The guard was alert and held his AK-47 at the ready.

That was the bad news. The good news was that the guard post was concealed in underbrush. It kept the post from being seen by unsuspecting visitors until they were fired upon by the sentries waiting within. However, if someone knew the post was here, knew how to approach it from the rear, the situation would be different. Armed with that information, a lone man could sneak around the guard post and attack from the rear. It would require stealth, but that would be second nature to a former Green Beret. Even a wounded former Green Beret.

The sentry never knew what hit him. He was unconscious before he even realized he was being attacked. Barry dragged the guard into the woods and left him there, bound and gagged.

One down, God only knew how many more to go.

Barry continued his trek to the Liberty's Torch compound. His wounded leg ached, but he moved swiftly and silently through the forest. *Next time*, he thought as he limped his way through an area of particularly heavy growth, *I want the wings*.

The first the troop convoy knew of any danger was when Colonel William Thom saw the missile shooting out of the sky toward them. Then, before he could even point to it or alert his men, Thom heard the sound of the incoming missile.

His second-in-command, Captain Maheras, also heard that sound and recognized it. An ashen white shroud came over Maheras's face as he looked in the direction of the sound. Then he too saw the TOW missile streaking toward them.

He barely had time to begin what he believed would be his last living prayer when the missile abruptly veered off course, shot over them, and struck the ground scant yards beyond them. The sound of the explosion rang in his ears, the harbinger of a killer headache. He would welcome it.

After all, you couldn't take a couple of aspirin to make death go away.

The officers looked in the direction from which the missile had come. At first, they saw nothing. They could hear the sound of gunfire, but whatever was up there was too far away to be seen.

Then, as suddenly as the shooting started, it stopped. Thom gave the order for the troops to evacuate the convoy and seek cover in the woods.

Maheras watched the sky for the second missile they were sure would come, so it was he who saw the object first, coming at them from the sky to the north.

Except it wasn't an object. It was a man.

A man in a red and white costume was flying down at them in an erratic, evasive path. Thom did not recognize the man's uniform. He could only assume the attacker to be a high-tech advance scout, coming to do the job the missile had failed to accomplish. Behind the man, confirming the colonel's fears, a Cobra assault helicopter was approaching, its turret cannon blazing.

Thom gave the order to fire.

The Falcon heard the first bullet whiz by him. *Perfect*, he thought, *the soldiers are shooting at me.* He had the Cobra coming up his exhaust and now the very men he was trying to protect were trying to shoot him out of the sky, too. Of course, they couldn't know he was trying to save them, but that knowledge did little to comfort him at the moment. He had to beat the Cobra to the convoy and launch his counter-attack. And, as he was still flying at maximum speed, he *really* needed to take a quick breath or two.

The Falcon came in, moving like a moth flitting around a light at over two hundred miles per hour. He stayed above the convoy, too high to offer the soldiers a good target, but close enough for his purposes. He looked over the convoy as he flew, searching for the one item he was sure was there. Flying from vehicle to vehicle in a wild evasive pattern, his eyes moved about anxiously. He knew he was running out of time. And then he spotted what he needed for his plan.

After doing a quick loop over one of the trucks, he swooped in quickly, abandoning his evasive pattern, banking on the fact that he was moving too fast for the soldiers to fix their aim on him. He flew toward an open-backed truck filled with soldiers of various nationalities. Though the soldiers were armed, they did not aim their weapons nor attempt to fire them. That confirmed that they had what the Falcon needed.

He flew in, passing directly over the heads of the confused soldiers. He reached down, grabbing a rifle from one man. He pulled the rifle free and then zoomed back up into the sky and at the swiftly-approaching Cobra.

The Cobra was almost upon the convoy, almost close enough that it could fire its TOW missiles and be sure of hitting something. The Falcon couldn't allow it. He flew in close to the chopper, hovered in front of it for a second and took aim with the rifle. He squeezed the trigger.

The Falcon's shot hit the front window of the Cobra's canopy. The round exploded on the reinforced glass with a soft *splut* and a glob of pink paint spread across the windshield.

The Falcon flew around the Cobra, firing again and again. The paint balls—originally intended to mark hits in the war games—now served another purpose.

Splut! Splut! Splut!

With each shot, more of the canopy was covered with the pink paint. The Falcon flew from the left to the right and back again, firing over and over. He emptied the rifle at the Cobra and, when he had finished, the glass canopy was completely covered in the sticky wet paint. Neither the pilot nor the gunner could see out through the windows to aim their weapons or fly their craft.

The Cobra banked, turned, and started to fly away from the convoy. The Falcon looked back to see that everything was all right below and then followed the fleeing copter.

The gunner had opened the cockpit door and was directing their flight. They didn't go far. When the Cobra passed over a clearing some distance away from the troop convoy, the pilot brought the helicopter down. They could escape before their intended targets could reach them. There was one flaw in this plan.

The Falcon waited for the them to exit the chopper, then flew over them.

"Gentlemen, I suggest you surrender."

The only response was the sound of gunshots as each of the two men drew and fired their handguns.

They didn't have a prayer of hitting the Falcon. He was too high and moving entirely too swiftly for them to aim their weapons effectively. He flew above them, avoiding their shots easily, until each man had emptied his gun's clip and was, pathetically, dry firing at him. He swooped down and hovered in front of the panicked militiamen.

"Are you going to make me repeat it?" the Falcon asked.

The pilot rushed at the Falcon like a charging bull. "I ain't gonna be captured by no—*uhf!*"

The words died in the man's throat, probably because the Falcon had flown forward and grabbed him by the neck. He picked up speed as he flew and slammed the pilot into a stately, sturdy oak tree. The man hung on the tree for a moment, defying gravity, and then fell heavily to the ground.

"Man, I was *hoping* you'd do something stupid like that," the Falcon said, still hovering a few inches above the ground to keep the weight off his broken heel and toes.

The Cobra pilot wouldn't be conscious anytime soon. Turning, the Falcon saw the gunner bolting for the trees at the opposite end of the clearing. He waited until the second before the man would have escaped into the relative safety of the woods before he grabbed him by the collar and flew him above and through the tops of several trees. The man shrieked in terror.

It was music to the Falcon's ears.

• • •

It was a strange sight that greeted Colonel Thom and Captain Maheras as they looked into the sky. The Falcon descended before them, the two unconscious men thrown over his shoulders. He dropped them the few inches to the ground with a satisfying thump.

From this distance, the officers had no trouble recognizing the hovering Avenger.

The Falcon held out the paint gun. "Please give this back to the man I borrowed it from—with my thanks. As for this garbage," he said, sweeping his hand over the unconscious men on the ground, "well, if I weren't a Christian, I'd suggest digging a very deep hole. But, that being the case, I'll ask you to hold them for the FBI."

Colonel Thom didn't know quite what to say. Shortly after he had become an officer, one of his superiors, a career solider who had served under General Thaddeus "Thunderbolt" Ross, had told him of watching the Avengers battle the Lava Men. The man had said it was both awe inspiring and intimidating to stand face to face with a super hero. Now, all these years later, Thom finally knew what his commander had meant.

"Is there anything else we can do for you, sir?"

"Sir?" the Falcon responded, suppressing a laugh as he shook the colonel's hand. "Just make sure these mutts are uncomfortable. That and loan me a radio. I need to check in with someone, let him know the info panned out and that I got here in time. But, hurry," he added, a mix of concern and determination in his voice. "The rest of these losers have a friend of mine and I'm not going to let them keep him a second longer."

21

THE VERDICT

I t was a moment Taylor Douglas had been anticipating eagerly and he wanted to savor it for as long as he could.

"Gentlemen of the jury, as I call on each one of you, you will stand and deliver your verdict." Douglas smiled. He looked to see if there was any reaction from the defense table. He saw none and was felt momentarily disappointed. It passed quickly.

Fine. Let the sanctimonious fool and his lawyer pretend they aren't worried. We'll see how long they can maintain their calm as they listen to the verdicts.

The desired reactions, he was sure, would come soon enough. This was a glorious moment. As each guilty verdict was returned, it would be a nail in the coffin Captain America knew was waiting for him at the end of the trial. And, as each additional nail was pounded in, the smugness would surely fade from the face of that star-spangled betrayer.

"Juror Number One, in the matter of *The People* v. *Captain America*, how do you find the defendant as to counts one through fifteen? Guilty or not guilty?"

Here it comes, thought Gruenwald. He wasn't so naïve as to believe he could escape the fate awaiting Captain America. They were both dead men. If the contempt of court charge wasn't enough for Douglas to sentence him to death, he was sure he would be found guilty of some other imagined crime against the people and put to death just the same.

The defense attorney studied the jurors. Courtroom experience had taught him that one could often read a jury and predict the probable verdict before it was delivered. Jurors about to convict frequently found it difficult to look the defendant they were about to condemn in the eye and instead stared at the floor while the verdict was read. Jurors about to acquit would look a defendant in the eye to share in the defendant's joy.

Juror Number One was looking directly at Captain America, attempting to stare the Avenger down. From the obvious malice in the juror's eyes, Gruenwald suspected the conventional wisdom would not hold true in this court. These madmen wanted to watch the Captain as they delivered their verdicts. They longed to see him cower as they condemned him.

"Guilty," the first juror said.

"Juror Number Two, how say you, guilty or not guilty?"

The second juror stood and smiled sadistically at the Captain.

"Guilty."

"Juror Number Three, how say you, guilty or not guilty?"

The third juror glared at Captain America. "Guilty," he said, without a moment's hesitation.

"Juror Number Four, how say you, guilty or not guilty?

The room turned its undivided attention to Sherman Fairchild. At first, the old man did absolutely nothing. Then, he coughed, a nervous cough, but did not stand. Still sitting next to Fairchild, Norm Paris leaned forward and rested his arm on the jury box. His impatience was apparent.

The militia colonel turned his head slightly, looking at Sherm Fairchild out of the corner of his eye. Fairchild could see his growing anger.

"Juror Number Four," Taylor Douglas said pointedly, unexpected irritation spoiling his once-placid demeanor.

Sherman Fairchild looked Captain America directly in the eye. He wore an odd expression, the discomfort of a man attending the funeral of someone he doesn't really know and feeling quite out of place. Then, without standing, the elderly militiaman looked away and mumbled something.

"What was that? I couldn't hear you," Douglas said.

"Yeah, speak up, Gramps," Paris added. "Why not share your freakin' wisdom of the ages?"

"Guilty, Your Honor," Fairchild repeated in the weak voice of what he had become: a frightened old man. Whatever courage he once possessed was nowhere in evidence.

• • •

Gruenwald saw the satisfied look that passed between Douglas and Juror Number Five then back again. Juror Number Four had been Cap's only chance. The intimidation of the burly man sitting next to him had worked. It was all over now.

"Juror Number Five, how do you say, guilty or not guilty?"

The burly man stood up as if he had been shot from a cannon. He turned his whole body, instead of just his head, to face Captain America, as if he were challenging Cap to a duel.

"Guilty! Guilty! Guilty as hell! And the only thing I'm only sorry about is that I ain't gonna be pulling the trig—"

Douglas's gavel banged down to interrupted the man in mid-word. "Thank you, Juror Number Five," Douglas said, reestablishing the order of his courtroom before continuing.

"Juror Number Six, how say you, guilty or not guilty?"

The next juror rose to his feet then looked around. Gruenwald had seen other lawyers with that look: he obviously wanted to make sure that all eyes were on him, that the fifth juror hadn't robbed him of his moment in the spotlight. When he seemed satisfied that, for now, at least, he was the center of the universe, he announced, "Guilty, Your Honor."

"Juror Number Seven, how say you, guilty or not guilty?"

Number Seven stood, said his "Guilty," and sat down as quickly as he could.

"Juror Number Eight, how say you, guilty or not guilty?"

The overweight man in the eighth seat looked uncomfortable in his suit. He also offered a quick verdict: "Guilty."

"Juror Number Nine, how say you, guilty or not guilty?"

Number Nine stood up, adjusted his tie, and pulled on his jacket to make sure it hung properly. "Your Honor, it is with great pleasure that I say, guilty."

Douglas started to say something, then stopped. Then he looked at the Captain. Gruenwald had to suppress a smile at the look of disappointment on the judge's face. Obviously, the leader of Liberty's Torch had expected the Captain to look devastated rather than sitting calmly awaiting his fate. *Better men than you have tried to intimidate him and failed*, Gruenwald thought. Douglas then turned back to the jury box and asked Juror Number Ten for his verdict.

"Guilty," the tenth juror said, after standing.

"Juror Number Eleven, how say you, guilty or not guilty?"

John Richards stood up and opened his mouth to speak. Then he stopped. He looked around at the other men in the jury box. He saw the hate in their eyes and realized he felt none of his own. He saw no disquiet in their faces over this Roman circus that had passed for a trial. Whatever it was that the men in this courtroom wanted, he no longer wanted it. But he wasn't sure he was strong enough to do the right thing.

Richards looked at Captain America, looked at the Avenger's face and deep into his blue eyes. Those eyes did mirror that man's soul and, in them, flashed the courage that lived unconquered within, the courage that filled and defined the man.

The Captain returned the look, fixing his eyes on Richards. The juror found that, somehow, the strength within Captain America was passing between the two of them— moving from the Captain to him and filling him as well. And John Richards found within himself the courage to say:

"Your Honor, I find the defendant not guilty."

The twelfth juror had already started to stand in anticipation of delivering the satisfying final verdict. He stopped abruptly and, in doing so, tripped over his own feet. As he fell clumsily to the floor of the jury box, his expletive was lost in the shocked cries of surprise that echoed through the courtroom.

Norman Paris turned crimson, shaking visibly. He bolted from his chair, lunging toward Richards. He literally snarled at the object of his rage, "You son of a—"

He finished neither curse nor lunge. Both were swept away in a blur of red, white, and blue.

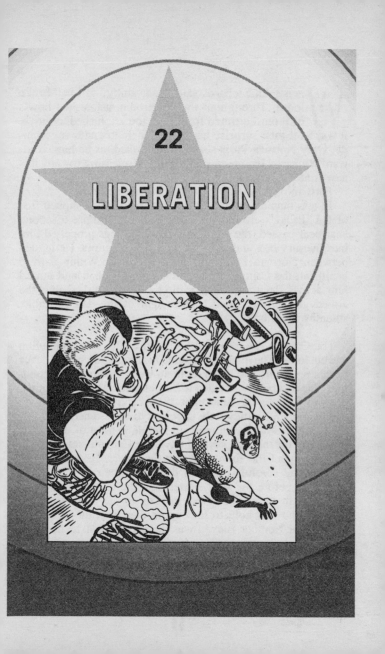

22

LIBERATION

When John Richards said, "not guilty," all hell broke loose. Throughout the courtroom, astonished howls of protest erupted from men too astonished to move. It was as if their surprise had turned them to unmoving granite. Only Norman Paris seemed unaffected, as he lunged toward Richards intent on making his displeasure toward this new traitor a physical reality.

Paris moved quickly. Another moved quicker.

In less than a heartbeat, Captain America had slipped free of the shackles around his arms and legs. Before a second heartbeat passed, the Captain's powerful legs propelled him into the jury box and over the first row of jurors. He landed between Norman Paris and John Richards. Within a third heartbeat, the Captain lifted Paris from his chair and hurled him across the room. The militia colonel crashed into the armed guard who stood to the right of the defense table, stunning them both.

The Captain was relieved he could finally stop pretending and cut loose. The manacles around his arms and legs had never been a problem. The locks on them were shoddy and second-rate. The lockpick concealed in his belt buckle had made quick work of them on the first night of his captivity. After that, he had fixed them so they only appeared to be fastened.

Although Marcus Gruenwald had done most of the actual trial work for the past several days, the Captain had not been idle. He spent the time studying the jurors. He had looked at each one carefully, gazing deep into their eyes. He had suspected before the trial started that the red-haired man in the eleventh juror's seat was the key to the trial. When he testified and was able to look more clearly at the jurors, he knew Juror Number Eleven was the one. Indeed, he had prepared his closing argument specifically for that juror.

He may not have realized that he was going to return a verdict of "not guilty" until he actually heard the words coming from his mouth, but the Captain had known it far earlier and prepared accordingly. He figured the lone "not guilty" would, at least momentarily, paralyze the people in the room, and he readied himself to act in that moment.

When it came, he moved quickly.

The guns were the most important thing. The Captain had noted each man in the room who had a gun. He knew which weapons were out in the open and which were in concealed holsters, necessitating that extra second before they could be drawn and fired.

Even as the astonished militiamen watched him throw the fifth juror across the room to slam into the guard, Captain America was moving. He leapt from the jury box and over the judge's bench to land squarely on Taylor Douglas. With a fluid move, he sprang off of Douglas, driving Douglas's head into the bench and Douglas into unconsciousness, and grabbed his shield from the wall. He pushed off the wall, executing a perfect backflip that carried him to the floor in front of the bench. While still upside down, he threw his shield across the room.

The shield smashed into the head of the second armed guard, rebounded and slammed into the head of the armed man who had sat behind him and Gruenwald, and then ricocheted back to Cap's hand as he completed his flip. Both men would be out for the duration of this soirée.

The Captain threw his shield again. It struck the bailiff, even as the man was drawing his gun and knocked him unconscious, bouncing back to its master in a perfect arc.

He quickly scanned the courtroom. The remaining militiamen were beginning to move. Most were heading for the doors at the rear of the room, afraid to face the Captain's fury; others were advancing on him. They would have to wait.

The guard to the right of the defense table had recovered and was aiming his rifle at the Captain. Faster than a human eye could follow, the shield flew from the Avenger's hand and struck the AK-47. It shattered in the guard's hands.

The Captain picked up the rifle the other guard had

dropped at his feet, smashing it against the table so it could pose no further threat. As he did, someone slammed into his back.

Before the Captain could recover from the blow, a second and then a third man jumped on him. They buried him under their weight like linesmen piling on a quarterback. The Captain tried to shake them off, only to be taken aback as more men threw themselves on the pile.

"Stand him at attention, boys." The Captain recognized the malevolent snarl of Juror Number Five.

Several men pulled Captain America to his feet, holding his arms so tightly behind him that even he could not break free. The Captain stood helplessly as Juror Number Five aimed his gun at him.

"I'm gonna salute the flag."

The door into the Liberty's Torch compound was exactly where Phillip Barry had been told it would be. Even better, there was only one guard at the door, again as he'd been told. He studied the setup.

Although the door itself was concealed, there was nothing near it to cover Barry while he snuck up on the guard. With his bad leg still slowing him down, he would never be able to rush the door before the man had a chance to react. This time, there was no other choice. From his hiding place, Barry unslung his rifle from over his shoulder. He aimed carefully and fired.

The guard jerked up when the tranquilizer dart struck him in the neck. He reached for it, trying to pull it out and staggered around as if he were drunk. That was the problem with tranq darts. Bad spy movies not withstanding, they weren't really instantaneous. A target could do things, even sound an alarm, before succumbing to them. Still, the instructions Barry and the Falcon had received had asked him not to kill unless absolutely necessary and he felt honor-bound to comply. He had taken the tranq rifle and a sidearm, the latter to be used only as a final resort.

The guard was dizzy, but remained cognizant enough to reach for the alarm button. That was when Barry emerged from his hiding place and rushed the door. The guard attempted to fight back, but was too woozy to be effective. Before the man could lift his own rifle, Barry was on him.

A single punch knocked the man down. Then, the dart finally took full effect and the guard slipped into senselessness. By the time he came to, it would be over—one way or another.

Barry grinned as he activated the door access code supplied to him. At least, he mused, if the darts weren't instantaneous, they were equalizers, slowing down his enemies enough that his wound no longer put him at a disadvantage.

The door slid open quietly. Barry wasn't surprised to see the empty corridor before him. The instructions had told him that would be the case, that the other compound dwellers would be in the courtroom. Barry checked the map again; it charted a course that would allow him to navigate the labyrinth of the Liberty's Torch headquarters without difficulty.

Barry chuckled softly to himself. It was like getting a triptych with all the points of interest, not to mention access codes, already highlighted. Triple-A should consider adding this service. As castle-stormings went, this was the way to go.

According to the map, he was getting close to the courtroom. That was confirmed when a door at the far end of the corridor swung open and several men came running out of it. They looked like extras in a Godzilla movie. The men ran past him, barely noticing that there was an intruder in the compound. They only cared about one thing: getting out before Tokyo fell on them.

Barry continued down the corridor, slowed somewhat by the men bumping into him in their mad flight. Then, while most of the corridor still separated him from his destination, he heard a gunshot. He limped along the corridor as best he could, but, by the time he reached the courtroom, it was already too late.

• • •

Captain America knew he would never be able to break free of the men who held his arms before Juror Number Five fired his gun. He didn't even try. Instead, he did what they weren't expecting him to do.

He jumped off the floor, bringing his legs up over his head as he did. With his captors still holding him, he extended his legs and kicked the gun as it discharged. The shot went harmlessly into the ceiling.

The Captain continued his maneuver in one swift motion. He somersaulted backward, rolling over and breaking free of the men who held him.

The men whirled around to grab the Captain again, but he wasn't there. As soon as his feet hit the ground, he had jumped again. He executed a flip over the militiamen and landed in front of Juror Five.

The juror was bringing his gun down to fire again when the Captain's shield smashed into his face. Blood poured from his ruined nose and he crumpled to the floor.

The five remaining militiamen surrounded Captain America. They all rushed him at once—and learned that there was no safety in numbers when they faced this warrior.

The Captain vaulted over his first attacker, pushing off the man's head with his hands while simultaneously kicking his legs out to each side of his body. Each of his feet struck a militiaman in the face, one on the left and one on the right. The two men were unconscious before they hit the floor.

Even as he did that, the Captain directed the lunge of the man he was vaulting over, forcing him to plow into the man directly behind the Avenger. By the time either could recover, their former captive had landed, driving his shield into the gut of the fifth man. That man doubled over, only to straighten up when the Captain's right uppercut sent him reeling backward and out of this fight for the duration.

Taylor Douglas regained consciousness just in time to see his master plan falling apart. All around the courtroom, several of his most valuable followers lay senseless, while Captain America was easily dispatching those few who remained. Douglas reached for his gun, but the cursed Avenger was moving too swiftly for a clear shot. The realization came that this might be the proper moment to exercise the proverbial better part of valor. The way to the rear door was clear; he started to run for it.

The two remaining men flanked Captain America, one in the front and one in the rear. As they charged, the Captain saw Taylor Douglas running toward the rear door. He started to calculate how he could defeat his remaining attackers and still stop Douglas from escaping. He formed his plan instantaneously.

The Captain reached out and grabbed the man in front of him. He fell backward, pulling the man to him. He placed his right foot on the man's chest and executed a back roll, carrying his victim over him and then throwing him into the man behind them. The two militiamen collided with a loud thud.

Even as the Captain executed this maneuver, he turned his head and saw Douglas running past Gruenwald toward the rear door and freedom. With a quickness belying his scrawny body, Gruenwald slid to the other side of the defense table. He shot his left foot out and tripped Douglas.

The would-be savior of America fell forward, his face hitting the hard concrete floor with loud and satisfying crack. The Captain suspected the militia leader would be taking all his meals through a straw for the next several months.

Gruenwald's action allowed the Captain to freely concentrate on the last defender of Liberty's Torch.

"I guess we can chalk up another one for the 'International Zionist Conspiracy,' " Gruenwald quipped. Then his face became more serious. He looked down at the unconscious Taylor Douglas and then over at Captain America. "Thanks, Cap. Thanks for everything."

The Avenger merely nodded in reply, then looked down at the two groaning militiamen at his feet. "Gentlemen?" he said. The two men sat up and put their arms behind their heads in surrender.

The Captain went to the defense table. "Are you all right?" he asked Gruenwald. The attorney was slumped forward and looking a bit haggard.

"I'll be fine in a second, Cap. All of a sudden, I seem to be a little wasted. Just let me catch my breath."

"It's the adrenaline rush," the Captain explained. "Now that the fight is over, your body isn't pumping adrenaline into you any more. It, and you, need to recover."

The Captain glanced back at the two still-conscious members of Liberty's Torch. They still sat in the middle of the floor, showed no further signs of resistance. They might not have had adrenaline pumping through them, but, like Gruenwald, their strength was spent and they were no longer interested in fighting.

The Captain saw a bearded man limp into the courtroom through the rear door. He walked to him with his hand extended in friendly greeting.

"Phillip Barry, I presume?"

Barry took the offered hand and said, "Yup."

"The Falcon?" Captain America asked.

"He checked in with me just before I entered the compound. He accomplished his mission, too. And," he continued, "the Army and the FBI should be here any second. They'll pick up any stragglers they find running through the woods. A few of them might escape, but I doubt they'll be much trouble in the future."

Barry looked down at the manila envelope in his hand. "Of course, you probably have their home addresses, don't you?"

"As a matter of fact, I do."

The two men laughed. The Captain then asked if Barry had any trouble finding the place.

Barry waved the envelope in the air. "Are you kidding?

With all the info *you* supplied? About the only thing you didn't include in here was how many stars the compound mess rated.''

"Not a one," answered Gruenwald as he walked up to them. The Captain introduced Gruenwald to Barry, then told the lawyer how he had supplied information that allowed the Falcon to thwart the real objective of Liberty's Torch.

"*You* supplied the information?" Gruenwald gasped. "How did you manage that?"

Suddenly, the Captain looked uncomfortable. For a moment, he stared at the floor, unable to meet Gruenwald's gaze. He took a deep breath and raised his head.

"I, ah, I would break out of my cell at night and collect it. I couldn't tell you about it, Mark, and I'm sorry about that. But I couldn't risk tipping my hand before I was ready."

"What? Why didn't you just break out and take me with you? That would have made *my* week a lot easier."

Captain America's tone was apologetic as he explained what he had done and why he had done it.

"Douglas was using my trial as a diversion to distract the authorities from the air strike he was planning. I had to use it the same way. As long as Liberty's Torch had me and the trial was proceeding, they thought their real plan was secure. And they were laying low during the trial, foregoing any attacks on any of their usual targets. That first night, I contacted the FBI and told them *not* to rescue me. It was better for the country if I let myself stay a prisoner while I uncovered what was really going on."

The Captain's face reddened. He looked Gruenwald directly in the eye, hoping to find forgiveness there. "Mark, if I caused you any discomfort, I'm truly sorry."

"Considering the results, I guess I can't complain." Gruenwald said, pausing for a long moment. "But, I warn you, you're going to be the one feeling discomfort when you get my bill."

Gruenwald smiled at Captain America and laughed. The

Captain returned Gruenwald's smile eagerly. That the lawyer forgave him was, after the news that the Falcon had stopped the helicopter strike, the best thing he'd heard all day.

"Oh, no," Barry interjected, "you don't get off that easy. How did you get your mitts on that information?"

"It wasn't difficult," the Captain said with self-effacing modesty. He used the lockpick in his belt buckle to get out of his cell at night. Having seen that the security cameras didn't move, he knew they weren't working yet. And there weren't many people in the compound. Once he was out of his cell, it was a simple matter of sticking to the shadows.

He had figured to do that for all his excursions, but he got lucky that first night: he found a spare Torch uniform. Taylor Douglas had ordered he not be unmasked, so no one knew what he really looked like. When he put on the uniform, he appeared to be just another member; no one paid any attention to him.

"Why didn't they?" asked Gruenwald. "Even in that uniform, you were a stranger to them."

"It's an old trick," the Captain said. "If you act like you belong wherever you are, everyone assumes you do belong and leaves you alone. The fact that many of these men were unsociable loners anyway made it even easier than usual."

Over the next two nights, Captain America had collected the information he needed.

"I got most of it from Douglas himself," he said when Barry asked where the info had come from. "He thought his computer was secure, but I'm pretty good at encryption codes. His weren't even that hard to crack."

Just that morning, a couple hours before down, the Captain had discovered Douglas's real objective. If he was going to prevent the helicopter strike, he didn't have any time to waste. He risked leaving the compound to get the envelope to Barry and the Falcon. "I knew you and Sam could handle it," he added.

This time, it was Barry's turn to blush.

• • •

Later, the Falcon joined Captain America and the others as the Army and the FBI cleaned up the Liberty's Torch compound. Under the Captain's direction, all the information on Taylor Douglas's computer and every other computer in the compound was downloaded onto disks that could be turned over to the federal prosecutor. Barry commented that the information they were finding, along with the papers found in Douglas's office, would insure that the leader and most members of Liberty's Torch would be needing, "lifetime subscriptions to *Better Bars and Gardens*."

Then Barry blanched. He turned to Gruenwald and asked, "It *will* be admissible, won't it? Tell me Cap wasn't committing illegal search and seizure when he hacked into the big kahuna's computer? I'd hate to see these guys get off on a technicality."

"It wouldn't matter if he did. The FBI would have found the information legitimately anyway, during this raid. That makes it all admissible."

Captain America continued to supervise the info retrieval from the compound. He stopped only once, when he saw Juror Number Eleven, the man he had since learned was John Richards, being led out in handcuffs.

"One moment, Private," the Captain said, walking up to the soldier escorting the manacled Richards. "Can I have a word with this prisoner?"

The private smiled, apparently thrilled to his boots that Captain America was actually talking to him.

"I guess so. My orders are to not let any of these prisoners talk to anyone until they've been questioned, but I'm gonna assume you outrank me, okay?"

The Captain smiled his thanks to the soldier.

"Mr. Richards, I just wanted to thank you for what you did in that courtroom this morning."

"Thank *me*?" Richards said incredulously.

"That's correct. Our country was founded by people who went against England, sometimes even against their friends and family, to fight for what they believed was right. This morning, in that madness Douglas spawned, you served the *real* America in that most proud of traditions. I wanted you to know that I will be there to testify on your behalf.'' The Captain snapped to attention and saluted Richards. ''Thank you, soldier.''

Though his movements were restricted by his handcuffs, John Richards returned the Captain's salute before he was led away to a waiting van. The cooperative private shook his head as he marched Richards down the corridor. The private probably didn't know what had just happened here, but he would, someday, have one hell of a tale to tell his kids. And his grandkids.

Later still, with the mop-up operation winding to a finish, the Falcon found Captain America in Douglas's office. His friend was staring at a tattered American flag on the wall.

''Steve? Are you all right?''

''I'm fine, Sam. I'm just thinking about men like Douglas and what could turn them so wrong.''

''In his own twisted way,'' the Falcon said, ''I suppose he thought he was being loyal to America.''

The Captain shook his head sadly.

''No, Sam. I don't know what country Taylor Douglas thought he was representing, but it was *never* America.''

The Captain walked to the door, turned back for one last look, and switched off the office lights. He stared into the darkness for an instant more.

''Let's get out of here, Sam.''

23

THE TRUE LIGHT

"**A**shes to ashes . . ."

He hated funerals.

It was John Donne who said, "Any man's death diminishes me, because I am involved in mankind," but it was Captain America who lived it. Few had more firsthand experience with the sentiment than did he. Throughout the Captain's career, death had been the one constant. He'd had many partners—Bucky, the Avengers, the Falcon, Rick Jones, D-Man, Diamondback, and others—but, too often and as contradictory as it seemed, death seemed his only lifelong companion.

His childhood, what should have been a time of innocence, had been marred by the death of his father. And even though was still too young to understand what death truly meant, he could see what it did to his mother and know it was bad. Then his mother died and a young man who should have been discovering girls and playing baseball and studying for exams had instead learned how to fend for himself.

As a young adult, he was thrust into a war where the lives of young men were discarded as easily as spent cartridges. He missed the end of the war but, when he returned to the world after his decades of frozen sleep, nothing had really changed. Although the country he loved was technically at peace, he was still Captain America. He still fought and saw death far too often.

It didn't matter whose death—they all affected him deeply. Even when Baron Zemo died, the Captain took no comfort from the fate of the Nazi responsible for the death of Bucky and so many others. He even regretted that he had been, however indirectly, responsible for the man's death and ashamed he had been too slow to save him.

"Dust to dust . . ."

He had seen too many deaths. He had seen too many funerals. From the simple Potter's Field service for his father to makeshift battlefield rites to the elaborate affairs for presidents and heads of state, he had seen all kinds of funerals and had never taken comfort from a single one of them.

This one was as bad as any of them.

People had come from all across the country to the small Iowa cemetery where Colin Maxwell was being buried. His fans and fellow writers from both coasts, even some from overseas, had journeyed to pay their last respects to their fallen comrade. Many of the writers spoke to honor Maxwell and did so eloquently. The Captain heard the words and appreciated them for what they meant to Colin's other friends and to Barbara Maxwell, who wore her widow's black as well as could be expected.

The Captain wished he could have said something, but it was out of the question. He was there not as Captain America, but as Steve Rogers. To reveal the special bond he shared with Maxwell might put Colin's family at risk.

Sam Wilson had come with him to Iowa and Steve was grateful for his friend's presence. The Falcon had not known Colin well, but, even if the writer's murder had not brought them into battle against Liberty's Torch, Steve knew Sam would have been by his side for this. It helped fill the void that Colin's death had left within Rogers.

But only a little.

Steve looked down at the coffin, just the simple box Barb had requested, but covered with the American flag he had arranged. It was hard to imagine his friend in there and Rogers found himself thinking of happier times they had shared.

That first meeting when they had stayed up all night talking and walking around New York. Their hours discussing the 1940s, that era Colin never tired of learning about and Rogers never wanted to lose. The pool halls they had frequented. Their quest for quaint jazz clubs or eateries stuck in a time some five decades earlier.

Their relationship had changed somewhat when Colin and Barb were married. Colin would still come to New York to do research, but now there was a part of his life more important to him than his work. Still, Rogers wouldn't have changed anything, not even going back to the way it had been, for the joy he had experienced meeting Barbara and attending her and Colin's wedding. Or the greater joy he felt looking at those first treasured snapshots of their son, Nicholas. His friends were living what he looked on as the "all-American family" dream, a dream forever denied to Steve Rogers by dint of who he was, what he could do, and all those other Americans who depended on him.

Steve was abruptly brought back to the present by the sound of the twenty-one gun salute, followed by the military bugler playing "Taps." He came to attention and saluted until the song and the service was over.

After the service, as family and friends were saying goodbye to Barb Maxwell, he stayed in the background. What he had to say to her had to be spoken in private. As Rogers waited, Sam Wilson came up to him.

"Steve, I know Colin served in the Army, but he was never in combat. Did you call in a few favors to arrange this full military funeral?"

Steve Rogers looked at the hole in the ground and, beyond it, at the cemetery workers waiting with their shovels for the bereaved to leave. He glanced over at Barb, taking note of the flag folded over her arm, the flag that had draped her husband's coffin. He turned back to Wilson.

"You're wrong, Sam. In his own way, and in the sacrifice he made, he was most definitely a soldier. He was a casualty of the war against every bigot, every dictator, every madman who denies the worth of all men. Colin Maxwell and all the courageous citizens like him who are just as willing to stand up for what's right—they are the real soldiers in this war. They are the true torches of liberty. Their example lights the way for all men. We needed to remember him for what he was, for all that he was."

Sam smiled. "Fair enough." Then he laughed. "Shoulda known I'd get a speech."

Steve shared the laugh, welcomed it in this sad time.

When Barb Maxwell was finally alone, Steve walked over to her. She held up her hand before he could say a word.

"Don't, Steve," she cautioned him.

"Huh?"

"You were about to apologize to me, weren't you? To tell me you're sorry that you weren't in time, that you couldn't save him from those men? You might as well be wearing a sign. Well, kindly stop beating yourself up. There was no way you could have known and nothing you could have done. Your guilt isn't what Colin would want you to take with you from his graveside. He'd want you to take the happiness and the good times you shared. And he'd want you to remember always that you gave each other friendship."

In a lifetime of service, Captain America had learned many things. Chief among them was how to control his emotions so they wouldn't interfere with the task before him. But that lifetime of training did him little good as he embraced Barb and said goodbye to his friend.

One of the Captain's tears was caught by the dry Iowa breeze. Landing on the casket, it glistened in the sun for a moment and, in the heart of liberty, for all eternity.

The next evening, Captain America was back in New York. The Weather Channel had said it would be a glorious night, warm with a refreshing breeze coming in off the Hudson. A night to make London and Paris and Rome envious. A night to stay up late and take in everything that the city that never sleeps had to offer.

Several blocks from the Hudson, Captain America sat at his computer in the basement of Avengers Mansion. He had entered the latest encryption codes many hours ago, but was hard at work on something far more difficult. Still, though it was hard work, he thought it well worth the effort.

After all, the Captain reminded himself, he couldn't very well dedicate his autobiography to Colin Maxwell until he had finished writing it.

Tony Isabella has been called "America's most beloved comic-book writer and columnist." He has also been a comics editor, retailer, distributor, lecturer, and show promoter. His writing and editing credits range from *The Amazing Spider-Man* to *Young Love* and include memorable work on *Daredevil*, *Ghost Rider*, *Harlan Ellison's Dream Corridor*, *Hawkman*, *Justice Machine*, *Luke Cage: Power Man*, *Satan's Six*, *Star Trek*, and *What If*. His most popular creation, and his personal favorite, is *Black Lightning*, an inner-city super hero created for DC Comics in 1976, and revived, to critical acclaim, in 1995. Currently, he is writing a daily online column of reviews and commentary for World Famous Comics—which can be found at http://www.wfcomics.com/Tony—and a weekly column for *Comics Buyer's Guide*. Captain America is one of Isabella's favorite heroes, not only because of the values for which Cap stands, but because of the legendary comics creators who created him and all those who have shaped him over the past fifty years.

Bob Ingersoll may be the senior appellate attorney in the Cleveland, Ohio, Public Defender Office, but his real love is writing in and about the four-color world of comics. In his regular column "The Law Is a Ass" for *Comics Buyer's Guide*—which has been quoted by such writers as Harlan Ellison and Ron Goulart—he examines, with tongue firmly in cheek, the way the law is portrayed in comics so as to entertain and enlighten people on how the law really functions. In addition to his column, Bob has written numerous comic books, including stories for *Star Trek: The Next Generation*, *Lost in Space*, *Quantum Leap*, *Sentry*, *Hero Alliance*, *Green Hornet*, *Justice Machine*, *Mickey Mouse*, and *Donald Duck*. Bob's seventeen years of experience as an attorney served him well in writing *Captain America: Liberty's Torch*; it told him everything a court could do that was wrong, so that he knew exactly what Liberty's Torch would be doing.

Mike Zeck has been drawing comics for more than two decades. Some of his Marvel artistic highlights include launching *The Punisher* to stardom with a five-issue miniseries, the *Secret Wars* maxiseries, and the acclaimed "Kraven's Last Hunt" story arc in the Spider-Man titles. Recently, Mike returned to the crime genre with the miniseries *Damned* from Homage Comics. With Phil Zimelman, he has provided covers for the various Marvel anthologies published by Byron Preiss Multimedia Company and Berkley Boulevard Books, as well as the covers to the Marvel Super Thrillers published by BPMC and Pocket Books. Next on his plate is to provide illustrations to Adam-Troy Castro's upcoming Sinister Six trilogy of Spider-Man novels. Mike and his wife, Angel, reside in Connecticut.

Bob McLeod was born in Tampa, Florida, in 1951 and now makes his home in Emmaus, Pennsylvania. He attended the Art Institute of Fort Lauderdale in Florida, then moved on to an apprenticeship at Neal Adams's Continuity Studios. Starting out as an inker for Marvel in 1974, he moved on to pencilling in the early 1980s, working on several Spider-Man titles. In 1983, he cocreated *The New Mutants* with Chris Claremont, and worked on the title first as penciller, then as inker. His numerous credits include *Action Comics*, *Venom: The Enemy Within*, *Spider-Man: The Lost Years*, *The Ultimate Spider-Man*, *The Ultimate Super-Villains*, *X-Men: Empire's End*, and inking Mike Zeck's work on "Kraven's Last Hunt."

CHRONOLOGY TO THE MARVEL NOVELS AND ANTHOLOGIES

What follows is a guide to the order in which the Marvel novels and short stories published by Byron Preiss Multimedia Company and Berkley Boulevard Books take place in relation to each other. Please note that this is not a hard-and-fast chronology, but a guideline that is subject to change at authorial or editorial whim. This list covers all the novels and anthologies published from October 1994–March 1999.

The short stories are each given an abbreviation to indicate which anthology the story appeared in. USM=*The Ultimate Spider-Man*, USS=*The Ultimate Silver Surfer*, USV=*The Ultimate Super-Villains*, UXM=*The Ultimate X-Men*, UTS=*Untold Tales of Spider-Man*, and UH=*The Ultimate Hulk*.

If you have any questions or comments regarding this chronology, please write us.

Snail mail: Keith R.A. DeCandido
          Marvel Novels Editor
          Byron Preiss Multimedia Company, Inc.
          24 West 25th Street
          New York, NY 10010-2710
E-mail: KRAD@IX.NETCOM.COM.
          —Keith R.A. DeCandido, Editor

X-Men & Spider-Man: Time's Arrow Book 1: **The Past [portions]**
by Tom DeFalco & Jason Henderson
    Parts of this novel take place in prehistoric times, the sixth century, 1867, and 1944.

"The Silver Surfer" [flashback]
by Tom DeFalco & Stan Lee [USS]

The Silver Surfer's origin. The early parts of this flashback start several decades, possibly several centuries, ago, and continue to a point just prior to "To See Heaven in a Wild Flower."

"In the Line of Banner"
by Danny Fingeroth [UH]
This takes place nine months before the birth of Robert Bruce Banner.

X-Men: Codename Wolverine ["then" portions]
by Christopher Golden
The "then" portions of this novel take place while Team X was still in operation, while the Black Widow was still a Soviet spy, and while Banshee was still with Interpol.

"Spider-Man"
by Stan Lee & Peter David [USM]
A retelling of Spider-Man's origin.

"Transformations"
by Will Murray [UH]
"Side by Side with the Astonishing Ant-Man!"
by Will Murray [UTS]
"Assault on Avengers Mansion"
by Richard C. White & Steven A. Roman [UH]
"Suits"
by Tom De Haven & Dean Wesley Smith [USM]
"After the First Death . . ."
by Tom DeFalco [UTS]
"Celebrity"
by Christopher Golden & José R. Nieto [UTS]
"Pitfall"
by Pierce Askegren [UH]
"Better Looting Through Modern Chemistry"
by John Garcia & Pierce Askegren [UTS]
These stories take place very early in the careers of Spider-Man and the Hulk.

"To the Victor"
by Richard Lee Byers [USV]
Most of this story takes place in an alternate timeline, but the jumping-off point is here.

"To See Heaven in a Wild Flower"
by Ann Tonsor Zeddies [USS]
"Point of View"
by Len Wein [USS]
   These stories take place shortly after the end of the flashback portion of "The Silver Surfer."

"Identity Crisis"
by Michael Jan Friedman [UTS]
"The Liar"
by Ann Nocenti [UTS]
"The Doctor's Dilemma"
by Danny Fingeroth [UTS]
"Moving Day"
by John S. Drew [UTS]
"Out of the Darkness"
by Glenn Greenberg [UH]
"Deadly Force"
by Richard Lee Byers [UTS]
"Truck Stop"
by Jo Duffy [UH]
"Hiding"
by Nancy Holder & Christopher Golden [UH]
"Improper Procedure"
by Keith R.A. DeCandido [USS]
"Poison in the Soul"
by Glenn Greenberg [UTS]
"Here There Be Dragons"
by Sholly Fisch [UH]
"The Ballad of Fancy Dan"
by Ken Grobe & Steven A. Roman [UTS]
"Do You Dream in Silver?"
by James Dawson [USS]
"A Quiet, Normal Life"
by Thomas Deja [UH]
"Livewires"
by Steve Lyons [UTS]
"Arms and the Man"
by Keith R.A. DeCandido [UTS]
"Incident on a Skyscraper"
by Dave Smeds [USS]

"A Green Snake in Paradise"
by Steve Lyons [UH]

      These all take place at various and sundry points in the careers of Spider-Man, the Silver Surfer, and the Hulk: after their origins, but before Spider-Man got married, the Silver Surfer ended his exile on Earth, and the reemergence of the gray Hulk.

"Cool"
by Lawrence Watt-Evans [USM]
"Blindspot"
by Ann Nocenti [USM]
"Tinker, Tailor, Soldier, Courier"
by Robert L. Washington III [USM]
"Thunder on the Mountain"
by Richard Lee Byers [USM]
"The Stalking of John Doe"
by Adam-Troy Castro [UTS]
"On the Beach"
by John J. Ordover [USS]

      These all take place just prior to Peter Parker's marriage to Mary Jane Watson and the Silver Surfer's release from imprisonment on Earth.

Daredevil: Predator's Smile
by Christopher Golden
"Disturb Not Her Dream"
by Steve Rasnic Tem [USS]
"My Enemy, My Savior"
by Eric Fein [UTS]
"Kraven the Hunter Is Dead, Alas"
by Craig Shaw Gardner [USM]
"The Broken Land"
by Pierce Askegren [USS]
"Radically Both"
by Christopher Golden [USM]
"Godhood's End"
by Sharman DiVono [USS]
"Scoop!"
by David Michelinie [USM]
"The Beast with Nine Bands"
by James A. Wolf [UH]

"Sambatyon"
by David M. Honigsberg [USS]
"Cold Blood"
by Greg Cox [USM]
"The Tarnished Soul"
by Katherine Lawrence [USS]
"Leveling Las Vegas"
by Stan Timmons [UH]
"If Wishes Were Horses"
by Tony Isabella & Bob Ingersoll [USV]
"The Silver Surfer" [framing sequence]
by Tom DeFalco & Stan Lee [USS]
"The Samson Journals"
by Ken Grobe [UH]
   These all take place after Peter Parker's marriage to Mary Jane Watson, after the Silver Surfer attained freedom from imprisonment on Earth, and before the Hulk's personalities were merged.

"The Deviant Ones"
by Glenn Greenberg [USV]
"An Evening in the Bronx with Venom"
by John Gregory Betancourt & Keith R.A. DeCandido [USM]
   These two stories take place one after the other, and a few months prior to The Venom Factor.

The Incredible Hulk: What Savage Beast
by Peter David
   This novel takes place over a one-year period, starting here and ending just prior to Rampage.

"On the Air"
by Glenn Hauman [UXM]
"Connect the Dots"
by Adam-Troy Castro [USV]
"Summer Breeze"
by Jenn Saint-John & Tammy Lynne Dunn [UXM]
"Out of Place"
by Dave Smeds [UXM]
   These stories all take place prior to the Mutant Empire *trilogy.*

X-Men: Mutant Empire Book 1: **Siege**
by Christopher Golden
X-Men: Mutant Empire Book 2: **Sanctuary**
by Christopher Golden
X-Men: Mutant Empire Book 3: **Salvation**
by Christopher Golden
    These three novels take place within a three-day period.

Fantastic Four: To Free Atlantis
by Nancy A. Collins
"The Love of Death or the Death of Love"
by Craig Shaw Gardner [USS]
"Firetrap"
by Michael Jan Friedman [USV]
"What's Yer Poison?"
by Christopher Golden & José R. Nieto [USS]
"Sins of the Flesh"
by Steve Lyons [USV]
"Doom²"
by Joey Cavalieri [USV]
"Child's Play"
by Robert L. Washington III [USV]
"A Game of the Apocalypse"
by Dan Persons [USS]
"All Creatures Great and Skrull"
by Greg Cox [USV]
"Ripples"
by José R. Nieto [USV]
"Who Do You Want Me to Be?"
by Ann Nocenti [USV]
"One for the Road"
by James Dawson [USV]
    These are more or less simultaneous, with "Doom²" taking place after To Free Atlantis, *"Child's Play" taking place shortly after "What's Yer Poison?" and "A Game of the Apocalypse" taking place shortly after "The Love of Death or the Death of Love."*

"Five Minutes"
by Peter David [USM]
    This takes place on Peter Parker and Mary Jane Watson-Parker's first anniversary.

Spider-Man: The Venom Factor
by Diane Duane
Spider-Man: The Lizard Sanction
by Diane Duane
Spider-Man: The Octopus Agenda
by Diane Duane
> *These three novels take place within a six-week period.*

"The Night I Almost Saved Silver Sable"
by Tom DeFalco [USV]
"Traps"
by Ken Grobe [USV]
> *These stories take place one right after the other.*

Iron Man: The Armor Trap
by Greg Cox
Iron Man: Operation A.I.M.
by Greg Cox
"Private Exhibition"
by Pierce Askegren [USV]
Fantastic Four: Redemption of the Silver Surfer
by Michael Jan Friedman
Spider-Man & The Incredible Hulk: Rampage (Doom's Day Book 1)
by Danny Fingeroth & Eric Fein
Spider-Man & Iron Man: Sabotage (Doom's Day Book 2)
by Pierce Askegren & Danny Fingeroth
Spider-Man & Fantastic Four: Wreckage (Doom's Day Book 3)
by Eric Fein & Pierce Askegren
> Operation A.I.M. *takes place about two weeks after* The Armor Trap. *The "Doom's Day" trilogy takes place within a three-month period. The events of* Operation A.I.M., *"Private Exhibition,"* Redemption of the Silver Surfer, *and* Rampage *happen more or less simultaneously.* Wreckage *is only a few months after* The Octopus Agenda.

"It's a Wonderful Life"
by eluki bes shahar [UXM]
"Gift of the Silver Fox"
by Ashley McConnell [UXM]
"Stillborn in the Mist"
by Dean Wesley Smith [UXM]

"Order from Chaos"
by Evan Skolnick [UXM]
> *These stories take place simultaneously.*

"X-Presso"
by Ken Grobe [UXM]
"Life Is But a Dream"
by Stan Timmons [UXM]
"Four Angry Mutants"
by Andy Lane & Rebecca Levene [UXM]
"Hostages"
by J. Steven York [UXM]
> *These stories take place one right after the other.*

Spider-Man: Carnage in New York
by David Michelinie & Dean Wesley Smith
Spider-Man: Goblin's Revenge
by Dean Wesley Smith
> *These novels take place one right after the other.*

X-Men: Smoke and Mirrors
by eluki bes shahar
> *This novel takes place three-and-a-half months after "It's a Wonderful Life."*

Generation X
by Scott Lobdell & Elliot S! Maggin
X-Men: The Jewels of Cyttorak
by Dean Wesley Smith
X-Men: Empire's End
by Diane Duane
X-Men: Law of the Jungle
by Dave Smeds
X-Men: Prisoner X
by Ann Nocenti
> *These novels take place one right after the other.*

The Incredible Hulk: Abominations
by Jason Henderson
Fantastic Four: Countdown to Chaos
by Pierce Askegren

"Playing it SAFE"
by Keith R.A. DeCandido [UH]
> *These take place one right after the other, with* Abominations *taking place a couple of weeks after* Wreckage.

"Mayhem Party"
by Robert Sheckley [USV]
> *This story takes place after* Goblin's Revenge.

X-Men & Spider-Man: Time's Arrow Book 1: **The Past**
by Tom DeFalco & Jason Henderson
X-Men & Spider-Man: Time's Arrow Book 2: **The Present**
by Tom DeFalco & Adam-Troy Castro
X-Men & Spider-Man: Time's Arrow Book 3: **The Future**
by Tom DeFalco & eluki bes shahar
> *These novels take place within a twenty-four-hour period in the present, though it also involves travelling to various points in the past, to an alternate present, and to five different alternate futures.*

X-Men: Soul Killer
by Richard Lee Byers
Spider-Man: Valley of the Lizard
by John Vornholt
Spider-Man: Venom's Wrath
by Keith R.A. DeCandido & José R. Nieto
Spider-Man: Wanted Dead or Alive
by Craig Shaw Gardner
"Sidekick"
by Dennis Brabham [UH]
Captain America: Liberty's Torch
by Tony Isabella & Bob Ingersoll
> *These take place one right after the other, with* Venom's Wrath *taking place a month after* Valley of the Lizard, *and* Wanted Dead or Alive *several months after* Venom's Wrath.

Spider-Man: The Gathering of the Sinister Six
by Adam Troy Castro
Generation X: Crossroads
by J. Steven York

X-Men: Codename Wolverine
by Christopher Golden
> *These novels take place one right after the other, with* Codename Wolverine *taking place less than a week after* Crossroads.

The Avengers & the Thunderbolts
by Pierce Askegren
> *This novel takes place many months after* Wreckage *and* Countdown to Chaos.

X-Men & Spider-Man: Time's Arrow Book 3: The Future [portions]
by Tom DeFalco & eluki bes shahar
> *Parts of this novel take place in five different alternate futures in 2020, 2035, 2099, 3000, and the fortieth century.*

"The Last Titan"
by Peter David [UH]
> *This takes place in a possible future.*